Darkness Visible

The Complete Short Stories

LEON STEELGRAVE

Published by Ice Pick Books

ISBN 978-1-8384435-0-4

Books by Leon Steelgrave

Europa City 1: White Vampyre
Europa City 2: Though Your Sins Be Scarlet
Europa City 3: The Violet Hour
Europa City 4: A Life Owed

Europa City One-shot: Cocoa Psycho Killer
Europa City One-shot: Smack Upside The Head

Darkness Visible: The Complete Short Stories

CONTENTS

AUTHOR'S NOTE

The following stories were written between 1993 and 2013, the first 25 of which were previously published in two separate eBook collections: *More Stories About Drugs, Sex & Violence* and *Phantasmagoria*. The remaining stories are presented here for the first time.

They run the gamut from horror to crime noir, touching on the points of fantasy, surrealism and science fiction in-between. Where necessary I have applied a fresh lick of paint to some of the older stories that they may stand proud with their fellows. Hopefully none of the original spirit has been lost in the process.

Leon Steelgrave

March 2021

PREDATOR/PREY

Picture a singles bar. You don't need to know its name or location, we are all familiar with these types of cattle market and no greater definition of the club is required.

The woman is tall, sinuous and beautiful, in a cold sort of fashion. She moves with the primeval grace of a great cat, for that is what she is — a hunter.

'Will she pick me?' you wonder. The answer is, of course, no. You are too tall or too short, too thin or too fat. Your gender is wrong, unsuited to the direction in which her sexuality is swinging this evening. The capricious favours of her bed will not be yours tonight. You instinctively know this to be true.

The man, sipping a gin and tonic at the bar, is equally suave. The dark intelligence in his eyes shows that he is more than equal to the woman's lust. If such a thing were possible, one suspects that his desire may run even deeper than hers does. But surely no one is that carnal?

Their eyes lock, a stream of unspoken dialogue passes between them, then they close in for the kill. You watch, a little ashamed of your voyeuristic behaviour. It's not as though you couldn't find a trap of your own. God knows you could have your pick of any of the people in this sleazy den. The night is still young and you have plenty of time to try a few moves of your own. In the meantime, you might as well enjoy the floorshow.

Their interaction fascinates you. You've seen all the tricks before, but rarely performed with such intensity. The woman accepts a drink form the man and giggles (that laugh's much too young for her) as she dips a finger with an exquisitely manicured nail in the clear liquor. She traces her finger around the rim to produce a single, ringing note. Whenever she looks at him it is through lowered lashes, showing him deference and hinting that she is willing to surrender herself to his power.

The man smiles in return (I bet he's sucking in that gut) and reaches across to retrieve an ashtray from the bar, his hand brushes against her breast seemingly by accident. The woman remains ice-maiden cool. Yes, you can touch me but it's going to take far more sophistication than that to win the game.

She asks for a cigarette and he obliges. When she leans forward to accept a light she is careful to show off her breasts to their full advantage. The movement causes her to lose her balance on the high barstool and she reaches out, her hand grabbing the man's thigh. It lingers there a fraction too long to be purely accidental or decent.

'Hi. I couldn't help noticing you were sitting alone. I don't wanna to be presumptuous, but you look kinda lonely. Perhaps you need a friend?'

The voice makes you turn, your anger flares momentarily at this interruption to your enjoyment of the floorshow. You smile; this suitor is rather attractive. A sense of irony makes your smile wider, for it would seem that you are now the prey. Your uninvited guest takes this as a sign of acceptance and sits nervously beside you.

The man returns his lighter to his pocket with a well-practised movement. His eyes never stray from the woman during the operation. He is thinking that it is all too easy. The prey is naïve and falsely confident in its abilities. It is a pity there is no greater sport to be found.

The woman exhales and carefully crosses her legs, showing the maximum possible amount of thigh. Her thoughts run in a similar vein to that of the man. She is picking up overconfidence and an excess of ego. It lends a rank odour to the air around her and makes her savour the thought of destroying both confidence and ego.

You offer a drink, conversation, but your attention is rarely focused on your conquest. The man and woman at the bar continue to fascinate you. They draw your attention from your partner at every given opportunity. Your inattention does not go unnoticed, but you gloss over it with saccharin pleasantries. Then the man and woman are moving, weaving through the crowds, heading for the exit. Shocked by your own actions, you find yourself on your feet, mumbling feeble apologies about some forgotten prior appointment. You hustle your way across the room without a backward glance. Your limbs feel stiff and leaden. Perhaps you're getting old? Ha!

You give the cloakroom girl your ticket and wait impatiently for her to find your jacket. Each second of delay decreases your chances of being able to pick up their trail. Though what you intend to do when you find them you do not know. Will you follow them home to his or her apartment? Will you wait afterwards and follow whoever leaves to their abode. If you do, what then? This is madness. You have clearly lost your mind.

'Hey, are you gonna to take your coat or are you just gonna stand and stare all night?' the girl grouses. Glaring at her impertinence, you snatch your jacket and hurry out to the street.

Outside it is dark and cold drizzle is falling, making the sidewalk slick underfoot. Despite the weather the street is relatively crowded. You walk a few paces to your left, your head weaving from side to side like a cobra getting ready to strike its prey. You turn on your heel with a silent curse and head back to the right. Something catches your eye. Is it them? Yes. Necking in the harsh sodium glow of the streetlights. You slow down and will them to go on so you can continue to follow them. Your breathing is harsh and you're surprised to find yourself sweating heavily despite the chill night air. Perhaps you're coming down with a virus? Maybe that's the source of your madness?

They disengage and move off down the street. Your heart skips a beat when they pause at the edge of the road, if they should hail a cab you will have no chance of following them. But no, they are waiting for a break in the traffic. Your heart slows — it's all right — you can continue your pursuit.

They cross the road and step into a garbage-strewn alley that stinks of urine. It makes you apprehensive to find yourself in the city's seedy guts, but you can't seem to stop yourself from following them. You have embarked on a journey of self-discovery from which there is no turning back.

A hand grasps your ankle and you cry out. The old derelict stares at you with bloodshot eyes as you hurry past. With luck, they will not have heard you.

From the alley to a viaduct beneath the road and then back to another alleyway, you follow them until they arrive outside a cheap motel, the kind that rents rooms by the hour. Not that you are familiar with such places.

You watch them through the glass doors of the reception as they check in. Your wheezing breath reminds you of an elderly relative whom you watched sicken and die. You ask yourself what you should do now the hunt is over. You're fevered. You really should go home now that there is no more to see. Yes. Go home, back to your warm, comforting and safe little life.

Taking your own advice, you are just about to turn away

when a light illuminates one of the downstairs windows. The blind rolls up and the woman stands framed before you. You watch as the man, now naked, comes up behind her and grabs the straps of her dress. His muscles ripple as he tears the fabric to ribbons, which hang about her waist. Her breasts rise and fall in rhythm with her quick, shallow breaths.

The man is strong and handsome. The woman is firm and beautiful. How you crave to feel that ripe flesh against your own, and how you envy them. Ensnared, you continue to watch as the man tears the remaining scraps of fabric from the woman and steps in close, to encircle her from behind. She shudders. The muscles in her thighs and belly ripple.

You're sweating heavier than ever and each breath burns like fire as you struggle to draw oxygen into your starved lungs. You ignore your growing malaise and continue to watch.

The woman's breasts flatten against the glass as the man forces her against it. Her palms and spread fingers press against the window as she braces herself. With horror you realise she is staring straight at you, just like the man who, with fingers knotted in her hair, looks over her shoulder. Their eyes seem to ask if this is what you came to see. You don't know. You've been struck mute. A growing sense of dizziness threatens to rip you from consciousness. You stare in terror at your wrinkled, liver spotted hands and scream silently in fear and incomprehension. Your vision dims and the last thing you ever feel is the sickening lurch in the pit of your stomach as you fall.

The woman sighed. 'Was it good for you, darling? Such a gorgeously filthy id, I feel quite bloated.'

'Yes, I knew the moment I felt those eyes watching us in the bar that we'd found the one. Almost too easy. This city's full of the desperate and the needy. But we're only doing to them what they do to themselves.'

THE DOG TRAINER

Bennett glanced at his watch and cursed; he was late for the interview. He dropped a gear and accelerated into the bend of the narrow lane. As the car straightened it hit a patch of leaf mulch and the rear end fishtailed. An invisible hand grabbed hold of Bennett's chest as he eased off the accelerator and steered into the skid. The tyres screeched in protest but held the road and the car was suddenly back under his control. He gave a nervous, brittle laugh as the panic left him and resolved to drink no more than two pints with lunch from now on.

The rest of the journey passed without incident and ten minutes later he pulled up in the gravel drive of a slightly dilapidated country house. This was the residence of Sarah Farquerson-Brown, whom his editor had once daubed "the most wicked woman in Britain". That had been back in the eighties when Bennett was a junior reporter and her clients knew Ms Farquerson-Brown as Madam Sin, proprietor of a high-class brothel that delivered a heavy side order of bondage and flagellation, all wrapped up in faux occultism. Just the kind of mix of sex and perversion that titillated the public. One made all the more potent by the fact that several of her clients were high-ranking members of the

Cabinet. Sarah received six months for running a house of ill repute, following which she promptly vanished from the public eye and consciousness.

That was twenty years ago, and besides, it was a different century. Public taste had changed and BDSM was far more openly accepted. By some, anyway. Bennett found it hard to comprehend masochism. Indeed, he required the F7 key to spell it. But personal taste should not be a bar to a good story, nor in his experience inconvenient details such as the facts. Madam Sin had risen again and her club nights were big business. It was the Holy Trinity of tabloid journalism — money, sex and filth! And Bennett was determined to get the headlines.

Sarah stood in the door waiting for him when he stepped from the car. She wore a simple white blouse, tweed skirt and riding boots. Her blonde hair scraped back in a tight ponytail to expose sharp cheekbones and intense green eyes. The eyes remained hard when she smiled and said, 'Do come in, please. The kettle has just boiled.'

Bennett let her lead way, admiring the sway of her hips. Quite tasty for a mature bit of flange. He normally avoided any woman past the age of thirty-five. He knew from experience that some terrible things lay at the wrong end of gravity's well.

'I've poured the water — that's all I do. Help yourself to tea or coffee.'

Bennett started guiltily at her voice and tried to cover it up by smiling. 'Thank you,' he said, dropping a teabag into a chipped mug.

Sarah continued to talk as he waited for the tea to soak into the water. 'You might find the tea tastes different — all my water comes from a natural spring — so it's free from all that chemical nonsense.'

Bennett nodded distractedly as he searched for somewhere to place the tea bag. He spotted another used bag resting on the stainless steel of the draining board and dropped his own beside it. His host stood a little too close for comfort as he completed the operation by adding three spoons of sugar and a splash of milk.

'Ready? Good. I should warn you that when we go through to the lounge you will see two dogs lying in the corner. You're not to look at them, nor are you to speak to them. Is that understood?'

'If you say so. I'm not really a dog person.'

Sarah subjected him to a penetrating gaze. 'Oh I think you may be more of a dog than you realise.'

The lounge, like the kitchen before it, was surprisingly normal. Bennett was not sure what he had expected, something more dungeon-like, perhaps. A wood burning stove on a granite hearth acted as the focal point of the room, with a leather recliner situated to the right of the fire. It faced the exterior wall of the house, allowing the occupant to stare through the window into the garden. A two-seater sofa sat directly opposite the fire and Sarah indicated to Bennett that he should take a seat.

Bennett sat and placed his mug on the small coffee table before him. His eyes slid casually over the remainder of the room while he fished in his pocket for the tape recorder. A large woollen blanket had been spread beneath the window behind the armchair on his left. Sarah's "dogs" lay curled together on the blanket. Bennett stared, swallowed and then stared some more. The two men were naked except for leather jockstraps. Their well-toned muscles gleamed with oil as they stretched sinuously in their sleep. Bennett, for the first time in many years, found himself lost for words. It had to be some form of elaborate put-on for his benefit, Madam Sin courting the outrage of the press to help promote her club through controversy. Two could play at that game.

'An interesting breed. I'm not sure I've come across it before.'

'They're quite magnificent specimens, aren't they?' Sarah's face shone with pride as she continued, 'I've had them since they were children. It's the best way, you know.

You have to dominate them from an early age, make sure they know who's the boss. It's all about being pack leader. That's where so many people go wrong in relationships. Dogs don't understand kindness. They view it as weakness. They're cunning brutes if you let them get away with it. The key is all in the psychology.'

'Really?' Show or not, this was even better than Bennett had hoped for. He pointed to the tape recorder. 'Do you mind?'

'Not at all.' She gave him another piercing look. 'I wouldn't want to be misquoted, would I? Where was I? Ah yes, dog psychology.

'Are you married, Mr Bennett, or perhaps you have a girlfriend?'

'I see women from time to time, yes.'

'And I bet they're always pleased to see you? Greet you as soon as you come through the door with a great big hug and a kiss. All that fuss makes you feel important, doesn't it? Let's you know that you're the one in charge.'

'I suppose so. I've never really thought about it.'

'I don't suppose you have, and neither have the women. Society has taught them to perpetuate a role, ingrained it almost down to a genetic level. They let you have the run of their homes, make decisions for them, and then reward you with affection. All of which only reinforces your dominance.'

'I think that's a bit of an over simplistic view of it, and a trifle harsh.'

'My methods are strict, I don't deny it. But they get results. And my two lads are happy. There's no doubt or confusion in their minds. When I call them their first thought is how they can please me.' Sarah picked up a lighter and a silver cigarette case from the hearth. 'Do you mind if I smoke.'

'No, I'm dying for one myself. Do you have an ashtray?' Sarah indicated to the sideboard behind him and he swivelled round and spotted a leaf shaped ashtray. His fingers shook as he took a cigarette from his pack, lit it and drew the nicotine deep into his lungs. The old bird was frighteningly convincing, enough so that he almost believed her. So matter of fact about the whole business. But it was too absurd to be true. The whirr of the tape caught his attention and he realised it was time to continue the interview. He scrabbled for a leading question, something that would eventually cause her to expose the charade.

'What about your friends, how do they treat your dogs?'

'They either accept my methods or they don't call round. It all comes down to dominance. Those two in the corner don't move because they know when someone enters the room nothing is going to happen. My visitors ignore them because they are here to see me. The dogs are not important. You have to reinforce that at every opportunity. Their natural instinct is to go round everybody in the room until their presence has been acknowledged and they have worked out their place in the pack. Is that not what you do, Mr Bennett, when your girlfriend has visitors?'

'Yeah, I suppose so, but that's just being social. Everyone does it; you introduce people to your partner. It would be rude not to.'

'Perhaps. But if you were to be honest with yourself you would admit that it is more your need to feel important, to be in charge of the room, that drives you. Especially when other females are present. You need to sniff around, check out the legs, hips, lips and tits. Don't you?'

The interview was rapidly spinning out of Bennett's control. He found Sarah's questions insulting and simultaneously arousing. She was making a fool of him and yet he felt powerless to prevent it. In an attempt to rally himself he countered with the time-honoured, 'I'm the one asking the questions here.'

Sarah nonchalantly flicked the ash from her cigarette and ran the tip of her tongue across her lips. 'If you say so, Mr Bennett. I was simply trying to explain my methods. I find it works best if I relate it to the listener's personal experience.'

'Whatever. This prank of yours has gone on long enough. You've made your point. You can tell your friends in the corner to get up. We both know they're not dogs.'

'Reality is a very subjective thing, Mr Bennett. I can assure you that to all intents and purposes that they are dogs in a very real sense.' She snapped her fingers. 'Max, Rutger, come here!'

The two men stood immediately, walked across the room and sat down at the foot of Sarah's chair. She ruffled both men's hair and they stared adoringly at her. 'See? It's all in the training.'

Bennett felt nauseous, felt some deep seated wrongness. It oppressed him with a sensation akin to drowning. Years of journalistic instinct screamed at him that this was no act, while his rational mind tried desperately to back away.

'But why? Why in God's name would you want to do that to another human being?'

'Why not? They are fed, cared for and loved, but all on my terms. Look at them, simply being in my company makes them happy. What is so immoral about that? It's all a question of perception. Dogs need a firm hand. Deep down they don't actually want to lead. They are happiest when you treat them firmly.'

'I'm sorry. I just can't see that.'

'That's because you don't know any better. Give yourself over to me and I will teach you to be happier than you ever thought possible.'

'Don't delude yourself. You could never break me like that.'

'No?' For the first time Sarah smiled with real warmth. 'We'll see. If you're right, then you'll go away with the story to end all stories about crazy Madam Sin. If you're wrong… Well, you might just never leave. Unless you're scared, of course?'

'Of you? I don't think so,' Bennett blustered. His denial of his fear made him rash and he exclaimed, 'Let's do it!'

'Such impatience. I see I'm going to have my work cut out with you. That's the problem with an older dog. There's so much will to overcome. So many bad habits to break. But break you I will.'

Sarah led Max and Rutger out to the garden and locked them in their kennel. When she returned she had a rope leash in her hand fashioned in a running noose. She looped it over his head and said, 'Strip.'

'Now wait a minute…'

Sarah gave the leash a quick, sharp tug and the rope contracted painfully about Bennett's throat. 'There's no point doing this unless you're prepared to co-operate with my methods.' She gave the leash another gentle tug. 'So take off your clothes and kneel on the table. I need to examine you.'

Bennett grudgingly took off his shoes, shirt and trousers. He looked hopefully at Sarah but she indicated that he was also to remove his pants and socks. Once he was in position Sarah walked around the table in a slow circle. She prodded the hanging bulge of his stomach. 'You're a bit on the plump side, aren't you? Too many treats and not enough exercise, but we can sort that out.' Next, she ran her fingers through his thinning hair. Flakes of dandruff fell to the table. 'Coat's a bit scruffy, too. Been spending a bit too much time indoors, I think.'

Bennett flushed with a mixture of rage and embarrassment. 'If you've quite finished humiliating me, then I'd like to get down.'

Sarah gave the leash another swift tug. 'You'll get down when I say so and not before. Do you understand?' Bennett nodded frantically as he clawed at the rope. 'Good. I've still to complete my examination.' She ran her hands up and down the muscles of his arms and legs and felt the muscles of his neck and shoulders. Bennett, despite his predicament, became aroused. Sarah saw his erection and glared at him. 'Put that thing away, now!'

'I can't help it,' Bennett pleaded.

Sarah gestured meaningfully with the leash. 'I suggest you jolly well try and help it. That's not acceptable behaviour. If you can't control yourself I'm afraid I shall have to have you neutered, and that makes for a fat, lazy dog, which I'm not fond of.'

Bennett stared at her, unsure if she was serious or not. For the first time he wondered what he had let himself in for, the glow of the lunchtime alcohol having dissipated. He had assumed it was all going to be a bit of playacting, an insight into the stage show. Now, naked and with a rope burn around his throat, he wouldn't put it past the crazy bitch to cut his balls off. Probably best to go along with her until he saw an opportunity to escape.

Sarah pointed to the floor and said, 'Off.' Bennett climbed down from the table and looked at her. 'Sit.' He hunkered down on his haunches. 'Good boy. I think that's enough for your first day. Time to bed you down in your kennel.'

The thought of being left naked outdoors proved too much for Bennett. 'Now wait one minute!' he exploded. 'This game has gone on long enough. I'm not staying in no bloody kennel. I've got deadlines to meet and my girlfriend is expecting me home tonight.'

'I'm afraid your deadlines are going to have to wait. You should have thought about that before you entered into our arrangement. As for your mistress, I'm sure she'll be more than happy to wait for you a few days, especially when she sees what a well behaved dog you are afterwards.'

'Jesus, woman, are you out of your mind? This is kidnapping. You can't keep me here against my will. If you don't let me go I'll… I'll make sure you end up back inside being fisted by all the bull dykes!'

'For goodness sake, don't be such a drama queen. Remember you agreed to this. Surely you're not backing out already? I thought you had more integrity than that. Of course if you don't want the story…'

Bennett searched her face for some telltale sign that

would inform him of how far she would go. Whatever twisted desire she had to be avenged on the press she had to know she couldn't get away with harming him. Didn't she?

'All right, I'll go along with it for now. But just so you know, there are limits.'

'There are no limits. That's the whole point.' The wicked gleam in her eye sent a chill through Bennett's bones. He only hoped the story would be worth it in the end.

The kennel was a wooden shed with a concrete floor, surrounded by a large chicken-wire mesh run though which Bennett and Sarah entered by means of a slatted gate. Max and Rutger lay curled up together on a pile of cushions. Rutger opened one eye and stared disinterestedly at his new companion for a few moments before going back to sleep.

'I'm afraid you've just missed the evening feed so you'll have to wait 'til morning. Not,' she added with a glance at his belly, 'that it will do you any harm.'

'That's it? You're just going to leave me here until morning? What if I need the bathroom?'

'There's a bucket in the corner. I take it you're house trained?'

Bennett stared at her incredulously, 'You expect me to shit in a bucket?'

Sarah shrugged. 'That's up to you, but it's going to get very unpleasant in here quite quickly if you do it anywhere else. Goodnight.'

Bennett sat hunched in the corner for long minutes after Sarah left. The sun had started to set, the temperature dropping in accord. Lying naked on a concrete floor, chances were he would die of exposure before morning, but he would be damned before he curled up like some dog with Sarah's pair of freaks. Better a night of cold discomfort than giving himself over to whatever depravity Max and Rutger had in store for him.

His resolve lasted until the early hours of the morning when, shivering with cold, he made his way over to the cushions and curled up below the two men. Max sensed his presence and wrapped an arm about his shoulder to draw him closer. Bennett tensed at the touch but the warmth was so comforting it overcame his fear and he finally drifted off into a fitful sleep.

'That's what I like to see, my pack bonding together.'

Rutger and Max woke instantly at the sound of Sarah's voice and moved swiftly to her side. Bennett, still half-groggy with sleep, only vaguely aware of what was going on, felt the rope tighten about his neck. Sarah gave the leash a gentle pull and he staggered to his feet. 'Time for walkies!'

Afterwards, Bennett was only able to recall the vaguest details of the trek through the surrounding woodland. For more than an hour, Sarah forced him to walk at her side. Branches whipped his naked flesh while sharp stones and thorns tore at the soft soles of his feet until each step sent a wave of pain through his body. Sarah seemed oblivious to the growling protest of his stomach or the yelps of pain that occasionally escaped from between his clenched teeth. As long as he walked behind she was content to ignore him. Only once did Bennett make the mistake of trying to take the lead at a narrow point in the path. Sarah let the leash go slack and allowed him to walk a few paces forward before violently hauling the noose tight. Bennett thought his head was going to come off as the rope constricted around his throat. The noose slackened by itself as she walked on, forcing him to scrabble quickly after for fear of being throttled.

Feeding time further served to remind Bennett that he was now number four in the pack. Breakfast was chunks of cold steak in thick gravy, served in large bowls on the kitchen floor. The cold, hunger and nakedness had so dispirited Bennett that he did not hesitate in making for the nearest bowl. Max and Rutger stepped in front of him and bared their teeth. Ludicrous as the display was, Bennett felt too tired and sore to argue. He waited until they had eaten before starting on his food. The gravy ran down his chin and dripped through his fingers as he shovelled the overcooked pieces of meat into his mouth and swallowed them almost whole. Bennett thought it one of the best meals he had ever eaten and felt a sudden surge of gratitude towards Sarah for feeding him. Then he caught sight of her watching with a satisfied smirk and realised how close she had come to breaking him in less than a day. He pushed the bowl angrily aside and stood up.

'You sick, twisted bitch! You're enjoying this, aren't you?' he said, ripping the rope from his neck. 'You want discipline? I'll give you discipline.'

Bennett waved the leash threateningly and suddenly Rutger and Max were standing between him and Sarah. 'I ought to warn you, Mr Bennett, that they are very protective of me. So I wouldn't do anything rash if I were you.'

Rutger gripped him by the throat and growled to reinforce his mistress's threat. Bennett did something then he hadn't done since he was a toddler; he felt the warm trickle of urine run down his leg and pool about his feet. Rutger sniffed distastefully and hurriedly moved away from the rapidly expanding pool.

'You dirty dog!' Sarah moved quickly, catching Bennett off guard. She grabbed him by the scruff of the neck and ushered him to the kitchen door. 'Out you filthy beast, get out!'

The door slammed behind him and Bennett found himself lying on his hands and knees on the gravel of the drive. A few metres away from where he crouched, he saw the familiar outline of his car. He glanced over his shoulder at the kitchen door and then ran for the car. The driver's door was open and he climbed inside. Keys? Where were the bloody keys? An image formed in Bennett's mind and his heart sank. The keys were in his trousers inside the house. He looked through the windscreen but saw no sign of Sarah or her freakish companions. His freedom couldn't last much longer. He needed to make a decision and he needed to make it fast. His eyes flitted frantically round the inside of the car and alighted on his old pair of trainers on the back seat. Time to make a run for it.

Adrenaline dulled the worst of the pain as Bennett sprinted down the drive and out through the gates onto the road. Blood pounded in his ears and each breath burned in his lungs as he forced himself onwards, desperate to put as much distance between him and any pursuit. Twice he staggered and fell to the road, ripping the skin from his palms, but the pain only made him run harder. Panic held him so firmly in its grasp that he never heard the rattle and thrum of the truck. A sudden impact, the sound of splintering bone (his bone, he thought distantly) and a sickening moment of weightlessness. Then darkness.

The pickup truck screeched to a halt and the old farmer looked at his wife and said, 'Stay here while I go and see what we hit.' He stepped from the truck and walked a hundred paces back down the road to where Bennett's shattered body lay in a ditch.

'What is it, George?'

'Nothing too much to worry about. Looks like we hit one of Lady Sarah's dogs. Guess we better go up to the house and tell her.'

SALVATION

Stillness lies over the world. The cars and trains have stopped running, planes no longer fly and the ships do not sail. Clocks have ceased their second by second measuring of life and the idle chatter of merchants and patrons has ended. The tall spires of the deserted churches and the imploring fingers of the crumbling high-rise tower blocks reach towards the heavens in mute accusation. A thousand broken windows stare back at me like so many empty souls. I am utterly alone in the still twilight. One last act remains before I consider my work perfected. A final whimper at the end of all things. I raise the gun to my head and my finger tightens on the trigger.

It began with a murder, my thoughts long bent towards revenge. Sometimes slow. Sometimes quick. Always satisfying. On that occasion, as on so many others, the man's breath stank of stale beer and fried food. He pushed me face down onto the dirty mattress as his fingers clawed at my belt. My trousers were pulled to my ankles and I heard him unzip his flies. I knew what was to follow, as it had followed so many times before. I vowed on each occasion that it would be the last time that he used me in this way. Ripped and torn to satisfy the twisted desire of the monster

I had once thought my friend. Harker systematically abused me, like a receptacle for all that was filthy and unclean in his head. Four long years I suffered this extracurricular activity with my personal tutor in my private hell.

It started innocently enough with my mother hiring a retired teacher to coach me after school. Mother, always so obsessed with the good of the family name and the perfection of her children; how was she to know she'd given me into the hands of a sick pervert? One who cunningly drew me in, asking what I thought of girls, knew of sex, offering to educate me. It started with an examination of what was to become the instrument of torture. First a touch and a stroke, then mutual masturbation. I knew it was wrong and when he wanted to go further I refused and threatened to tell. Harker laughed, told me I was a filthy little beast, that no one would take my word over his, and that my family would disown me for telling such lies. Such humiliation could be avoided by doing as he asked. My sense of shame as much as Harker's threat kept me silent, made me complicit in my own abuse. Would you have known any better when you were ten?

I was powerless to stop these advances at first, but as I grew older and stronger my hate grew accordingly until I was able to take my revenge. And how I took it!

My teeth sank deep into the flesh of his forearm as I twisted in his grasp. Hot blood trickled down my throat as I spat out gobbets of flesh. Blows rained about my face and my body unheeded, numbed by adrenaline's rush. Harker's throat was soft beneath my fingers as I tightened the noose of my grip. His eyes bulged and foam flecked his fat lips as tongue protruded from mouth in a gurgling cry. That horrible rattle of life's final breath possessed music of its own, made me squeeze all the harder while his face turned first purple then blue, swollen and grotesque. A shudder as he shot his final load, warm and sticky on the flesh of my belly. I felt my stomach heave and hot bile spattered across Harker's body, his fingers entwined in the filthy sheets. It was then I realised I had concentrated on my revenge for so long that I had never seen beyond this moment, considered how to hide my crime.

I found a paraffin stove in the corner of his dank bed-sit and emptied its contents over the body and bedding before pilling a stack of old newspapers about the stove. The fire destroyed not only the room but also a good portion of the tenement. Though there were suspicions in the beginning, the inquest finally recorded a verdict of accidental death. I lived for many months with the fear that some chance clue would reopen the investigation and expose me as a killer. But as the months slipped by and my fifteenth birthday came and went I grew increasingly confident. Harker's face and whispering voice, which had haunted my dreams for so many years, finally receded and I began to look to the future, to reclaiming the life he had stolen from me. It would take time, though, and learning. As Harker had so aptly demonstrated in his twisted manner, a man was little in this world without education, which served often as a mask for crime and perversion.

Fate, however, seemed determined to keep me in firmly in my place. My father lost his job with the civil service and had to take a lower paid position as a bank clerk. The family felt this drop in income almost immediately. Enough that my mother began work part-time to provide some luxuries for my brother and myself.

Peter was always the favourite and, although it was not his fault, I hated him for this. He being the better student, it was tacitly understood that I would leave school and get a job to contribute towards his education. It occurred to me then that if I wanted to continue my own learning I would have to trim the fat. It should be understood that I didn't bear him any real hostility. Peter was simply the victim of circumstance. Inherently soft, I doubt he would ever have amounted to much. Others would always have put themselves before his ambition. When looked at logically, killing him was a kindness, sparing him from a life sure to be full of disappointment. I know this must seem harsh and extreme, but after long weeks of deliberation and examination of the family finances, the basic mathematics of the situation remained inescapable — one of us had to go and I had lived through too much for it to be me.

Peter was an early riser and always first in the bathroom, which provided me with an opportunity. One evening, after everyone had gone to bed, I removed the earth bonding from the shower and loosened the live feed. Taking no chances with his electrocution, I replaced the fuse wire with a steel pin, swapping it back during the ensuing panic and confusion. I swear the body smelt like burnt pork as the medics carried it out on a covered stretcher. Burnt meat and singed hair. Roasting human flesh is an odour that once experienced is never forgotten. It made his murder more real in a manner I hadn't anticipated. Believing, as I did, that I'd feel no more guilt for his death than I had over Harker. But Harker had been a twisted piece of scum that had no right to life. His death left the world a better place while Peter's left a raw wound that never healed entirely. An act that brought me closer to Harker than I cared to consider. Enough that I swear I heard his perverted laughter as the ambulance drove away and thought I saw his face peering back at me from the glass.

My parents became grossly overprotective of their last surviving son and naturally expected of me that I should go on to great things. For my part, I threw myself into my studies with a single-minded determination. As much to honour Peter as to drown out the whispering voices in my head that attacked me when my thoughts were idle. Regardless of the motivation, this work ethic soon pushed me into the top ten of any class I attended. I also began to excel in other areas outside of school such as electrical, mechanical and civil engineering. When you have a clear understanding of how the world around you is put together it becomes increasingly easy to arrange for "accidents" to happen, although it was some years before I found it once again necessary improve my circumstances by means of a carefully timed death in the family, but I'm getting ahead of myself.

Theology and biology occupied my thoughts in tandem during my final year at school. Could the life force of a living being be detected by dissection? Was the great secret of life really contained in the double helix? Where did spirit dwell within the biological idiom? I could not fathom it, so felt compelled to delve deeper and deeper, driving myself as though chased by the very Devil himself. As much I learned, there always seemed more to discover. Spending so much time on my studies made it impossible to hold down even a part time job. The government was cutting grants and my debts began to mount at an alarming rate. The time had come once more for tough, affirmative action. Time to hasten my parents along. There was not a lot to choose between them — the insurance was more than adequate on either one, and I was confident that I would be able to wheedle whatever I required from the survivor. The real problem was that while one accident may have been considered unfortunate and a second an unlucky coincidence, three would have been suspicious, which is why I decided the next accident would have to be the last. The way I saw it, whoever I chose, the other would have pined away, so I killed them both together — an act of kindness. They had lived a reasonably full life, more than many. When I asked if they had suffered the ashen-faced police officer told me it would have been almost instant. The car having piled into the side of a petrol tanker when the brakes locked during a fatal skid. So little of the bodies were recovered that it was barely worth cremating them again. But is it not written that you should honour thy mother and father? The tears I cried were real — I wasn't some monster, cold and devoid of compassion. If father had only retained his job and been able to contribute to my upkeep, or mother had worked a little harder, their deaths might have been avoided. As it was, given how hard they pushed me in my studies, I'm sure it would have been a comfort to them to know their life assurance was contributing to that all-important education.

I graduated a year later with a doctorate in molecular biology. Extracts from my thesis were published in all the major journals and I enjoyed a period of minor celebrity as the new wonder-child of my field. My star was in the ascendancy and I was determined that I should benefit from my years of monastic study. I lived a life of luxury in those few hours when I was not working. Fine wine, food and beautiful women, I sampled them all and then carelessly threw them aside. Money, as has been asserted elsewhere, is power; it is also an aphrodisiac, as I quickly came to realise by the amount of hangers-on I started to attract. The women amused me at first with their flirtations and vacuous conversation, but none of them offered any real companionship and I quickly discovered there were more immediate ways of gratifying my sexual urges. And if I had other desires, what of it? No one cares about a beaten up whore except her pimp who sees in her bruises and cuts a loss of earnings, and that could always be compensated for. Yes, I was on the gravy train and the drive of my ambition began to slacken. What had seemed urgent in youth could now wait a few more months or even years. I was working to nobody's timetable but my own. I suppose it was inevitable this should happen — that the good times weakened my initial resolve. But something was always lacking. I never knew complete fulfilment, whether from sex, drugs or the accolades of my peers, there was always an underlying sense of failure. It seemed to me as I looked in the mirror, my reflection growing fat and grey, that day by day I was starting to look more and more like Harker. In word and action we became almost inseparable, with our lies, promises and threats. Sometimes, when I spoke to my crying, screaming victims, I heard the phrases, no the very words, Harker had once said to me. Until, at last, I knew I would have no peace until I got back to the job in hand.

The one I had sworn myself to all those years before in Harker's grubby bedsit.

Even with the knowledge I had accumulated it took many years to succeed in my aim. The virus had to be airborne, highly communicable, one hundred percent fatal and relatively painless. It also required a further weeding out of the field. That said, I never killed indiscriminately, even when provoked by the ill-informed opinions of my colleagues, and I always tried to make it as clean as possible. But occasionally the need for promotion forced my hand and a rival or a superior suffered some act of ill fortune. The police, contrary to what most of us would like to believe, are not stupid. They can spot a pattern, particularly when linked to someone in the public eye, which is why I ceased to harm those that stood in my way by direct means. One suffered a breakdown after the death of his wife; the victim of an apparently random hit and run. Another took an indefinite leave of absence after her son died from an overdose. Nothing too tangible, more a case of cause and effect that worked in my favour; realised over months, sometimes even years. At times it tried my patience to the limit, especially when I knew one well timed push during rush hour would solve my problem with clinical precision, but I had to avoid all suspicion.

During this time the by-product of my research spilled over into many fields — genetics, stem cell research, organ cloning. I helped save thousands of lives and eased the suffering countless others, made the world a better place, though I never felt satisfied with the limit of my progress. My renown grew until the public came to view me as part genius, part saint. If only they had known the real purpose of my research! But I was always careful to hide my true face in public. My mask could not be allowed to slip, not until everything was ready.

Then came the day I perfected the virus. Only one thing prevented immediate action — the desire to witness what I unleashed. It took another ten years to create a vaccine, but it was worth every second of that time and besides, selfish as it was, I was not yet ready to give up all I had worked for. I felt entitled to enjoy a little more of life's pleasures.

It started slowly, spreading through the city like ripples in a pond. Panic set in as the hospitals filled and one by one the doctors and the nurses fell beside their patients. Cars and trains transmitted the plague across the land, while air passengers carried my doom over the seas and oceans to other continents. Rioting and looting were widespread as civilisation collapsed across the globe in a matter of weeks. The satellites went down and the news channels stopped broadcasting. Deep within their bunkers the men of power sat and cowered as they waited for the Horsemen of the Apocalypse.

The annihilation of the human race was only a matter of time. Four weeks, six days, twelve hours, twenty-three minutes and seventeen seconds, according to the computer model I'd created to track the spread of the virus. Mankind had less than five weeks to live from the moment I removed the stopper from the vial in that crowded shopping centre. Air travel was banned within a week, but by then it was too late. By day twelve the police, the military and the government had effectively ceased to exist. The final television broadcast came after two weeks, leaving dead air in its wake.

On the thirty-forth day I walked through the gutted remains of a city thick with the stench of decay. The carrion birds had gathered to feast upon the uncollected corpses of the fallen. They eyed me warily as I stalked the charnel streets, a lone figure in a dead land. A sense of relief filled my being as I looked on the bodies, burnt out cars and broken glass. This was what I was born for. This was what I had worked so long for, an end to human misery and suffering. No more paedophiles preying on children. No more abusive spouses beating their partners. No more crooked politicians fleecing the public. No more wars fought for oil and greed. No more greenhouse gases frying the planet. I had put an end to pain and starvation and injustice. But the voice, Harker's mocking voice, refused to be silent. He seemed to gloat louder than ever now that we were alone. Telling me how alike we had grown over the years, that I was his son and heir. Lies of course. A further distortion of the truth. But that was okay. I knew how to shut him up for good: the gun to my head, my finger on the trigger.

DEATH AND TAXES

Campbell lifted the glass and took a sip of the ice-cold champagne. A snap of his fingers lowered the lights, while a spoken command kindled the music centre to life; LED's pulsing sequentially across the fascia as the first strains of music filled the room. It had been a good year, one worth celebrating. Profits were up. The company had increased its market share and looked set to expand and diversify. Even without his creative accountancy, they were showing healthy margins, both in manufacture and on site. The problem being that it was never enough for a man of Campbell's tastes. While the proles worried about keeping up with the Jones, he was careful to ensure he kept ahead of them. But luxury, like all vices, took money to feed, and the more he fed his habit the more it grew, out stepping the bounds of his director's salary and his conscience. Not that he considered himself a thief, being of the opinion that for a crime to be committed there must be a victim. If the taxman was not receiving his share entirely up front then he was making it back through a score of stealth taxes.

A sharp rap on the door jarred Campbell from his enjoyment of the moment. He wondered as he crossed the room how his unannounced visitor had bypassed the penthouse's security. Wilson, he thought bitterly, was probably asleep on the job. If so, it was for the last time. Only last week he had been interrupted by some grotty little urchin door canvassing. It really was too much.

The man on the opposite side of the door did not look like a salesman. Tall and thin, he wore a grey suit with a grey overcoat that matched his grey hair and grey complexion. His heavy lidded eyes flitted from Campbell to the room behind before coming to rest upon Campbell once more. 'In future, sir, you might want to consider using your door chain. Can't be too careful in this day and age — you get all sorts round these parts.'

'I'm sure you do. Mr?'

'Murray,' the grey man intoned, producing a CID warrant card from his pocket. 'Detective Inspector Murray.'

Campbell felt the blood drain from his face. The urge to confess rose up from the pit of his stomach only to be ruthlessly strangled by a reflex reaction of the brain. He had not got where he was today by caving in at the slightest sign of trouble. There was any number of explanations as to why a CID officer should choose to call upon him. He stepped aside and waved Murray inside with a saccharine smile.

Murray continued his frank appraisal of the room while Campbell buzzed nervously round him, offering to take his coat, asking him to sit, and enquiring if he wanted a drink and a cigar. The CID officer refused them all with an impassive shake of the head, his eyes expressionless slits.

'Fifty inch plasma screen — now that's nice. Bet that set you back a pretty penny. I've always fancied one myself, but you know how it is on a policeman's salary.'

Campbell's reaction was to say, 'Take it, it's yours,' but the same reflex caught the first treacherous movement of his tongue and he said, 'Just a boy's toy, really, the benefits of the bachelor lifestyle. One of these days I really must find a wife.'

'Ah, yes. It is a truth universally acknowledged…'

'I beg your pardon?'

'Jane Austin — Pride And Prejudice — a single man in possession of a good fortune must be in want of a wife.' Noting Campbell's expression the Inspector said, 'Not much of a reader then, sir?'

'Only of the financial section. Some, no doubt, would say there's fiction enough contained in there.'

'Would they indeed? Now that is interesting.'

Campbell bit his lip and cursed silently for broaching the very subject he had been trying to avoid. He shuffled nervously over to the crystal decanter on the sideboard and poured a large whisky. His hand caressed the soda siphon and then he thought better of it. He needed all the help he could get.

'Are you sure you don't want a drink?'

'Not while I'm on duty, sir.'

'Duty.' Campbell mulled the word over in much the same manner as he had the malt. 'Perhaps you'd be so kind as to enlighten me as to the nature of your business? I assume you're not here to discuss an overdue speeding ticket?'

'No, sir. I am here on behalf of the Inland Revenue. It would appear that there are some irregularities concerning your tax returns for the period between 1998 and 2004.'

Campbell felt as though he were falling. A ringing noise sounded in his ears and his body temperature seemed to drop by several degrees. His voice little more than a squeak, he repeated, 'Irregularities? I can't imagine why, and I'm afraid I can't help you either. I leave all that to my accountant. Perhaps you should speak with him, Inspector?'

Murray permitted himself a faint smile. 'I already have and it was a most interesting conversation. Most interesting.'

Campbell took another gulp of whisky and spluttered as it caught in his throat. 'How so?'

'They say it's a thin line between tax avoidance and tax evasion, but you, Mr Campbell, appeared to have crossed it to the tune of some one point two million, give or take a couple of thousand. A man could buy a lot of plasma screens with that kind of money.' Murray's eyes flitted around the room. 'And more besides.'

'But, but,' Campbell stammered, 'I'm innocent. Don't you see? My accountant must be trying to frame me.'

'Now why would he do a thing like that, sir? By all accounts, if you'll pardon the pun, he's done rather well out of his association with you. Four bedroom semi in Cheltenham, villa in Spain, and an Aston Martin in the driveway. Mr Penfold has no reason to rock the boat, as it were. Of course, he has no desire to go to prison either, which is probably why he squealed like a little piggy as soon as my colleagues starting interviewing him.' All trace of friendliness had vanished from the Inspector's voice. 'Had quite a lot to say about you, Mr Campbell.'

Campbell dropped into a heavily padded leather armchair. 'Of all the ungrateful bastards, I ought to wring the little runt's neck for him!'

'I think you'll find you're in enough trouble as it is without adding a murder to the proceedings.'

'I was speaking figuratively,' Campbell tried to reassure the Inspector.

'If you say so, sir, but from where I'm stood at the minute you're a man with little to lose. Her Majesty's government takes a very dim few of such matters. Chances are you'd do less time for fiddling with a few kiddies — judges are always looking to understand that sort of thing. Greed needs no explanation.'

'You're arresting me?'

Murray nodded. 'Michael Paul Campbell, I am arresting you on suspicion of tax evasion. You do not have to say anything…'

The breath whooshed out of Murray as Campbell jabbed him in the stomach with his elbow before clambering over the armchair. He stood at bay for a second and then darted towards the bedroom. Murray took an uncertain step forward and then pitched onto the armchair. By the time he recovered Campbell had locked himself in the bedroom.

Campbell's chest felt tight and a cold sweat had broken out on his forehead. This whole business had to be some ghastly mistake. He couldn't possibly go to prison — he had a lunch reservation at the Ritz for Christ's sake! But the Inspector hammering at the door was all too real, as was the prospect of being the bitch of some fat, unwashed, hairy-knuckled psychopath. Indulging in a spot of mutual masturbation with a bit of rough down King's Cross was one thing, forced anal intercourse quite another. Prison was unthinkable. The deprivations would kill him as surely as a noose around his neck. Better to end it here and now, cleanly and quickly.

Campbell's hands shook so much it took him three attempts to open the gun cabinet. He selected a Purdey side by side, broke the gun and loaded it. Murray's imprecations became more forceful and strident: Campbell could hide but he couldn't run.

Campbell snapped the shotgun closed and laid it on the bed before pulling off his right shoe and sock. An irritated tick twitched at the side of his mouth when he noticed the smear of gun oil on the cream coloured sheet, then he realised it no longer mattered. He sat on the edge of the bed, placed his big toe through the trigger guard and jammed both barrels under his chin. At the next knock on the door he pressed down with his foot. Blood and brain matter rained down like confetti.

Murray's fist paused in mid knock and the colour drained from his face. His voice soft and uncertain, he called out. 'Mr Campbell? Michael? Jeremy Banks, Network Nine. You've been had...'

CHARLIE SAYS

friend introduced me to Charlie at a party. One of those chance meetings that seems unimportant at the time but goes on to change your life — usually not for the better. Charlie was smart, witty and intelligent. The life and soul of the party. She had the kind of charisma that drew you in and held you tight. Anything was possible when you were with Charlie. I can't explain it. Something about her took you over completely. She made you happy, made you feel powerful, made you a little crazy in the head. Only afterwards, in the cold light of day did you look back and wonder what you'd been thinking, wonder where all the hours and all the money had gone. Promised yourself that this would be the last time (until the next time).

After that first meeting I started bumping into Charlie more and more frequently. At first it was only at the weekend, down the clubs, usually on a Friday. Then, as Charlie's influence grew, it became Friday and Saturday, sometimes Sunday too. The more time we spent together the more I wanted to go out. Soon I was hitting the pubs as well, two or three times through the week, and wherever I went Charlie went too. She was my party bitch, a match made in heaven. I wondered how we had escaped one another's attention for so long. We liked the same music, the same bars and clubs and, in the beginning, shared the same friends. With so much in common you would have thought that we'd have become soul mates long before we did. I guess it's one of life's little mysteries.

Dianne, my partner, didn't like Charlie, which I guess was understandable, Charlie being everything she wasn't. I'm sure she felt threatened but Charlie was only a friend. At least that's how things were in the beginning. But like I said, Charlie had a habit of taking over. I wanted Dianne and Charlie to get along. Actually, like most men, I wanted Dianne and Charlie period. For a while I got my wish and it was great. But something had to give and in the end that something was Dianne. She didn't say a word, didn't even leave a note. I got home one day, or should I say one morning after a night out, and she was gone. Not just her but her clothes and half of my record collection as well. To be fair to her, I think Charlie had something to do with that. Records, books and comics had been disappearing from my collections for some time. I didn't really notice. I was too busy having a good time. Sweat running down my back, t-shirt clinging to my flesh, reaching for the lasers, night after night after night. The crowd was alive, a pulsing sentient being that responded to every nuance of the DJ's art. He was the puppet master and we were marionettes, dancing to a different beat. If you've ever been clubbing you'll know exactly what I mean.

Dianne wasn't the only one who had a problem with Charlie. A number of my friends told me to stay away from them when I was with her. It has to be said that she tended to accentuate my less desirable character traits. Agro was never far away when Charlie was about. One minute I'd be enjoying a quiet drink and next everything would start kicking off. An off the cuff remark would be taken to heart and the fists would fly. At least I think that's what happened in most cases, by then I was normally well pissed, which helped 'cause I was relaxed when I hit the ground. But hey, it's all character forming, right?

I drifted away from my old of friends. They were lightweights, not like the people Charlie introduced me to. They were for real. Admittedly a few of them were on the shady side, petty crims and hustlers regardless of gender. But they all loved Charlie and, more importantly, they knew how to party. Relationships were free and easy in Charlie's circle. Alliances and partnerships came and went, some lasting only as long as a night of fucking, while others stretched into weeks. And Charlie? She stood at the centre of our depravity, facilitating our carnal desires and our little wars of ego. No matter how messed up things got no one ever thought to blame her. Charlie was as pure as the driven snow. Charlie was Teflon coated. Blame slid right off her. Just one of her many talents.

The non-stop partying inevitably affected my work. I started turning up late and making silly mistakes. The product of fatigue and the fact I simply couldn't be arsed any more. My line manager hauled me up and asked me what was going on. He couldn't understand the drop in my performance, wondered what was going down in my personal life. I fed him a line about taking my break up with Dianne hard. Told him I was going through a slump, but that I'd pick myself up soon. He looked at my latest set of bruises and shook his head before telling me that the next time I screwed up he would have no choice but to issue a formal written warning. I thanked him for his concern and then got straight on the phone to Charlie and organised a night out. I was rattled. The mortgage payments were already crippling me and if I lost my job the bank would be sure to foreclose on the loan. I needed Charlie to help me think straight. She always came up with a solution.

The answer was simple, for someone who wasn't standing up close to it. So simple I couldn't believe I hadn't thought of it for myself. Some friends of Charlie had a spare room they were willing to let me crash in, so I sold the flat, jacked in my job and took a sabbatical paid for by the equity.

Everybody at work thought I'd gone mad. Dave tried to talk me out of it but I'd made up my mind. Naturally I had some doubts, but Charlie soon talked me round. Pointing out that the flat had too many memories of Dianne to be good for me. That work was cutting into my socialising. An intelligent bloke like me could get another job anytime he wanted. A better one. My boss had never appreciated me or given me the credit I deserved, the same as Dianne and the rest of my family and friends. None of them knew or understood the real me. They were jealous because they lacked the balls to follow their dreams. But not me. I was through with being a wage slave. Done with sucking corporate dick and tugging my forelock to a bunch of middle class wankers. I was going to write film scripts; gritty docu-dramas that were going to lift the lid off the club scene. I was going to be famous.

But first I had to do my research. If I wanted to write an exposé on the club scene I would have to immerse myself in it totally. I had to hit rock bottom. That's what Charlie told me and I knew she was right. Life experience is invaluable to a writer; it's what gives his or her work value. The public may be fickle but they aren't stupid, well not all of them. They can spot a fake a mile off. What I needed was authenticity. I wanted my work to exude reality, and not the pretty kind. They say you should be careful what you wish for, and they, whoever they are, are right.

Seventeen thousand pounds seems like a lot of money when it's sitting in the bank, particularly when your rent consists of little more than chipping in for bills and doing the odd favour for your flatmates. It should have lasted me a year, but somehow I got through it in less than two months and had to sign on. After food there was barely enough left over from my government pittance to buy in a bevy at the weekend. It certainly didn't cover going out, not in the manner I'd become used to, and it wasn't enough to keep up with Charlie. Not that it stopped me trying.

At first my new friends were happy to lend me money

to go out or to stand me a ticket and a few drinks, but they became increasingly hostile when it became clear that I had little or no intention of paying them back. Getting a new job was the obvious answer and I even interviewed for a couple. But people get the wrong idea about you when you don't have money for a haircut or a razor. The other problem I had was being behind with the rent, which meant I spent more and more time running errands by way of paying my debts. It became something of a full-time occupation. Not that I minded, because I usually ran into Charlie on my rounds.

It's funny how you can love and hate someone at the same time. The more time I spent with Charlie the more I felt she was taking a loan of me and yet I wanted to see her even more. A blind man could've seen that she was using me but I felt powerless to walk away. After each encounter I vowed that we were through, that I was going to move on, only to find myself in search of her before the day was out. Completely insane, but as my world and prospects shrank, she became more and more important to me. Charlie was the only thing that mattered. Charlie took the pain away and made me forget my worries, for a time at least. Charlie held me captive and I hadn't enough self-respect left to care. As long as I had Charlie I was happy.

Every obsession runs its natural course or else external events intrude. I moved out of the flat and started sleeping rough. Mainly because I owed Charlie's friends too much money to stay, but it also made it more difficult for my other creditors to keep track of me. I was into some heavy people for serious money by then. How heavy I didn't realise until they sent a couple of the boys round one evening. A pair of West Coast nutters who had done a long stretch in the Bar-L for a spot of grievous, during which, far from being rehabilitated, they had honed their skills. They broke four of my fingers with a hammer and told me my bollocks were next if I didn't pay what I owed within the week. I may not have been getting much use out of my bollocks but I didn't want to part company with them either. But if my association with Charlie's friends had taught me anything it was if you couldn't earn or blag it then you steal it.

My crime spree lasted four days and if I hadn't been caught I reckon I would have been close to clearing my debts. I started small with some opportunity thefts, car stereos, iPods, mobiles and purses. It's amazing what the public will leave unattended, if only for a few seconds, which is all you need. I'd made the acquaintance of a fence that worked out of the Barras some months back and he gave me top whack on the stuff. I should have been more cautious, but as soon as I had a bit of cash I couldn't stop myself going in search of Charlie. A couple of bars later and there she was, as beautiful and sweet as ever. I promised myself I'd only stay for a couple but one thing led to another and before I knew it I'd blown most of what I'd made from thieving. Stupid. I should have known better but it was too late by then, the damage done.

Time was running out and purses and electrical goods were small change. I needed to hit something big. I got an evil looking fucker of a knife off Big Jim and decided to do the all-night garage near the motorway, reckoning the day's takings would be more than enough to save my worthless knackers. I would have got away with it too if it hadn't been for some have-a-go hero. The attendant, a spotty student on minimum wage, pissed his pants when he saw my blade. Poor cunt couldn't give me the money quick enough. I was on my way out when some fucker with more muscle than brain tackled me to the ground and twisted my arm up my back until it almost broke. Then the alarm went off and the next thing I knew I was being bundled in the back of a meat-wagon.

A jury of my peers took all of ten minutes to find me unanimously guilty of armed robbery and nineteen other acts of theft. I tried to explain it was all Charlie's fault but they wouldn't have it. I guess none of them had ever been in the grip of an all-consuming passion before. The judge gave me seven years, which I thought a bit excessive for a first offence, but there you go. Prison wasn't so bad once I got used to the absence of Charlie. Looking back, I kind of wonder what all the infatuation was about. The anticipation always greater than the pleasure. Anyway, things aren't so bad. Not since I met Mr Brown.

LEDA

The kick inside made Leda gasp. She placed a hand upon the swollen mound of her belly and uttered comforting sounds to sooth the unborn infant. Her time was close, perhaps as little as two weeks away. Then her daughter would make her squealing entrance into the world and with her birth would come a reckoning.

Leda's husband stirred beside her, turned over and muttered in his sleep. Shame and anger awoke in her heart as she stared at his dark head of hair resting on the pillow beside her. The child she carried belonged to another, a man who had taken her by force. Power, they say, is an aphrodisiac, and perhaps she was not quite as cautious as she might have been, but that did not give him the right. Regardless of wealth, influence and power, no man was entitled to take what he had taken from her. And yet, when confronted, he had contrived to make it her fault, casting her in the twin roles of temptress and whore.

As a senator's wife Leda had grown used to the constant political wrangling and seemingly endless succession of fundraisers. Few arenas were quite as hostile as the cocktail party. Here what you wore, who you spoke to and, most importantly, what you donated were closely monitored, with your political stock rising and falling accordingly. A wife was required to look decorous, to hang upon her husband's arm, upon his every word, as he made the circuit of lobbyists and wealthy oilmen. Leda had played the role many times but that evening the host had attempted to add a twist by making the event a masked ball.

Leda wore a feathered half mask that barely hid her identity; her husband, in his red leather Il Capitano, looked like the very Devil himself in evening dress. But of all those assembled it was the swan who caught her attention. Dazzling white tuxedo topped by a full head mask of soft feathers, there was still no mistaking the President of the United States. His invitation to dance could not be refused and Leda had to concede that there was something absurd and simultaneously alluring about the swan-headed figure.

Up close the smell of bourbon was unmistakeable and the speech that delivered inappropriate endearments slightly slurred. The feet, however, knew their steps, moving with a surefooted grace even as his left hand wandered downwards from the small of her back. Each time she moved the hand it slid slowly, caressingly, back into place. Once she caught her husband's eye but instead of coming to her rescue he offered up a helpless shrug. The waltz continued and so did the slow progress of the clock towards the midnight unmasking.

Drawing close to the president's wife, Leda excused herself before making for the bathroom. The house was unfamiliar and it took one of the serving staff to direct her to the top of the curving double staircase and a white painted door at the end of the upper hallway. There, to the accompaniment of a dripping tap, Leda contemplated her situation. She could not hide in the bathroom for the remainder of the evening without being missed but as soon as she returned the president would doubtless commandeer her again. The thought repulsed and excited her in equal measure, for she could feel the eyes of the crowd following them across the dance floor. The lingering and jealous gazes of the great and the good spoke to her of power. If she failed to exploit this one off opportunity she would likely regret it for the remainder of her days, and it was not as if she did not have her husband's tacit approval.

Stepping out of the bathroom, Leda walked straight into the arms of the president. He took a hold of her arm, squeezing painfully, and steered her towards one of the bedrooms.

'There you are, Leda. I thought you'd left without saying goodbye.'

'Let me go, you're hurting me!'

'I think you like being hurt. It gets you hot, doesn't it? Makes you want me.'

'You're drunk. You don't know what you're doing.'

'Au contraire, my little one. I'm making an executive decision. This is what we both want, only you're too afraid to say it out loud.'

As he forced her onto the bed, a knee between her thighs, Leda made one last attempt to prevent what was coming. 'Please don't do this to me. I swear I won't say a word, not even to Troy.'

The president opened his fly and drew Leda's dress up to her hips. 'I know you won't, darling. Because if you do I'll tell him you led me on and you'll be out on the street.'

Leda lived with her indecision for three days before reporting the rape. The detective listened impassively before cautioning her against giving a false statement. His lips curled into a disdainful sneer when she refused to withdraw her complaint and he told her to sit tight.

Two hours later a Secret Service agent calling himself by the name of Smith entered the interview room. He placed a folder on the table and flipped back the cover to reveal a series of photographs taken on the night of the ball. Leda dancing with the president. Leda drinking a cocktail. Leda smiling and laughing. Flirtatious, giggling, these were images of a woman who enjoyed being the centre of attention, one that in Agent Smith's opinion now sought further attention. Or perhaps, with next year being the end of the president's first term, she simply hoped to sabotage his chances of re-election.

'I don't care about some damned pictures taken in public — he raped me!' Leda protested.

'Then why didn't you go to the hospital and have a rape kit done? Why didn't you report the alleged crime immediately instead of waiting three days?'

'I wasn't thinking straight. I went to the bathroom. I just felt so dirty that I needed to wash away all trace of what he'd done to me.' Leda started to cry. 'I was frightened and didn't know what else to do. But when I got home I realised I had to keep the dress. That's evidence. You can test it, right?'

'Say we do test this dress and let's say, for the sake of argument, that we find the president's DNA on it. That in no way implies rape. It doesn't even confirm that penetration took place, let alone sexual intercourse without consent. You have no bruises. The president, I am assured, has no scratches, bites or other marks indicative of a struggle having taken place. If you were raped you didn't put up much of a fight.'

Leda's voice was a tiny whisper. 'But I said no.'

'Maybe you didn't say it loud enough. Maybe no sometimes means yes. Frankly, it's not my job to judge or care. If I were you I'd do my country and my husband a favour and go home. So far only a handful of people outside of this room know of your infidelity. Do Senator Troy a favour and keep it that way.'

Sickened and disgusted as Leda was, she had to admit defeat. The case would never go to court and while she could damage the president's reputation the harm done to her family would be much greater. Justice was a fickle beast, particularly when the Supreme Court was full of appointees put there by the guilty party.

Faced with this knowledge, Leda tried to put the rape behind her only to discover a few weeks later that she was carrying her attacker's child. An abortion seemed the only option and she even went as far a making the appointment but when the time came she found herself unable to go through with it. The life growing inside her was innocent of the sins of the father. Troy was delighted when he found out she was expecting, their previous attempts at starting a family having failed. His happiness proved infectious and for a time she was able to believe that everything would be all right. Almost but not quite. Deep inside Leda knew her anger was only sleeping.

Leda felt the kick inside and smiled to herself. She laid a gentle hand on her belly and whispered, 'Hush now, Helen. Save your strength, my little one. Yours shall be the face that brings this nation to its knees. You will take their lust and greed, turn it back against them and use it to destroy all that they hold dear.'

CARBON

Wayne had been channel surfing for over an hour, flicking through the seemingly endless succession of cable programmes and advertising. A Zen-like trance descended on him as wave after wave of bland, anodyne sales pitch washed over him. This was the sound of one hand clapping; the noise that issued from the lips of eternally youthful bit actors. Some of their surgeons were so good you could almost detect expression in the stretched, flawless skin. The adverts rolled on.

Here at Carbon Forty-Two Laboratories we offer a unique service for you and your loved ones — a lasting memorial to the deceased full of inherent beauty. After cremation, the ashes of the dearly departed are heated to extract the carbon and then pressed in our laboratories to form a brilliant diamond. Where nature requires millennia, our industrial presses take only months, depending on the size of the stone required.

All the diamonds produced by Carbon Forty-Two are fully authenticated and can be laser etched with a personal inscription along the girth of the diamond. This is a unique memorial that will be treasured by you and your family for generations to come. Our monthly payment plan allows you to take advantage of our services at today's prices, allowing you to plan comfortably for the future!

Further details and prices are available on our website, and don't forget to check out our new service for pets!

Wayne crumpled his beer can and reached for another. A quick reconnaissance of the area surrounding the couch turned up only empties. 'Kathleen, fetch us some more beer, honey.'

Repent all you sinners and step into the light of Jesus!

I know many of you folks out there are probably thinking what would the Lord want with the likes of me? But I am here to tell you that Jesus is willing to accept all of you, so long as you are prepared to listen to the Word!

I know it's hard to imagine looking at me now, but there was a time when the Reverend John Brown was just plain ole Joe Brown. And I was much conflicted, yes sir, I was! I drank hard liquor, I smoked marijuana, and I got myself in trouble with the law! Yes, I was a bad man, a misguided man. I don't mind admitting that to you now. But then the light of Jesus came into my life and I listened to the Word, His Word, and I was saved! Yes, saved from a life of evil. Now that once wretched and pitiable man is a good husband and the devoted father of two beautiful girls, for whom I give thanks to Jesus daily. They are my little angels, for none are so precious as the children — they are our future!

And now I am here to tell you that you too can be saved! But salvation has to start with giving. Only in giving do we free ourselves from greed and possessiveness. Entry into the spiritual realm has to start by freeing yourself from the material, so call now and make a donation on...

What was taking that fat lazy bitch so long? He ought to take off his belt and give her a good whupping. Or maybe he should just throw her worthless ass out on the street. Better still, in the dumpster with the rest of the garbage. 'Didn't you hear me, woman? I need a beer.'

When you buy a used car you want reliability and here at Alamo Motors we aim to make sure you never find yourself in a last stand situation! That's why all our vehicles come with a six month guarantee that covers all parts and labour. That's six months free parts and labour! Subject to terms and conditions. So don't let yourself get bushwhacked — remember the Alamo!

Wayne stabbed his finger down on the standby button. 'Kathleen!' he shouted, 'How many times do I have to ask if we got anymore beer?'

Kathleen threw down her bag of chips and swivelled round from where she'd been watching a portable television set in the kitchen. 'How the hell should I know? I'm busy. Get your ass up off that couch and go look in the icebox yourself.'

'You're in the kitchen, why can't you look?' That damned woman always had some excuse for ignoring him. 'You're closer.'

'God damn it! Do I have to do everything in this house?' Kathleen stormed. 'No, we're out of beers. You'll have to go down to the mall.'

'Can't — I've been drinking.'

'And when's that ever stopped you before? Take the back roads. You can drive real slow. And make sure you take the coupons and get some groceries. Some of us here need to eat — we can't all live on beer and chips.'

'And don't it show,' Wayne muttered under his breath, adding, 'Can't you do the shopping? I hate using coupons — the grocery clerks all look at you like you're some kinda insect. Bunch of pimply-faced no-hopers!'

'You're a fine one to talk, Wayne. If you'd get your lazy

ass off that couch and get a job I wouldn't need to clip coupons!'

'Kathleen, you know that's not fair, honey. I have me a bad back. The doctor said so. You were there, remember?'

'If you didn't have that big jelly-belly straining it, it might get better a damn sight quicker! And don't forget to see the supervisor on your way out. I've already told the fat jerk that he needs to look at the fire. I keep getting those headaches. Tell him I'm gonna sue if he don't fix it soon.'

'Fine. Whatever.'

Wayne kicked his empties aside and grabbed his cut-off denim jacket from the hook by the door. Kathleen appeared as he was pulling the various bolts on the door. She handed him a wad of coupons, which he stuffed into his jeans' pocket before slamming the door behind him. He took the back stairwell down to the ground floor. It stank of stale urine and vomit as usual. Reaching the bottom, he remembered Kathleen's instruction and knocked on the supervisor's door.

'Mr Sipowitz, it's me, Wayne, from three-thirteen.'

There was the sound of mumbling, the jangle of keys and then the door opened to reveal a balding, swarthy-skinned man. 'What d'you want, Wayne?'

Wayne looked apologetic. 'It's Kathleen, Mr Sipowitz. She keeps going on about the fire. Would you look at it? Just to put her mind at rest. You know women, when they get an idea in their head, they just can't shake it. It's not like you can't smell gas, is it?'

'All right, I'll see what I can do. But,' Sipowitz wagged an admonishing finger, 'this is the last time. She ain't happy after this, she can find herself another apartment. Is that clear?'

Wayne put the truck in reverse and backed out of the driveway. The winter sun was already low in sky as he turned onto the freeway and headed towards town, driving with a drunk's exaggerated care. Early Sunday evening, light traffic and no sign of any cops. All the same, he felt safer cutting across country on the old road. Nice and quiet on the back road, just wilderness on either side as far as you could see. A man could be alone with his thoughts here. And Wayne was a man who needed to be alone, his thoughts being of the criminal variety.

Kathleen had to go. He couldn't recall when he first thought about killing her but the idea had been maturing for several months now. When you weighed it all up, there wasn't much he was going to miss. She wasn't much of a cook or a homemaker and the sex had all but dried up. Not that he was interested in her anymore. She'd really left herself go over the last couple of years. He patted is beer gut. Different with men, everyone expected you to spread out a little. Only natural, a sign of prosperous living. But a wife, well surely she had a duty to keep herself looking sweet? A man wanted a woman he could show off to his friends. You didn't ask her to be smart and you certainly didn't want her earning more than you, so the least she could do was keep herself pretty, right? Her welfare cheque was hardly worth the bother and certainly not the aggravation, but her life assurance was fully paid up. Yeah, once he got Kathleen out of the way the good times would come around again. He would get himself some new duds, a new truck and have himself a vacation. With a bit of folding green to spread around he'd have no trouble finding some sweet little thing to see to his needs. What Kathleen didn't seem to realise was that there was always someone younger, prettier and dirtier. The bars were full of hotties looking for a man with a bit of experience. The kind of man that could throw a decent hump into them. Yes siree, once Kathleen was gone there would be plenty of fresh pussy for him to enjoy. All he had to do was make it seem like an accident.

Poisoning? Good for someone with experience but he didn't feel confident enough to risk it. It might show up at an autopsy or someone at the drug store would remember him. He needed something cleaner, something surer. They hadn't been out hunting for a while; accidents happen all the time. Beer and rifles, whatever the NRA might try to tell you, were never a good combination. No, too risky. Somebody might see, or worse, the cops might not believe him. They'd beat a confession out of him and for once they'd be correct. Shooting was good, but he needed something less direct. A burglary could work — make it look as if Kathleen had been shot after disturbing an intruder. He could easily get another gun off somebody from out of town. As long as the cops never found the murder weapon, he'd be in the clear. Wayne slapped his thigh. Boy, he sure was one smart sonuvagun!

Wayne found the apartment empty when he got back from the mall. The fire was on in the living room, creating welcoming warmth after the cold of the stairwell. He shouted for Kathleen and made his way to the kitchen when there was no reply. Kathleen wasn't there either, but there was a note. It said she'd gone round to Carrie's and would be back soon. Yeah, right, he thought. She would be drinking, bitching and gossiping half the night. He had half a mind to go round and drag her home to cook him something decent, like a good wife ought to, but the thought of souring things with Carrie held him in check. Now that woman was a fine piece of ass, even if she was the wrong side of thirty. Her dumb-ass boyfriend had run out on her last year and since then Wayne had gone out of his way to be neighbourly, considering it his Christian duty. The woman was thick as pig shit, mind you, but it wasn't conversation he had in mind. Anyhow, he wouldn't have to listen to her hillbilly gibbering while she was sucking his dick.

The frozen food stared sadly up at Wayne and any last doubt he'd harboured evaporated as he cracked open a fresh beer and shoved the plastic tray in the microwave. He would see about getting a gun next week and then it would be goodnight Kathleen. No more than the bitch deserved!

'That's a beautiful ring, if you don't mind me saying so. The stone is such a deep shade of yellow. What is it?'

Kathleen smiled as she stretched out her hand and said, 'It's a diamond. I got it from my husband. You might say it's a family heirloom.'

Her new companion tilted drunkenly on her barstool as she leaned closer. 'Gee, that's some size of rock. I guess he must really love you?'

'I suppose he did in his way, though he was always something of a diamond in the rough.' Seeing the woman's blank expression she continued, 'He passed away last year.' She gave a little sniff and wiped an imaginary tear from her eye. 'It was just terrible. The coroner said it was carbon monoxide poisoning. I tried to get the super to look at the fire but he was always too busy, the fat jerk! I was round at a girlfriend's one night and Wayne fell asleep in the living room and… Well, he never woke up.'

TWO MINUTES

Two Minutes: it's a long time to hang by the neck, as my father used to say. An apt enough aphorism, although I don't imagine the old bastard meant it too literally, at least not compared to some of his other opinions. Pakis, Chinks, Irish gits and queers — gay being the misappropriation of a perfectly good word — my father was never going to win any awards for political correctness, but somehow I always excused him. He was my father and I loved him, which is what sons are supposed to do. Not that I would have dreamed of telling him such. He was of that generation of men that didn't show affection, physical or verbal. Perhaps if there had been I would have turned out differently, but that's only an excuse, the usual display of moral cowardice. Standing atop the scaffold, why should I accept the blame?

The hood is claustrophobic, it clings to my face when I breathe in and makes me feel as though I'm suffocating, and that in turn makes me breathe all the harder. For all of its discomfort I'm glad I can't see the crowd, the snide whispering of which is torment enough without looking upon their self-satisfied expressions. At my trial the public gallery was filled with those who had appointed themselves judge, jury and executioner. The daily press fuelled their insatiable appetite for cheap sensationalism; three generations of a family murdered.

The rough hemp chaffs at neck and wrists, shoulders ache from arms being bound behind my back. According to the hangman my five foot nine inch frame weighs in at eleven stone, nine pounds and seven ounces. He employs precise mathematics in calculating the distance of my final drop. A clean break of the neck is required, is judged humanitarian. Too short and my spastic jerking might disturb the public. Too long and it will be death by bloody decapitation. Either result would be a black mark upon the spotless record of my executioner. He is not a cruel man but he takes a quiet professional pride in his work. I can't find it in my heart to hate him.

The drop: a lifetime in which to remember a life that might have been more profitably spent. Drunken brawls, petty theft in lieu of honest graft, and a hand that was ever ready to fly upon my wife and children at the slightest provocation. As the trap falls away and my bowels turn to water above trembling legs I want only a little more time. To see the sun climb above the dirty brick and broken slate of a rundown tenement called home, to hear the barking of the neglected dog below and blaring crackle of a radio turned too high on a summer's afternoon. Time to say I love you, to promise I'll never hurt you again. This time my lie is true.

THE MYTHOGRAPHER

No one knew for certain where the mythographers originated. Some said they were a secret society of tabloid journalists, others believed them an elite cadre of publicists. There were even those who proclaimed them nothing more than the paranoid raving of conspiracy theorists. Truth or lie, it didn't matter, for myth adapts to feed the needs of the society that creates it.

John Smith was typical of their type, a man of unremarkable height, appearance and manner. Mythographers created headlines; they didn't appear in them. A firm believer in the "build them up and then knock them down" approach, Smith had overseen the rise and fall of many a star. Smith, not unlike his name, considered himself robust and dependable. In a career spanning almost fifty years, he could honestly say that he had never given less than his best. Something that couldn't always be said of his clients. There was a time, not so long ago, that talent, charisma and life consuming passion were the prerequisites for celebrity. Now everything was reality this and reality that. People, in Smith's opinion had enough reality without televising the messy, the unglamorous and the workaday. The greats, such as Elvis, Bogart and Monroe, had no truck with reality, and what was good enough for the King was good enough for John Smith.

A sculptor, however, can only work with the material at hand. Skilled hands can create beauty from sandstone as easily as marble, though it is not as long lasting, his latest client being a point in case. Mike, or rather Michael McCann, as he now wished to be referred to, had carved out a niche as a junkie poet troubadour, with his songs of doomed youth and a yearning for a mythic England that had never been. Morrison and, to a lesser extent, Cohen, had travelled the path successfully before him, the vital difference being that in between the drink and the drugs and the women they had produced a back catalogue of classic songs. Smith, faced with the thankless task of propelling McCann towards fame, would gladly have given his eyeteeth for McCann to write a song he could hum. Critical acclaim was all well and good, but success demanded a broad spectrum of appeal. At present McCann's fan base consisted of impoverished students and an unfortunate collection of ne'er-do-wells that appeared more inclined to steal his music than buy it. Quite how Smith's line manager expected Smith to make McCann appeal to everyone from teenyboppers to high-powered executives remained a mystery, particularly when the unwashed delinquent insisted on undermining his every effort. Now being a typical point in case.

'I don't see how going out with this bird is gonna help me career.'

'Column inches, dear boy. Exposure in every tabloid and second-rate tattle rag in the land. Ms King, should you need reminding, is the country's premier catwalk model and has previously been linked with the rock cognoscenti.'

'Precisely me bleedin' point mate — I don't want nobody's bleedin' cast offs. Beneath all those layers of slap, I've heard her face is spottier than me arse. An' how old is she — thirty-six? Man, that would be like bangin' me granny.'

Smith pinched the bridge of his nose between thumb and forefinger and counted slowly to ten. 'Mike. Sorry. Sorry. Michael. The crux of the matter is not whether you have relations with Ms King, nor even is it necessary for you to like her, it's simply enough that the public believe you are an item.'

'I don't get it, man.'

'No, I rather fear you do not. Appearance is everything. All that is required is for the two of you to arrive at nightclubs, film premiers and concerts together. Once the paparazzi have had their fill the pair of you can, if so desired, go your separate ways. Hmm. It might work to our advantage for you to be seen leaving with someone else — there is a good deal of mileage in a suitably orchestrated love triangle.' Smith raised a thoughtful forefinger. 'Do you love the new woman? Does Ms King want you back? Perhaps she takes you back only for you to cheat again. Yes, a serial philanderer is something that should suit your image rather well.'

'Woah! Stop the bus right there, Johnny boy. I've not even met this bird an' already I'm bangin' some other chick? It's twisting me melon, man.'

Smith subjected his protégé to his most condescending smile. 'Michael, remember what your manager told you?'

'Dave said I was to trust you — said you was the man to take me to the top.'

'That's right.' The smile became benevolent. 'I will speak with Ms King's people and arrange matters. How about the new Johnny Depp premier on Thursday? It's an A-list event with maximum exposure.'

'Can't do Thursday, man, got a gig.'

'Are you certain? There's nothing marked on your itinerary.'

'That's 'cause it's one of me guerrilla gigs. We select some shit 'ole of a pub an' announce the address an hour beforehand on the net an' then I turn up with me acoustic and bang out a dozen songs or so.'

'You're organising free shows?'

'Not exactly free — the kids pay a fiver or whatever to get in. It's not strictly formal, more on a donation basis. You get me?'

'I rather fear I do and I'm afraid it will have to stop.'

'What?' McCann's limbs appeared to explode in all directions as he jumped up from the sofa. 'This is my thing, man. It's what I do. I'm famous for it.'

More like infamous, Smith thought. 'I'm sure Dave has already discussed this with you. You can't be seen to be funding your drug habit via the benevolence of your fans.'

'I resent that! That is so not true. You make me sound like some kind of junkie. Truth is, man, I can give up the pipe any time I want.'

'That's reassuring to know, Michael. So I shall pencil you in for Thursday?'

'No fucking way, you old nonce! I'm a performer — I write songs and play music. That's what me fans expect an' that's what I'm gonna give them. Forget all your media BS — I'm for real. The fans know that an' that's what's gonna take me to the top. If you can't get with that, that's your problem, man! Later, I'm out of here.'

Smith winced as the door slammed behind McCann. The throb of a tension headache had been building steadily behind his eyes for the past ten minutes and with a jagged flash of colour it exploded into a full-blown migraine. He crossed to the suite's kitchenette, ran a glass of water and extracted a pill bottle from the inside pocket of his suit. The little ingrate really was too much. And the language. Old Blues Eyes would never have used the f-word in that manner. Frank understood decorum. A real gentleman. Sadly, there were so few of his stamp left now.

Smith shook his head and hit the speed dial on his mobile.

'I'm rather afraid, sir, that we have a problem with McCann. Yes, I know I said I could handle him, but I rather assumed common sense would make him more malleable.

No, you need not remind me how much we have invested in him, but if I might make a suggestion?' Smith moved the receiver from his ear and winced at the angry bark from down the line. His line manager had very clear ideas as to how he, Smith, should resolve the situation. 'As you wish, sir. I shall apologise and move matters on accordingly.'

With the connection now dead, Smith stared at the receiver with an expression of disgust that would have been hard to match had he in fact been holding a lump of excrement. But Smith was primarily a pragmatist and he had not survived so long in a particularly cut throat business without knowing when to fold. His time would come. It always did. Until then, he would make nice with the little guttersnipe.

Smith hated nightclubs with a passion. Gin joints and cabaret clubs had soul, mystique and a certain class, while the modern nightclub seemed to exist purely to allow overpaid footballers and their awful wives to parade their vulgar wealth. Not for the first time, Smith pondered retirement. The world was not as it once was, as evidenced by the obscene amount of flesh, both female and male on display, and the pounding noise that passed for music. Michael McCann typified the rot Smith despised and yet here he was, acting as go between for the ill-mannered so-and-so.

'Excuse me, miss, the gentleman over there would like to buy you a drink.'

'You wot? Can't bleedin' hear meself think in here. Not that I do much thinking anyhow — haaw! 'Ere, is that Mike McCann sitting over there?'

'Yes.' Smith leaned closer to shout into the woman's ear and was rewarded with a lungful of rank perfume. 'He would like to buy you a drink.'

'He would, would he?'

Smith nodded. From here it would, if such a thing were

possible, all be downhill. Younger colleagues had frequently accused Smith of snobbery. Perhaps this was so, but some minimum standard had to be maintained. This wretched creature, with her peroxide hair, orange spray-on tan and white stilettos went far beyond the pale. Smith had served to ward off gold diggers often enough to recognise the type. To employ a particularly unpleasant euphemism: coarse as cat shit and twice as thick. On second thought, the young lady and McCann were made for one another — only the public did not wish to see him date some scrubber from Shoreditch. It was one of life's small blessings that McCann possessed the attention span of a goldfish. Something else pretty and shiny was sure to catch his eye before long and in the meantime it was Smith's job to dispense the prophylactics, thus protecting the future earnings of his client. Accidents did of course happen, at which point Smith's other talents came the fore. The smart ones accepted his first offer and did not come back for more. As for the others — an involuntary twitch pulled at the side of Smith's mouth.

The twitch settled and Smith took hold of the young women's elbow and steered her towards McCann's table. 'We don't want to keep Mr McCann waiting, do we?' His smile was saccharin but the hungry light in the woman's eyes remained blind to all but the slouched figure before her. Tracy Jackson's dreams were about to come true, but she might not have been quite so keen had she considered the flipside. Sometimes your worst nightmares also became flesh.

Smith's eyes lingered on the retreating back of the Inspector. New century, new cops. Time was when the boys from the Met could be seen off with a suitable "donation" to a fund of their choosing. This new university educated, sharp-suited breed of career office made Smith nervous, particularly as the majority no longer appeared to consider themselves above the laws they enforced. Not that McCann had anything to fear, he genuinely knew nothing about Ms Jackson's disappearance. Plausible deniability — safer for all concerned. Still, a regrettable incident. Events might have to be accelerated towards their natural conclusion. Unavoidable as it might be, the stakeholders would not be best pleased with such a result.

McCann's moon-faced features stared expectantly up at Smith from the depths of the sofa in which their owner reclined. 'That's the second time the pigs have been round, can't we charge them with harassment or something?'

'I don't think that would be wise in the circumstances.'

'But it's not like we actually did anything, is it? I mean you gave her money and put her in a taxi after our misunderstanding, didn't you? Crazy bitch probably disappeared to spite me.'

Misunderstanding. Smith turned the word over his mind. Even the most skilled of the company's bright and outstanding criminal lawyers would find it difficult to equate the rape of a seventeen year old girl to some form of mistake.

'She was coked off her tits — didn't know what she was saying. All that "no" crap was just a front. Certainly didn't mind hoovering up me gear, did she? Nice little story for her poxy mates — doing coke with Mike McCann and getting' banged good an' proper. Did that slag a favour an' no mistake about it.'

Smith felt the now familiar twitch at the side of his mouth as he reached into his pocket and produced a plastic bag of white powder. He dropped the cocaine on the coffee table with a derisive snort.

'What?'

'I didn't utter a word, Michael.'

'No an' you bleedin' well better not unless you want to find yourself standing in the queue down the dole office on Monday morning.' McCann snapped open the bag and dipped a long pinkie nail into its contents. 'I'm the fuckin' star here! Without me you an' Dave ain't got a bucket to shit in between you. It's my sweat, my talent, that keeps you in those faggot suits you ponce about in all the time. I'm tired of you looking down your nose at me. You think I'm stupid but I ain't. I got your number, mate, no mistake.' McCann snorted greedily and then shook his head. 'Fucking hell, man, this gear is shit! Make yourself useful an' go out and get me something proper.'

Smith turned on his heel and made for the door. The nervous tick in his cheek increased as he caught site of McCann in the mirror, head bowed over the coffee table, racking up long, fat lines. The ungrateful bastard wouldn't know quality pharmaceuticals from rat poison. His line manager and the stakeholders be damned! No amount of money was worth enduring McCann's lowbrow and loathsome company for a second longer. His retirement, long prepared for, would be comfortable enough, even without allowing McCann to reach his full potential. The demos he had put down in the studio last week were as good as anything so far released, which didn't say much, but that wouldn't prevent a posthumous release shifting a suitable volume of units. Then there was the footage of McCann in rehearsal for the upcoming tour — a bonus DVD for the deluxe box set, or in Smith's terms two cases of vintage Krug. A suitably mysterious death would enhance the legend and keep the conspiracy theorists guessing, which in turn would keep the money machine turning.

Smith paused in front of the lift and pressed the call button with an immaculately manicured finger. The tick in his cheek ceased and he permitted himself a briefest of smiles while adjusting his tie. In an hour's time, maybe a little less, Michael McCann's star would reach its apogee.

DOWN THE RABBIT HOLE

Rachel was eating breakfast when the doorbell rang. She sighed, wiped a smear of cream cheese from her lip and put her half-eaten bagel aside.

The postman smiled at her when she opened the door. Henry had only started last week but Rachel could not shake the suspicion he had been hanging around the background of her life for considerably longer. Perhaps it was the way his world-weary countenance reminded her of Humphrey Bogart, a resemblance accentuated by the fact he persisted in wearing a trenchcoat at the height of the summer heat. There was something peculiar about the postman, something incomplete. As though he were a character from an unfinished story, doomed to play bit parts in the narratives of more complete lives.

'Miss? Is everything all right?'

Rachel started guiltily and blushed. A sense of embarrassment stole over her as she realised she had been staring at her caller.

'Yes,' she said hurriedly. 'Sorry, guess I'm not quite awake this morning. What have you got for me?'

Henry produced a package eight inches square and wrapped in brown paper tied with string. He held out a pen and clipboard. 'You've got to sign for it, Miss.'

'Of course,' Rachel said, dashing off a quick signature. She handed the pen back and Henry gave her the parcel in return.

'I gotta scram, doll. Maybe I'll see you around?'

'Sorry?' Rachel blinked.

'I said I'll be off then, miss. Always plenty of work for postie.'

'Oh, right. Toodles, Henry.'

Rachel placed the parcel on the kitchen table and picked up her discarded bagel. She chewed thoughtfully as she examined the unexpected gift. According to the postmark and stickers it had been sent from America by airmail. But who had sent it and why? A sticker on the underside of the package identified the sender as Dr T. Leary. Rachel frowned. Did she know a doctor by that name? The surest way to unravel the mystery was to examine the parcel's contents.

Rachel discovered the string to be hopelessly knotted. She cut it with the knife she had been using to open her bagels. The binding parted with a zing and the paper folded back to reveal a tea caddy painted with psychedelic swirls of colour. The hand written label on its lid proclaimed the contents to be:

Dr Timothy Leary's Patented
Magic Herbal Brew
(Extract of psilocybe & amanita muscaria)

'Tea! How thoughtful. I'll brew a pot now — that'll round off breakfast just peachy. But I wonder why he sent it to me?'

The leaves looked very much like conventional tea but

gave off a pungent odour and produced a murky green brew when she poured in the water.

'Hardly Earl Grey,' Rachel muttered. 'But appearances can be deceptive.'

She looked out her favourite teacup while the tea finished brewing. It had an image of the Mad Hatter and March Hare from Alice In Wonderland on it and was curiously oversized.

Initially sweet on the tongue, the tea had a somewhat acrid aftertaste. Rachel, ever keen to try a new herbal brew, drank it all. She frowned, unable to decide whether she liked the tea. The overall experience was not entirely pleasant. Perhaps another cup would help her to decide. Midway through pouring, she caught site of the kitchen clock. 'Oh no! I'm late! I'm late!' she cried and rushed for the door.

Hurrying down the road, she ran straight into the arms of Henry the postman.

'You oughta slow down, sister. Way you're going you gonna have an accident.'

'Henry,' she gasped breathless, 'is that you?'

'It certainly ain't nobody else. I meant what I said — this ain't the sorta neighbourhood a gal should be wandering about unaccompanied.'

'Don't be silly, I live here. I've walked down this street a...' Rachel's voice trailed off as she took in her surroundings. Neatly set yellow bricks had replaced the tarmac and the houses on either side were now fields of apple trees. Stranger still was her own attire, a gingham dress and ruby red slippers.

'Henry, I don't think we're in London anymore.'

'That's what I've been trying to tell you, doll. This here burg's the realm of the King.'

'The King?'

'That's what I said. He's a real kook. But his wife's worse. Though the Mistress of Illusion's not half as bad as her big sister.'

'What's so terrible about her sister?'

'Baby, you've either been living on the moon or you are one dumb broad. I thought everyone had heard of the White Vampyre?'

'Well, I haven't, and that's no account for you to be rude.'

'Sorry. It goes with the job description, world-weary private eye wit' a smart mouth. That aside, I've been waiting for an opportunity like this for months. This could be my big chance to blow this joint. It's what all us unfinished story characters dream of — an ending to our tale.'

'Would you please try to make a little sense?' asked Rachel.

Henry eyed her sternly. 'Look, sister, now is not the time for explanations. If you've got an ounce of smarts you'll button your lip and follow me. Believe it or not, I'm the best shot you've got at returning to reality.'

'Humph!' Rachel stamped her foot. 'I can't say I like your attitude but I don't seem to have much of a choice here. You know, I preferred you when you were just a simple postman.'

'I'll take that as a yes. Come on, we're late.'

'That's right — I'm late, but what for? Everything seems so terribly muddled.'

'There at least I can help you, kitten. We've got to meet with the Dutchman and Dogstar. If anyone can help us against the King, it's those two phonies. They know how to work all the scams and rackets.'

Rachel became increasingly uncomfortable as she wandered through the realm of the King. Here, nothing looked quite right. The colours were too bright, the lines too simple, like walking through a child's painting. She decided some conversation might ease her disquiet.

'Henry, do you mind if I ask you a question?'

'As long as you keep hoofing it, sister, I'm easy. But don't tell anyone I said that. I've got my reputation to think of.'

'Fine.' Rachel smirked. 'Your secret's safe with me.'

'Glad to hear it. Now, what did you want to know?'

'All that stuff you said about needing an end to your story — I don't understand. Everyone has to go through life the best they can, don't they?'

'People like you, real people that is, do. But have you ever stopped to wonder what happens to the characters after you stop watching the film or reading the book? Do they just appear fully formed with a history only alluded to? What happens to them if there's no sequel, or worse still, their creator abandon's the story before it's finished?' Rachel looked blank. 'I'll tell you what happens — we have to fill in the blanks in other people's lives. The passing stranger who asks for directions, the passenger opposite you on the train — that's me and hundreds like me. Bit actors, encountered once and then forgotten.'

'But people in stories don't have real lives. They're just figments.'

'Yeah?' Henry gave her a bitter look. 'Then I hope for your sake that you don't run into Mr Zebra. Some people oughta take more care of the dramatis personae in their songs. Poor schmuck started out as a piano keyboard, copped a dose of anthropomorphic radiation, and wound up posing as a columnist in some fanzine. Believe me, sister, he's not a happy camper.'

'Now that's just silly.'

'Can it, sister,' Henry cut her off as a throbbing rumble heralded the approach of heavy traffic. He shoved Rachel to one side and leapt clear of the road himself as five bright red fire-trucks crested the hill and braked to a halt.

Rachel stared. She stared some more, unwilling to believe her eyes. The trucks were decorated with frilly black lace. Elasticised straps ran from the wheel arches to a central band of garter like ribbon, while another strap secured two half moons of diaphanous material across part of the headlamps.

The radiator grill of the lead truck performed an eye twisting movement, splitting apart like lips. 'Who's the fox, Henry?' it asked in a sing song voice.

'Her name's not important, Dennis. You should know better than to ask a question like that. Names have power.'

'Look, Henry, it's nothing personal. But if I don't carry out the King's instructions and take a census of everyone in his realm, it'll be a kilo of pure Tate and Lyle in me tank for sure.'

Henry shrugged, as if to say, 'This is my problem?'

'Come on, man. Give me something I can work with here,' protested Dennis.

'All right. Anyone asks, you tell them she's a friend of Dorothy. You got that?'

'That's cool. I can work with that. So where you headed?'

Henry tapped the side of his nose with his index finger. 'That's none of your beeswax. Now, clear the road, we're late for a very important date.'

The trucks revved their engines and rolled back onto the grass verges at either side of the road. Henry grabbed Rachel's arm and hustled her through the gauntlet of red steel. When his red-headed charge made to protest he tightened his grip and increased his pace, dragging her along in his wake.

'What the hell do you think you're doing?' Rachel snapped as soon as they were a safe distance from the illegally dressed trucks. She shook off Henry's now lax grip and glared up at him.

'Sorry, kitten, but that Dennis is a real heel. He's not to be trusted. I reckoned it best that we split as quickly as possible. Didn't mean to cut up rough wit' you.'

Henry's face became a mask of utter misery as she continued to glare at him, so much so that she finally relented. 'All right. Apology accepted. So how about telling me how we get home from here?'

'We don't — you do. An' right now, sister. It's too dangerous for you to stay here. I thought you could help me, seeing how I was jammed up. But I realise now I was just being selfish. So this is the short goodbye.'

'Wait, Henry! I don't mind, honestly, I don't. I can't just leave you here.'

'That's just what you gotta do, sister. An' don't go acting tough on my account.'

'But what will you do?'

'What I'm best at, I'll survive. But promise me one thing?' Rachel nodded. 'The next time you see a passing stranger on a train, think of me.'

Rachel looked earnestly into his eyes. 'I will,' she said. 'That's a promise.'

'Good. Now follow the yellow brick road until you come to Agent Orange's shack. There's an elevator inside that'll take you down.'

'And that will lead me home?'

'Damn straight, if you'll pardon the pun. Like Louis, I gotta go now.' Henry's body turned transparent as he spoke. By the time he completed his sentence he was no more than a pale outline. Then he was gone.

Rachel shrugged and started down the road. A jaunty tune sprang to her lips as she skipped across the cobbles and it occurred to her that her adventures with the mysterious Henry were only just beginning.

The following week Rachel received another package in the post, an old torch from a boy named Jamie. His letter said that he hoped someday she would be able to meet him and his dog Wordsworth.

TRACKS

Honey to trap a fly, smack to trap a junkie. It didn't take much common sense to realise I was walking into a set up. But the average addict is not renowned for straight thinking. It's all about the high. Don't let anyone tell you any different. Even when you've just scored, part of your mind is already working out how to pay for the next hit and where to find it. Too much but never enough, is how it goes. You learn to live with it after a while.

Normally I wouldn't have cared, at least not until my bones started to ache, but it so happened I'd been off that medicine for ten days. Going straight is never easy, not when temptation is all around. All my friends were junkies and even my dear old mother dealt a little now and again when things got tight. This is life on the Craiglochgar estate — no job, no future and precious little hope, except for the weed and those little bags of sweet brown powder. With the mines long since closed and the nearby heavy industries dead, me and my friends were second generation unemployed. My father hadn't held a job for as long as I could remember. My mother did what she had to in order to feed me and my sister when we were growing up, a subject that as I grew older got back to me in the form of snide comments and crude remarks that led to predictable outbreaks of violence. To be fair, I was never going to make much of the education system, so being expelled at the age of fourteen was hardly a bar to my career opportunities.

Don't get me wrong. I'm not expecting you to feel sorry for me, or making excuses for how my life panned out. Each of us has choices, even if we don't see them at the time. There were those who said no and had the guts to get out and make a life free from the poverty, violence and despair. They took the abuse, physical and verbal, and held on to their dream of a better life. But for every one who got out there were at least ten more in the process of being sucked under.

By the time I realised I was making a death style choice it was too late. No education. Criminal record. Raging heroin habit. Not the type of person an employer readily hires, or that a bank lends money. My rare moments of clarity were bleak enough to send me chasing after a fresh hit.

For a time I didn't care because nobody gave a damn about me, least of all myself. But it turned out that there were only so many corpses with a needle in their arm I could look at before wising up. The first one sent me after the strongest skunk and the cheapest vodka I could find — a case of uncomfortably numb. The second made me angry. How could this stupid bastard do exactly the same thing? Pure dead selfish, Jamie dying like that. Number three — my own sweet sister — seventeen years old, cold and blue. I couldn't run from this one, neither could I hate Annie for dying. Was the smack and force of habit that killed her and if I didn't kick it would do for me too.

Ten days. The longest I had ever been clean. Even during the worst drought, there was always something to be had. Weed, jellies, vallies and copious amounts of booze, usually ripped off from the local Spar, or paid for by the proceeds of begging.

'Hey, mistah, can ye spare ten pee fer a cup o' tea?'

If I ever find a café that sells tea for ten pence I might actually buy one.

So here I was, having gone through the sweats, the cramps, aching bones, vomiting and the inevitable result of finding myself with a functioning bowel. I felt proud 'cause I'd done it myself. None of that methadone maintenance shite which, to be honest, only tends to tide you over until you score some proper gear. I'm clean, both my blood and my outer body. I've eaten a decent meal, one that involves protein, carbs and even vegetables, instead of fizzy juice, crisps and chocolate. Ever the optimist, I'm thinking of going down the job centre to see what they have on offer, even though I know it'll be shit. That's when I run into Michelle.

The other consequence of being off the smack is I now have my libido back. There are definite stirrings in the trouser department, because Michelle is fit by most standards. She doesn't inject, hasn't been chasing the dragon long enough for her looks to go, and even has all of her own teeth. Granted some might find her a little skinny, but no more than most of them catwalk birds, or the ones on billboards advertising Calvin Klein.

Michelle is on the downside of a high, although not as much as she makes out. We go back to the flat she shares with three other soon to be hopeless cases and do the nasty. I regret to say that my newfound lust for life doesn't run to wearing a rubber. When you've been sharing needles as long as I have the risk of catching HIV from unprotected sex doesn't seem that real. But it is, particularly when your partner's sleeping with anything in trousers.

There I am enjoying the afterglow and congratulating myself on a spot of good timing, when Michelle lays it on me. She has this package she needs to collect on behalf of a friend of a friend. She'd do it herself only her mother is sick in hospital and this friend needs the package before four, but visiting hours end at four. So if I don't mind doing her a favour, she can visit her granny. Did she say granny? That's right. Both her mum and her granny are in the hospital. It's a really bad time for the family. I must have looked sceptical at that, because she wastes another two vital minutes giving me seconds. What can I say? It's been a long time.

Five minutes later, Michelle's putting her knickers back on and I'm holding the code print out from a left luggage locker with an address scribbled on the back, thinking this can only end badly. And that brings us back to where I came into this horror show. That this is some kind of set up is a given. Even high and desperate, I could work that out. The only question worth asking is what's in the package and is it worth the sting? If the cops are watching it'll be a bust in every sense and I can look forward to some serious jail time. Assuming the drop is kosher, I can ignore Michelle's instructions and look in the bag. Only maybe that's what she wants me to do. You don't ask a junkie to pick up a suspicious package for you and tell him not to peek without knowing it's the first thing he's going to do.

If it's money I could disappear. If it's drugs I can sell them on. Trouble is not knowing who they belong to I might make the mistake of selling them back to their rightful owner. Either option is likely to see me minus my kneecaps, and that's the best case scenario. I might just as easily find myself helping to support a flyover for the next forty years.

A smart man, a cautious man, a man that planned on having a future, would cut and run, leaving Michelle to face the consequences. But then I'll never find out what's inside the bag and I have to know. Curiosity. It killed the cat and it'll probably do for me. I reckon that's just how it is. I have the code to a left luggage locker at the train station, an address in the only estate in town with a worse reputation than Craiglochgar, and like a fool I intend using both. All this clarity and I'm breaking every promise that I made.

The train station is a squat Victorian affair, all blackened granite and wrought iron, the finer details obscured by years of over-painting. There's no sign of any meat-wagons or PC Plod, only a scattering of commuters and, God help them, tourists. And let's not forget the pigeons. Fat mutant bastards that roost in the canopy above platforms waiting to drop their loads on the unwary.

Everybody in the hall looks suspicious, or perhaps it's the other way round and they're wary of this rail-thin dodger, with his bad teeth and bad skin. Paranoia is the only sensible condition in this situation. I mark the tall figures, anyone with too neat a haircut or regulation shiny, shiny shoes. Maybe there's a business seminar in town, otherwise half the local CID are hanging around the concourse waiting to nick yours truly. Abort the mission. It's not like Michelle's that good a shag. It might be imagination but I'm sure my cock has started burning. There's a definite itch and if I'm lucky it'll only be crabs.

I head in the direction of Smiths, an ordinary guy stopping off for his morning paper, even though it's half past two in the afternoon. Halfway through the door, I turn and bolt in the direction of the lockers in a rapid and hopefully unexpected feint. I have to know what's in the bag, whatever happens. Heads turn in my direction, curious rather than vindicated. I skid to a halt in front of the bored looking fat bastard that staffs the counter. He checks my number and disappears through the back. My fingers beat on the counter while my feet perform a similar tattoo on the floor. Somewhere in the shadows a big bruiser of a pig is waiting to snap the cuffs on me. Any second now it'll all be over and I can look forward to free food and lodgings at Her Majesty's pleasure. Forced and brutal anal penetration will also be provided free of charge, courtesy of the other inmates.

The bag thumps down on the counter, a small black and white rucksack, seemingly innocent. I wonder if this really is the source of my all-consuming fear. Why would Michelle trust me to collect drugs or money on behalf of some unknown Mr Big? Perhaps there's nothing more sinister in the bag than someone's dirty sports kit.

'You gonnae tak' the bag, son, or jist stare at it?'

The luggage attendant's voice is a harsh jolt back to reality. Rucksack in hand, I turn and head for the exit. The muttered curse of, 'Fuckin' junkies,' follows me across twenty yards of unadulterated hell as I wait for a hand to drop on my shoulder. Then I'm free, outside the station and heading up the high street.

Stage one of my mission accomplished, I can breathe easy for a few minutes and try to think things through. I need to find somewhere private to open the bag. I can tell by the weight that it contains something heavier than tracky bottoms and smelly trainers. Heavier than cash or powder. I've got a bad feeling about this. Suddenly I'm no longer so keen on finding out what's inside the bag. Long redundant synapses are firing, telling me to wipe my prints off and drop the bag in the canal along with a couple of bricks.

Bag? What bag, Michelle? No, I caught these crabs off some other slapper. Must be somebody else's balls you remember slapping off your arse.

Coulda, shoulda, woulda, the refrain of the doomed. Five minutes later I'm in the public bogs at the foot of the hill leading to the Sheriff Court. The rucksack stares at me from the top of the cistern. I pull open the zip and fold back the top. There are four separate packages inside, three wrapped in plastic, the fourth and heaviest in an oily rag. One is a kilo of brown powder (hello Mama!). Two is a bundle of notes (come to Daddy!). Three appears to be meat, rancid and raw. I'm thinking somebody has forgotten their dinner when I realise that no pig, cow or sheep I ever saw wore a wedding ring. Breakfast, the food I was so proud of eating, splatters into the toilet bowl. When I think I can't possibly heave any more, my stomach spasms with a last load of bile. It's lucky there's no attendant, because I'm making a racket fit to raise the dead, but that doesn't mean some concerned member of the public won't see fit to call for help on my behalf.

Package number four has still to be opened. I should have taken Michelle's advice and kept my big nose out of things that don't concern me. Too late now. I'm proud to say that my fingers barely shake. Mystery prize number four turns out to be a meat cleaver and a gun. The cleaver is shiny and sharp, with the notable exception of a ding half way along the blade, such as might be caused by hacking through a wrist bone. The gun is black and evil looking. I sniff the barrel, like they do in the movies. Is that the smell of cordite, or whatever it is that propels a bullet into soft flesh?

There might not be any spare meat on me, but such as I have I'd like to keep intact. Years of abusing junk has made me an adept liar. I do it by reflex, without even thinking about it, or really needing to. Yeah, telling porky pies is as natural to me as drawing breath, the two frequently being linked. But do I have the balls to deliver the package as asked and pretend I know nothing about what's inside?

'Would ye mind standing oan this sheet, son? Doing a wee bit decorating, like. I'll just go an' get ye a wee bit something for yer trouble.'

Bang!

So I'm back to dumping the fucking thing in the canal again, minus the cash. There I go, lying again. Minus the cash and the drugs. Or, like a public spirited citizen, I could always go to the police. I didn't know what was in the bag. I was only trying to help a friend. Why did I open it? Thought I could smell something funny. Plausible enough, but in my heart of hearts I know it'll never fly. Michelle has fucked me good and proper. This is what happens when you think with the little head instead of the big one. God, that's itchy, and I'm certain I just felt something move. Like microscopic rats, even the crabs are preparing to abandon the doomed ship of my being.

Can't run. Can't hide. But I do have a gun, a cleaver and the address of their probable owner. How difficult can shooting a person be, particularly if they're not expecting it?

Point — squeeze the trigger — problem solved. Right? Although I imagine it probably helps if you know something about guns.

I fiddle about with the pistol grip and the magazine drops free. So free that it passes through my fingers and plops into the toilet. About then I realise I should have flushed after being sick. My prints being all over what I assume is a murder weapon, I have to fish the magazine out of the pan. Besides which, ignorant as I am about guns, even I know you can't shoot somebody without having bullets in the gun.

I give the magazine a good shake, dry it on the oily rag and shove it back inside the grip. It sticks about half way and I realise I have it arse about tit. Attempt two is more successful and the two pieces fit together. So far so good. A diet of action films has taught me you need to pull back the slide to fire the pistol. The resulting click is encouraging. There's a little lever on side, presumably the safety catch, and I push it upwards to cover a red dot on the side of the gun, which I hope is the on position.

Mutilated hand, meat cleaver, rucksack and bricks go in the canal as planned, and then I'm making my way across town. My route takes me past Michelle's flat and the same idle curiosity that landed me in the shit to begin with makes me go inside. The common close and stair stinks of piss as usual. Less normal is finding Michelle's door open. God gave brains to some, to others beauty, but by the time He got to me it seems the only thing left in the pot was stupidity.

Michelle is dead, the junkie's stigma of a needle hanging from her arm. I know her well enough to realise she didn't take the fatal hit by choice. Whoever owned the rucksack was clearly unhappy with her decision to subcontract. Now I've two problems: a dead body with a fanny full of my DNA and, more pressingly, a psychopathic dealer looking for his drugs and money. There's a good chance the aforementioned psychopath is watching the flat, so I really shouldn't hang about. Michelle and her flat mates were not what you'd call house proud, which kind of lowers the odds of finding any bleach I can "squirt under the rim" in the hope of destroying the evidence. I'll have to take the chance that the pigs mark this down as another OD — one less junkie scrounging off the dole and littering the streets. There's nothing to do but clear out. Take the overnight train to London and hope Mr Big is prepared to chalk this one up to experience.

Back on the street the paranoia runs wild. Every face is hostile, every shadow full of danger. I'm looking twitchier than usual, which is really an achievement. Can't think straight, let alone act and walk. The gun presses against the small of my back, a malignant tumour that needs to be excised. I'm no action hero. All I am is some snot nosed kid with a taste for junk. My courage has only ever come from the high of heroin or the desperation of withdrawal. Ten days clean. I really thought I was going to kick the habit. I had plans and stuff, the faint glimmer of ambition. Now all I want is a hit to smooth out the fear, kill my thoughts and make the world go away. It's stupid, but then so much of today has been stupid that it doesn't matter. How could I sell on the smack without first conducting a little quality control?

A lane of cut price B&B's runs behind the High Street. Normally used by eastern European migrant workers, they'll let a room for cash with little or no questions asked, by the night or by the hour, depending on your preference. I go for one just the right side of respectable in the hope of avoiding any more suspicion than necessary. The room has a sink, a battered chest of drawers and a bed with a mattress so soft I think I'm going to sink right through. But it's clean and smells relatively fresh. If it's not the Hilton, it's a damn sight better than the halfway houses and squats I'm used to.

I can watch the great and good of the town go about their business through the slats of the Venetian blinds. But I've not come here for the view. With the door locked and the curtains drawn, I set about cooking up my fix. My hands shake with anticipation, sweats runs down my face. I want this and hate it too. The gear looks very pure, probably from the same batch that sent Michelle on her final ride, so I cook about half my normal dose. The hunt for a usable vein proves difficult, but eventually I find one in my forearm and slide the needle home. This is my religion and here I am about to receive the sacrament, all I have to do to taste a little bit of heaven is push the plunger home.

Ten days. I could weep at the waste and want of it all. Too much but never enough, I send myself on another high. Who's to know? Maybe Jesus really does want me for a sunbeam. It feels as though every part of me is floating away, my flesh dissolving into light. This is good and sweet and pure. I don't care who I've hurt, cheated, stolen from or lied to. I would sell my soul a thousand times for this moment to last forever. All lies and bullshit, but in the glow of the morphine rush it's all true. My life means something. I matter. There is the possibility of hope.

It's dark when I awake, a good four hours dead and buried. I switch on the bedside lamp and wait for the shadows to resolve themselves in the dim glow of the bulb. Dresser, sink and squatting figure. Hold on a minute, what was that last? Before I can react, the bulbous snout of a silenced pistol points in my direction.

'You've been a naughty boy. Taking things that don't belong to you, shooting other people's drugs and spending their money. Where I come from we call that taking the piss and if there's one thing that makes me angry it's some wee Ned from the schemes who thinks he can get away with taking the piss.'

'Take the drugs and the money! I'll pay you back what I've used,' I babble, playing for time.

The man shakes his head but the pistol doesn't waver. 'You're gonnae pay all right, son. Same as that stupid fucking whore. Nothin' personal, just a matter o' business. Can't have people thinking they can steal from me. That widnae do at all.'

I scramble up the bed. My uninvited guest enjoys that, or at least I think that's why he smiles. Below me, pressed into the soft bulk of the mattress, I feel the cold metal of the pistol I took from the rucksack. Somehow, in my blind panic, I manage to snatch it up. This provokes further laughter.

'Dinnae be daft, son. You huvnae got the balls. Whereas myself…'

His gun tracks towards my heart but my hand squeezes the trigger before he can fire. The recoil jerks my arm and it feels like my wrist is broken. It takes another minute for me to realise I'm still alive.

Mystery man is quite dead. There's a neat puckered hole in the centre of his forehead, the majority of the back of his skull and brains splattered across the carpet. A wisp of smoke curls from the silencer of his pistol and I look across and spot the bullet hole in the door. Perhaps my luck is finally turning.

I want to run but some perverse instinct makes me go through his pockets. Inside his wallet, like some malevolent turd, I find a warrant card. Detective Sergeant John Murray has apparently been moonlighting as a smack dealer. I am royally fucked and my only consolation is things cannot possibly get any worse.

I pack my bag and do my best to wipe down everything I've touched. Loath as I am to pick it up, I shove the gun back inside the waistband of my jeans. Now I know for sure it's a murder weapon I need to dispose of it where no one will find it. I also take forty quid in notes from DS Murray's wallet. He doesn't need it anymore and I reckon I'm due it for the aggravation. Chances are it's as dirty as the rest of his cash.

Something's blocking the door. It takes all my meagre strength to shove it open. That's when I discover the body of the hotel owner, a ring of keys still clenched in his fist. I guess that explains how Murray got into my room. The chancing bastard must have been listening at the door hoping to hear something he could use to put the squeeze on the cop. One man's misfortune is another man's luck. With the only witness to my being in the hotel dead, I might actually make it out of this nightmare. I step carefully round the pool of blood and make my way down the stairs.

Ten minutes later I'm standing on the southbound platform of the railway station with a one-way ticket to London in my hand. I've the better part of five grand in my pocket and about ten times that in smack. Enough of a nest egg to start over and this time, God's truth, I'm going straight. Would I lie to you?

ANOTHER NAIL IN MY COFFIN

I lit a coffin nail and sucked the smoke deep into my lungs. They say these things will kill you and they're right. One more thing I don't have to be afraid of anymore. All my life I've been a coward. Avoided conflict. Taken the path of least resistance. Ran from fear of being hurt. But not tonight. Tonight is the night I finally come good.

The Glock feels big and clumsy in my hand but the weight is comforting. I pull back the slide, just like Big Gerry showed me. His voice sounds loud and clear in my head, 'That's you wi' one in the chamber, son. Ready to rock 'n' roll.' A man like Gerry can smell fear. Tell when a sale's liable to go south and come back and bite him in the arse. 'None o' my business, like, but you absolutely certain you need a shooter for this job o' yours?'

The fear is like ice water in my gut and for a second I think about handing the gun back. Then I remember what the doctor told me; remember what MacPherson did to Anne. I thrust the wad of notes in Big Gerry's face and catch the dangerous glint in his eye. He takes a moment to look me up and down and then dismisses me with a shrug. Sees me for the skinny wee bam that I am and reckons I'll probably end up shot dead with my own gun. Instead of a beating, he shows me how to eject the chambered round and runs through the operation of the safety lever in the trigger. 'Dinnae want you blowing your ain baws aff, son.' I make it all the way to my car before spewing my ring in the gutter.

The only light inside the car comes from the glowing tip of my cigarette. I smoke it right down to the cork and start to cough. The fit lasts all of two minutes, by the end of which I've got shivers up and down my spine and a burning pain in my chest. I ought to be home in bed, not freezing to death in an unheated car on a dark December evening, waiting for one of MacPherson's boys to show. And the fear is back again, whispering poison in my ear. Dad always said I was weak. The runt of the litter, if I was his at all. Like Mum ever had a chance to play around. She'd no sooner popped one out than Dad put another one in her belly. Doctor tried to warn him but my father wasn't a man to be told. Number eleven, my wee sister Mary, was the one that finally did for Mum. Seems she was weak too.

A shaft of light spills across the pavement as the fire exit opens. Shug Webster stands framed in the sickly glow of the emergency light. Big and bald, with the classic "mars bar" down the side of his face. Maybe it's a trick of the light, but he looks older, seems to be carrying more fat than muscle. Ugly and dangerous, but he doesn't scare me. A smile creeps across my face. I'm going to enjoy this. Certainly a lot more than Shug will.

He smokes his tabby and flicks it out into the road before letting the door swing shut behind him. From the way he staggers up the road I can tell he's had a good skin full. I offer up a prayer to a god I long since stopped believing in and start the car. Silly bastard is making this easy for me, but then he's the kind of man that others are afraid of. Doesn't cross his mind that someone might be out to get him. If his rep isn't protection enough, he knows he can rely on MacPherson. Nobody's stupid enough to fuck with him if they want to keep breathing. Difference is that I'm a dead man walking.

I drive with the lights off, relying on the sodium glow of the streetlamps. Shug stotts along the pavement, oblivious to the darkness following behind. He crosses the road at the corner and I seize my chance. Foot to the floor, engine gunning. The steering wheel judders in my hands as Shug bounces off the bonnet and slides across the roof. I use the handbrake to turn the car and kill the engine. Shug lies K-Oed in the middle of the road, his right leg bent at an angle nature never intended. Looks harmless enough, but I give him a good dunt on the back of the head to make sure before bundling him in the back of the car. His blood looks black under the lights.

Could be Shug is innocent of the crime in question. I don't much care, so long as he gives up those involved. And anyway, he's a nasty, evil fucker who's had this coming for a long time. Still, if I had to do it again, I'd buy a better pair of pruning shears. The meat's all right, but the pinkie bone proves surprisingly tough. I break the bone as much as cut it. Shug's eyes bulge near out of his head. I rip the duct tape from his mouth.

'Aaahyoufuuckingbaastarrd! Gonna fuckin' kill ye, you fuckin' cunt!'

Wrong answer. I start to cut off his ring finger and then decide there's no point dicking around and go for the thumb. Takes the strength of both hands to cut it off. Fucking Lidl's cheap shite, eh?

At least Shug seems to have got the message. He groans and moans and curses, but the fight's gone out of him. I've barely broken the skin on his other thumb before the names come pouring out of him like pish in a doorway after chucking out time. Johnny the Boy, Wee Malkie and the boss man himself, Jim MacPherson. They all took a turn, but MacPherson went first. Not Shug, though. He swears on his dear old Mum's life that he never had anything to do with that. I want to believe him but it stands to reason that a man in his position — stark bollock naked and tied to chair in a lockup underneath a railway arch — would say anything. I have to know for sure.

I break out the car battery and the jump leads. The nipples and his nutsack get me no further. Maybe he's telling the truth, but it's time for the acid test. A couple of drops in each eye gets the confession I've been waiting for. Turns out Shug's been lying to me all along. Gonna have to punish him for that. I tape up his mouth and pour the remaining battery acid over his head. His muffled screams follow me all the way to the door.

I cruise around the city, checking out the more disreputable pubs in search of Johnny and Malkie. Wee Malkie is in Lauders, nursing a pint of heavy. I get myself a half and sit nearby. He gets up and scratches the hairy gut that hangs over the top of his jeans. His eyes are sharp and mean as he makes his way to the toilets. I drain my glass and try to look casual. No one's watching. I pass Malkie's table on the way to the bar and pour the Rohypnol in his pint. By the time he returns, I'm back at my table with another half, my nose buried in a copy of the Racing Post.

Maybe I'm being too cautious, but I'd rather the wee shite didn't give me any trouble. Twenty minutes later, he's mine. I watch him stumble towards the door, easy meat. The fresh air hits and five yards along the street he goes down like the proverbial sack of tatties. Good Samaritan that I am, I'm at his side in an instant, hauling him to his feet. A quick glance confirms nobody is watching and I drag him into the car. He sleeps like a baby in the back, mouth open, bottom lip trembling. Doesn't look like a monster. Then I remember Anne. Cold and stiff in the bath, water cloudy with her blood.

I could wait for him to come round. Could torture him, make the wee bastard beg for his life, but MacPherson is the one I really want. Nothing happens in this city without his say so.

I fill Malkie's pocket with bricks, dump him in the Clyde and stand there until the bubbles stop floating to the surface. Rest in peace, fucker.

It's late. I'm tired. Can hardly drive for my eyes closing. If I'm not careful the polis will lift me. Might already be looking for me if Shug's been found. Maybe I ought to cut my losses and go straight for MacPherson, but that means letting Johnny the Boy have a free pass. Try as I might, I can't square that in my head. MacPherson will probably have heard about Shug by now, or at least have missed him and started a search. I want that bastard to know I'm coming for him. Want him to know fear the same way I used to. Not that he will. Fuckers like MacPherson think they're untouchable.

Johnny's a gambler, likes to hang out in the casinos, which means he could be there until the wee hours. I visit each in turn. Not like I need to worry about paying the rent next month. Eventually find the cunt in the Merchant City. Suited and booted, he has some peroxide blonde on his arm, doing the whole Bond thing. Could be a problem, seeing as she's got her claws in tight.

I sit there and wonder how I'm going to split them up. Maybe I should take out the Glock and do the bastard right here. Posing fuckwits would probably be so shocked that I could leg it before they twigged what just happened. But if I do that what are my chances of getting MacPherson? Admittedly, I don't have all the time in the world, but I've enough to be patient.

Forty minutes later I'm down fifty quid at the roulette wheel and Johnny and his WAG wannabe are getting ready to leave. Johnny's been hitting the champers which means he'll be looking to get a taxi back up the west end. I slip out behind them, knowing I'm fucked if he goes down Argyle Street. Luck, justice, or whatever the fuck it is that's guiding me, remains on my side. The randy bastard decides to slip up "Shoplifter's Alleyway" for a quick knee trembler. I give them long enough to get into it before walking up and pressing the Glock to Johnny's head. He stops mid stroke and Blondie, eyes closed in mock ecstasy, moans in protest. I pull the trigger and walk off. It takes her a good sixty seconds to get it together enough to start screaming, by which time I'm already back at my motor. Three down, one to go.

Fifteen, twenty minutes tops, and the polis will have the city centre locked down tight. Doesn't matter. I know where I'm heading now and nothing can stop me. I park up on Pitt Street opposite Police Headquarters. What's that shit they say about bearding the lion in his den?

The duty sergeant eyes me wearily. Little wonder. Haven't slept properly in the fortnight since Anne did what she did. On top of which I've been up straight for the last thirty-six hours, ever since I got the results back from the doctor.

My voice is little more than a croak but I get the words out anyway. 'Got some information on a shooting.'

The sergeant revises his opinion of me from harmless nutter to potentially dangerous nutter.

'You want to make some sort of statement?'

'Aye, but no' to you. What I've got to say is only for DCI MacPherson.'

The sergeant's eyes dart around the reception area in search of some help, but the uniforms and CID have already cleared out in response to the shooting. We have a bit of back and forth, mainly him stalling in the hope that reinforcements will arrive, and then he reluctantly calls MacPherson.

The lanky streak of piss recognises me immediately, puts two and two together and comes up with an answer as near to four as makes no odds.

He smiles that superior smile I hate so much. 'Been a busy boy, Danny.'

I nod and pull out the gun. MacPherson continues to smile. Even now, after everything I've done, cunt doesn't think I've got the bottle.

A phone starts to ring. Takes me a moment to realise it's mine.

'You going to answer that?'

'If it's important they'll leave a message.'

MacPherson shrugs as if to say he was only trying to be helpful. I want to ask him why, to find out if he has some sort of excuse or reason that makes sense of the whole mess. But the only reason Jim MacPherson ever needed was because he could. Councillors and criminals alike, they've all spent the last twenty years in his pocket. Give him is due, he's been smart. Never once lived outside of his means or left any kind of paper trail. I saw to that, being his accountant. Money's offshore, waiting for the day he retires. Less than two years away. Could have made it. Been a wealthy man. But he thought he had to prove a point to me.

I shoot him twice in the face and sit down. The desk sergeant rushes over to the body. It don't take a doctor to know MacPherson's dead, not when the back of his head and most of his brains are splashed across the floor.

There's a message on my phone. I navigate through the menu and listen to the apologetic voice of my doctor. Seems there was some kind of mix up at the hospital. Turns out I'm not dying after all.

THE KILLING OF JOE FLY

Word went out that Joe was dead and that he'd bought it in the library. I didn't want to believe it. Knew I wouldn't until I'd seen the body with my own eyes. My girl begged me not to go, but being young, quick and dumb I ignored her concerns and took wing. I could handle myself and when the time came I would look Joe's killer straight in the eye, that being the least I could do for him.

My people don't kill one another so we don't have any police, courts or prisons, but the absence of such things doesn't mean I can't speak on behalf of the dead. I'm not talking in spiritual terms; we don't have any more use for that than we do rules of law.

So let me tell you about the departed. Joe was a through and through gent with a streak of generosity a mile wide. There wasn't an open kitchen window or a lump of fresh excrement he wouldn't tell you about, because the way Joe saw it, the world was rich enough for us all to have a share. Don't get me wrong. I'm not some kind of liberal or socialist dreamer. Far as I'm concerned, a fly that doesn't graft isn't any fly at all. But there's no point sitting on a mountain of food you couldn't hope to eat in a hundred years and letting it go bad on account of the fact you were the one that found it. No point fighting over it either, there being plenty more where that came from.

I don't want you to go away thinking Joe was some sort of saint. He had his flaws like the rest of us, particularly when it came to the ladies. Couldn't get enough of them, as a consequence of which he had himself a regular brood of kids by a score of different mothers. That said I never saw him let down so much as one of those little maggots. If Joe wasn't the best of us, he was far from the worst. Now Joe's dead his kids will have to make their way in this crazy world without his guidance.

Now you have the background, let's get on with the story.

Baked by the sun of an Indian summer, the tarmac outside the library sucked at my feet as I paused to settle my nerves. The librarian gave me an evil look as I flew through the automatic doors, then went back to checking in books. A perverse silence hung in the air, the quiet afforded not to the dead but to readers of musty books and journals. Humans have been killing one another since Cain put Abel in the ground, so there's no reason think they'd act any different towards so-called "lower" species. To them it was only a little pest control, not even worthy of a raised eyebrow, but taking it on yourself to end a life, any life, is murder in my book.

Now maybe they've their own concerns. Let's face it, who would know what goes on in those big empty heads of theirs? I reckon the problem with humans is they spend too much time thinking about what they have or don't have and not enough time living in the now. Life, as Joe would no doubt testify, is short and cruel, so why waste time worrying about it. There I go again, offering opinions where they're probably not wanted, talking about me when I should be talking about Joe. You're right; I've put this off long enough, time to view the body.

Joe lay where he had fallen, below a south facing window. Being a little after midday, a beam of sunlight illuminated his broken body. The murder weapon, a rolled up newspaper, lay on the windowsill, the black of its print highlighted by the yellow smear of his guts. The irrefutable proof of Joe's death settled in my stomach like a lead weight. My friend was dead and for all my earlier bravado I was powerless to do anything about it. As flies go I count myself among the toughest, but I'm still only a fly. Inadvertently spreading disease is about as much as a bluebottle can do.

Buzzing my frustration, I flitted up to the ceiling and surveyed the room. The librarian's stamp clicked away as she checked out books to a wizened old woman. Was this blue-rinsed Methuselah the killer? The arthritic talon of her hand convinced me otherwise. A stronger, more limber arm had dealt the murderous blow. Perhaps the librarian herself was guilty. What darkness lurked beneath that cheerful exterior? More than one killer has hidden behind the mask of quiet respectability. Her travels round the aisles would have afforded ample opportunity to squash the life from Joe. Worth watching, I decided.

Turning from the desk, my multifaceted eyes lit on an acne-scarred youth. Flakes of dandruff spotted the shoulders of his shirt. Deep-set eyes and a vicious slash of a mouth completed his mean appearance, but if an unfortunate face were taken as proof of guilt then half, if not all, the human race should be locked up. I needed some further evidence. The desk he sat at was closest to the window with a rack of newspapers conveniently adjacent. A blank space confirmed my suspicion that this was the source of the murder weapon. The spotted youth, who stared so fixedly at the contents of some social networking page, possessed both means and opportunity. All I needed to discover now was the motive.

Confident as I was, a good detective reviews all the facts before drawing any conclusions. I could go head to head with this sorry specimen, push him right to the edge, but would such a tactic reveal the truth? Was I guilty of making the evidence fit the facts I wanted to believe in? Needing a safe heaven in which to think things through, I took myself to the window and hid behind the slats of the venetian blinds.

The library, being a public place, it was possible that Joe's killer had already come and gone in the same fashion as the old woman I'd already eliminated from my enquiries. Much as I wanted to ignore this conclusion I couldn't dismiss it, but to accept it would be to admit defeat, something I wasn't ready for yet. I would put the youth and the librarian to the test. If both passed, well and good, I would give up my search for the killer.

The librarian was first. Summoning up my loudest and most irritating buzz, I settled on the counter. When she took no notice, I crawled up onto the spines of the pile of books beside her and made my way to the top of their literary summit. The librarian reached over and lifted the first book. Our eyes met and I prepared myself to spring to safety.

'Away with you fly.'

She shook the book gently and I took the hint, flitting up to the ceiling and the harsh glow of the fluorescent lights. For all her distaste, she had no real hatred, so I pronounced her innocent and moved on to my prime suspect.

He turned at the sound of my first buzz and his lumpen features took on a look of antagonistic spite. Needing to be absolute, I alighted on top of his monitor and waited. Sure enough, his hand crept across the desk until it encountered a magazine. I ignored the folding of its pages and the slow drawing back of his arm. A cold smile twitched the killer's lips as he prepared to strike. Warned by the sudden displacement of air, I launched myself skyward, leaving the magazine to strike harmlessly against the screen. The librarian's disapproving shush followed the smack of the magazine like an echo, but held no interest for me. I had looked into the eyes of Joe's killer and beheld the unthinking and unseeing hatred that lived inside. There was nothing more for me here.

It felt good to be outside again, to feel the heat of the sun on my wings and air around me. But how was I to take my revenge? Would I call an army of flies to follow his every step until they drove him into the depths of madness? It was a difficult if not impossible challenge. I seemed the one most likely to be driven insane, or would have been if at that crucial moment I hadn't spotted a dog doing its business on the grass. The owner called it to heel and as they walked away I knew happy times were here again, because when all was said and done I was only a fly and this is what Joe would've wanted.

THE ARTIST

Kennedy had often heard the question asked, 'What value art?' Some claimed it to be in the eye of the beholder, others within the soul. There were even those without spirit who reckoned it in monetary value alone. Not Thomas Kennedy, he recognised art as a way of life. A window upon the world through which the artist might view the truth. He knew this to be indisputable, even though the critics had cruelly maligned his art. The column inches devoted to his work were lengthy only in their denigration. But he forgave the authors. For those who cannot do must criticise, or else they teach. No one is more bitter than he or she who has failed in their life's ambition. Time always proved kinder to the artist than the critic. The passage of years had yet to vindicate the acrimonious musings of a hack.

The public adored Vettriano in spite of, or maybe even because of, the disdain of the establishment. Tracey Emin literally displayed her dirty laundry in public. Regarded in his day as a ghoul and a freak, Doctor Gunther von Hagens' plastinated bodies were now viewed as sculpture of the highest order. He opened up bodies to destroy what humanity thought was difference and proved that regardless of colour or creed we are all equal. His autopsy, installation art of the highest order. Genius that took the public consciousness almost half a century to appreciate, by which time Gunther had passed through the plastination process. Why then did no one understand Kennedy's "Suicide Bomber" or "Foetus In Aspic"? They labelled his work derivative, but such accusations only highlighted the critics' paucity of imagination and caused the artist to suffer the agony of the misunderstood.

Somewhat less sweet was the reality of the impoverished artist. Some might consider starving for the sake of one's art noble but Kennedy remained of the opinion that a good steak dinner was preferable to credibility every time. Poverty, however, had its compensations. Living in the low rent part of town exposed him to sights and people that enriched and stimulated his mind even as they disgusted him. The addict, the alcoholic, the down and out; in each he saw a living canvas walking tall. To experience such things vicariously through documentary and newspaper was one thing, but they did not excite the imagination or inspire the muse until you personally smelled the rank body odour, the stale blood and the vomit. The pleading eyes of the malnourished child, the hard unyielding gaze of the mother and the brutal alcoholic fist of the father formed the unpalatable face of society. Hidden from the rich, the comfortable, the blind who refused to see, but exposed by Kennedy in canvas, oil, plaster, clay and marble. Each blackened tooth, every pustule-ridden scab and lice infested strand of hair depicted in glorious detail for the edification of an uncaring public. The middle class burghers, people who did not want their ignorance disturbed, derided this thankless task as amateur and naïve. His name became a joke, his greatest achievements defiled by ignorant opinion. Discredited and disowned, Thomas Kennedy might well have sunk into the alcoholism or drug addiction of his subject matter if not for his vision, enormous self-belief, and one solitary piece of good fortune.

This chance discovery of an old locket, inside of which resided three strands of hair, finally set Kennedy on the road to the public adulation he had craved for so long. Unable to trust to his good fortune, he spent many hours researching its provenance. Experience had taught him that the only thing more numerous and scurrilous than the critic was the sceptic; a breed so devoid of a sense of its own worth that it could find value in nothing. Not enough to eradicate uncertainty from his own mind; he had to prove beyond question to the world that his discovery was genuine. Only then would its fruit be of value.

Possessing time in abundance, only a lack of funds hampered Kennedy's research. Having cut his expenditure to the bone, necessity finally forced him to renege on paying his rent. Fortunately, the only thing more generous than his landlady's person was her nature. A born social climber, this rather simple and motherly woman enjoyed the romance of having an artist, however unsuccessful, in her building. Distasteful as he found it, Kennedy set about seducing the poor creature. As he lay beside her in the dark, the mingled stench of stale sweat and heavily applied perfume in his nostrils, he thought only of achieving his goals. In truth the sex was not as repulsive as he had feared, and a little went a long way. But whatever service she pressed his body into his thought always lingered on the locket and its precious contents. Perhaps it had been a gift to an admirer, else some item of mourning jewellery. Regardless of its original purpose, it remained indisputably his and the fragile remnants inside would one day make him famous. He had to believe that.

After many painstaking months of research the origin of the hair was certified, opening the way for Kennedy to progress with the next stage of the plan. The technology had been available for a number of years but, like most innovations of its type, remained prohibitively expensive for the private individual. Galling to be so near and yet so far from achieving his aim. A remedy, however, was at hand.

One that provided Kennedy with a certain perverse pleasure, particularly with regard to those who had branded his work derivative, whenever he thought about the manner in which he raised the necessary capital.

Kennedy had always found the term forgery ugly, unforgiving and suggestive of a lack of originality. Whatever else might be said of his output during this period it did not lack imagination. One thing to copy the style of an Old Master, quite another to compose an original piece based on their known influences and set it within an accurate historical context. First he had to obtain canvases and frames by unknown but contemporary artists that he could strip down and rework. Then there was the restriction of palette, for this could not deviate from the pigments then available. While this attention to detail would not fool the true expert, it was capable of passing the most basic of radio-carbon dating. A number of Kennedy's compositions thus passed into the grasping hands of private collectors. If all they cared about was Rembrandt, Titian and Monet, the credulous fools were welcome to their "discoveries", while Kennedy at last had the ironic satisfaction of receiving some recompense for his artistic endeavours, even, as it were, under a *nom de pinceau*.

This undertaking proved so lucrative, his illegitimate earnings laundered as the sales of his own art, that Kennedy began to have second thoughts about retiring. By this time he had dispensed with his lodgings, purchased a small apartment in the West End, and was enjoying the shallow affections of women he believed more suited to his upwardly mobile status. Something he could only have previously dreamed of, but this proved to be a hollow pleasure. The females he attracted were of a greedy and deceitful nature and it did not take long for Kennedy to discover that they loved neither him nor his talent. Money attracted these predators. His ego might have survived this self-deception had it not been for the theft. The locket, that prized container that never left his person, disappeared one night along with his latest lover. While the contents had since been safely stored, the Renaissance jewel was not without intrinsic value. Although pounds and pence paled beside the principle of being robbed by one to whom he had opened his home. Realising that his taste for luxury had almost proved his undoing, Kennedy quashed it ruthlessly. The time had come to put aside his brushes, rinse out his smock and proceed with the plan.

The process proved to be erratic, and for a time looked to be a failure, but the follicle of one of the strands finally yielded usable DNA. The material was subsequently introduced to an egg and used to create an embryo, forming a replica of the donor cells. Recent advances in accelerated growth, developed primarily for the meat industry, allowed it to reach full maturity within six months.

Despite advice to the contrary, Kennedy could not resist visiting the laboratory prior to the operation. The figure floating in the amniotic fluid was physically perfect, more so than the original, for the growth hormones and nutrients allowed the clone to reach its full genetic potential. Muscles exercised and toned by electrical impulses rippled across a torso to rival that of his greatest creation, and Kennedy recognised this living sculpture as a work of art in its own right. All that this superb engine lacked was a mind to power it, the brain, deprived of stimulus, being as undeveloped as that of a newborn. Seeing that body he wanted to possess it, but knew it might be another two decades before the technology existed to imprint his brain patterns upon that blank canvas. Kennedy was not prepared to wait for twenty years, particularly with no guarantee of success. He would have to settle for the next best thing instead. Even so, it seemed rather a pity to create such a marvel only to discard ninety-five percent of it as waste. That it had no formal intelligence offered little comfort.

Regardless of his doubts, he gave the order for termination and harvest. The ensuing operation proved long and painful, the gamble enormous. Even with the drugs there remained a high risk of tissue rejection, the result of which would destroy his only asset. But he had come too far to back out. The operation must go ahead, whatever the consequences.

Kennedy faced long months of physiotherapy on completion of the graft to counteract the loss of sensation and fine motor control. There were times as he struggled to hold a brush that he despaired and cursed himself for embarking on this mad scheme, when it would have been far simpler to continue creating his undiscovered masterpieces. Luxury, after all, carries its own allure. But the gradual knitting of bone, sinew and nerve continued apace; with each day a little more of his skill returned and with it fresh impetus to create. His first works were clumsy, reminiscent of his early years at Art College. However, they improved at an exponential rate until he found himself producing work the equal of his preoperative peak.

Confident once more in his abilities, Kennedy launched himself on the chat show and lecture circuit, displaying his work and his scars to an audience hungry for cheap sensation. The critics still hated his art but that no longer mattered. The public had voted with their wallets and that was all that counted. Kennedy's face peered back at him from a hundred different magazine covers announcing that he had finally arrived. The world had at last caught up with his greatness and embraced his art. Five years on from the operation the agony and the ecstasy was validated a hundred times over, making Thomas Kennedy the darling of the masses.

The reason for his transformation from an impoverished, struggling artist to household name was not due to any radical change in direction by Kennedy, such evolution being beyond him. His attention to the afflictions of the human body, if such a thing were possible, had become more obsessive in its detail. Nor was Kennedy's meteoric rise to fame and fortune, his work now regularly commanding eight figure sums, due to something as capricious as a shift in the public consciousness. It was not even due to a belated championing of Kennedy's art by the critics who had previously maligned and mocked him. Kennedy's fame and fortune rested solely on the fact that, as he repeatedly showed off on world-wide television, he now signed his work with the hand of Michelangelo.

THE PARADOX TRAP

Isaac Barrington squeezed the trigger of his pistol, causing a narrow beam of energy to burn a neat hole through the forehead of the man that had materialised moments earlier. He watched dispassionately as the figure spun through a one hundred and eighty degree arc before collapsing on its back outside the ruins of Harrods.

A flight of Russo-American bombers flew over the ruins of London as Barrington contemplated his next sanction. A single execution stood between him and a welcome return to his own dimension. Not that he had reason to complain; it was just that this particular mission had started to drag. But no matter how great the tedium became he could not afford to relax his guard for even the briefest moment. The controller who conducted his briefing had warned him that this particular alternative was highly unstable and prone to dangerous paradoxes. As an experienced operator, he was well acquainted with the inherent danger involved in travelling between realities. Most agents were lucky if they survived a dozen trips before losing their sense of identity or being driven irrevocably insane by the constant contradictions.

This was Barrington's twenty-third tour for the United

Nations Time Crisis Control and he fully intended for it to be his last. The lucrative bonus that went with the mission would allow him to retire from the Game, unless he chose to accept a post as a Controller. The incentives Geneva had offered him were considerable, but Barrington knew he had pushed his luck as far as it would go.

Barrington flicked irritably at a mote of ash that had settled on the lapel of his Armani. As he waited for his final target to arrive, he recalled the strange series of events of three weeks previous — the night World War II began. The same evening he had attended Adolf Hitler's birthday party. He smiled wryly as he recalled how the celebrated Austrian landscape artist had drawn him into an argument over politics. The diminutive painter became quite belligerent when Barrington suggested that it would be wise for the United Soviet States of Europe to sever its links with the Japanese Republic and sign a non-aggression pact with the Russo-American Alliance.

'Surely, Sir Isaac, you do not dare to suggest that we should abandon our allies to that fascist rabble? Not after all the aid we received from President Mitsubishi in the aftermath of the great hurricane of forty-three. It is both a preposterous and ignoble idea, quite unworthy of a gentleman of your breeding.'

Barrington raised placatory hands. 'I was merely suggesting that in the event of a war it would be better for the USSE to remain neutral, allowing us to maintain our new found prosperity by trading with the Russo-Americans. It's nineteen fifty-seven after all, how long are we expected to remain indebted to the Japanese?'

Hitler's eyes narrowed angrily as he flicked the diagonal sweep of his fringe from them. 'It is a question of ethics, not debt! It should be plain for all to see that the *Untermensch* cannot be trusted. They won't be satisfied until their New World Order has seized control of white civilisation. I, for one, agree with Premier Attlee's stand against their annexing of Canada. Trade sanctions have failed to force them to withdraw their troops — we must use military force to nip their expansionist tendencies in the bud. War, I am afraid, is inevitable.'

'But entering into such a war may well sunder the individual Soviets of Europe forever. Besides which, I'm sure President Eisenhower has no intention of invading the USSE.'

'And how you can be so certain of the Russo-American's intentions?'

Barrington swallowed hard as he glanced around for some avenue of escape, only to discover none. He could, he supposed, try telling Adolf the truth — this evening would herald the start of a bitter five year conflict between the Russo-Americans and the combined forces of Japan and Europe. Millions of lives would be lost before the USSE sued for peace, abandoning the Japanese Republic to Russo-American subjugation. If those facts were not unpalatable enough, what would Hitler make of the revelation that the UNTCC had sent him from an alternative future to ensure the outbreak of war? The Austrian would think him insane.

Having little other recourse, Barrington took an indignant stand. 'What does a mere painter know about world politics anyway?' A childish outburst, which he immediately regretted. 'I'm dreadfully sorry, that was most uncalled for. Please accept my apologies. Too much champagne and the heat of the moment.'

'I will do no such thing, Sir Isaac,' Adolf spluttered, working himself up into one of his infamous paroxysms of rage. 'You have the gall to insult me at my own party in front of all my guests and then expect to continue as though nothing has happened. I do not think so! That is precisely the kind of ill-bred ignorance that typifies the English race. It is little wonder you have the highest crime rate and unemployment level in the whole of the Soviet. Your women are slovenly and your men boorish, as you have just proven by your ill considered views!' He banged his fist on a nearby table, causing a tray of canapés to spill to the floor.

'Security, Sir Isaac has decided to leave early!'

Two members of the gallery security staff converged on Barrington and carried him bodily to the door, where they unceremoniously threw him into the gutter. He picked himself up and groaned as he regarded his mud-splattered clothing. It seemed a small consolation to have appropriated a bottle of vintage champagne while being escorted to the door. But the bottle proved quite useful later that evening as he mourned the loss of one of his Cartier monogrammed cuff links. Barrington was in fact quite drunk as he listened to Premier Attlee's speech on the wireless in his room at the Ritz.

A grave sounding Clement Attlee had announced, 'I regret to inform you that a formal state of war now exists between the European Soviet and the Russo-American Alliance. Since there has been no response to the United Nations' deadline, which required the immediate withdrawal of all Russo-American troops from Canadian soil, we have been left with no other option but to use military force to protect Canadian independence.'

Barrington had travelled to Japan next, where he executed the deposed Emperor Hirohito, whose planned rebellion might have resulted in the early capitulation of the Japanese. On returning to the now devastated London, he dealt with a similar threat posed by the British right wing. This had necessitated the assassination of their leader, the aged and near senile Winston Churchill, five days ago.

And that was how Barrington came to be standing opposite the ruins of Harrods as he waited for his next mark. He knew very little about the target save that he was the leader of a terrorist cell that intended to disrupt the flow of alternative Alpha Omega's history. Ironically, the terrorist had chosen to use the same wormhole between the alternatives as Barrington. But such idle speculations were a sign of distraction, a highly dangerous state for a man in his position. Fortunately, the arrival of the familiar, albeit detested, colourful figure of Gustav Debauch saved him from further ennui.

A twenty-second century playboy, Debauch's hedonistic and sybaritic tendencies were rivalled only by his penchant for 1960s kitsch. He was further renowned for having gatecrashed some of the most lavish and elaborate parties in history during his endless search for pleasure. Such wild adventuring had led him to become something of a thorn in the flesh of the UNTCC. Various attempts had been made to curtail his activities, all of which were thwarted by a loophole in the existing legislation governing privately owned time machines.

Barrington watched as the self-styled dandy wove a drunken path across the rubble. He hollered a cheerful greeting and waved a half-empty wine bottle as he stopped short of the pavement.

'I see you've decided to moderate your dress sense since we last met, Gustav.'

'Am I to suppose, darling, that you disapprove of my ensemble?' Debauch cried in mock astonishment. He gestured to his maroon bellbottoms, frilled lemon shirt and black velvet jacket. 'I can assure you they were quite the thing at Warhol's little soiree.'

'I'm sure they were. But exactly what form of chaos did you cause there, I wonder?'

'Oh puh-lease,' sighed Gustav, 'don't be such a bore, Isaac. You can't still be sulking about that affair on the Luna-Simone. Not after all this time.'

Barrington folded his arms and glared at the time traveller. 'Would that it was just the Luna-Simone. You have to admit that you have an alarming tendency to appear where you're least expected. And often with the gravest of repercussions.'

'I find that remark positively wounding. True, there has been the occasional spot of unpleasantness on my adventures, but nothing that can't be accounted for by coincidence. Besides, the party after Lucretia Borgia's wedding was an accident waiting to happen. Darling, I said to the chef, that fish is positively off! But would he listen? No. Simply had to have it all his own way and damn the consequences. There's no helping those that won't help themselves, that what I always say.' He held out his bottle. 'Now be a sport, why don't you, and have a drink with an old friend.'

Barrington glared at him again, whereupon the dandy offered up such a whimsical smile that his reserve melted entirely. He took a long pull at the bottle and said with a belch, 'All right, I'll admit you're not such a bad fellow after all, although I still think your dress sense leaves a lot to be desired.'

'You're quite proud of your own yuppie garb, aren't you?' Gustav riposted as Barrington returned the empty bottle.

'What of it? I'd be the first to admit that I still mourn the passing of Thatcher's Britain. The mid-eighties, my own period, were glorious times for the young entrepreneur. I made a killing on the stock market before Black Monday.'

'How deliciously ironic that you should now find yourself killing literally.' Barrington opened his mouth to protest. 'Now hold on, darling, I wasn't judging you. Simply commentating on how people become victims of circumstance. But enough of this purple tosh, I see our wine is finished. If you hold on one moment I shall retire to the cellars of Harrods and procure us another bottle.'

Barrington shook his head in bewilderment as he watched Debauch retreat into the ruins. *There goes one of life's last great eccentrics.* Perhaps, on his retirement, he would accompany the arch hedonist on some of his adventures.

A familiar shimmering in the air warned Barrington that he had almost missed the arrival of his target. He took aim and fired instinctively. Too late, he recognised his own features. A surge of nausea gripped him as the paradox formed a closed feedback loop.

Isaac Barrington squeezed the trigger of his pistol, causing a narrow beam of energy to burn a neat hole through the forehead of the man that had materialised moments earlier. He watched dispassionately as the figure spun through a one hundred and eighty degree arc before collapsing on its back outside the ruins of Harrods.

THE LETTER

Father McMahon had taught Mallory the Ten Commandments in Sunday school. Right now, "Thou shalt not steal" was foremost in his mind. Under the baleful glare of the old priest, Mallory had been certain as to the absoluteness of this command. In no manner was it subject to revision, amendment or the addition of any qualifying sub clause. He, Mallory, would surely burn in the hottest pit of Hell for the removal of so much as a crust of bread from someone else's plate without their permission. All-seeing and all-knowing, the Lord did not accept excuses. Well He knew what lay in the hearts of miserable sinners and reserved the right to punish them for their transgressions. As such, it struck Mallory as more than a little unfair that nowhere within His holy writ had the Lord found it necessary to advise its readers on what action to take on discovering one Commandment at odds with another.

Mallory thrust his hand into his pocket. Was it his imagination, or did the envelope feel hot, a foretaste of the fate that awaited him if he did not return it to its rightful owner? He pulled his hand free and used it to dash away the treacherous tears that sprang to his eyes. Boys don't cry

— not a commandment of the Lord but of the playground. Right as he was to fear hellfire, life had a whole host of humiliations to offer prior to eternal damnation. Being caught blubbing by the likes of Pat O'Rourke being one of them. He would never hear the end of it if such a thing were to happen.

His toe scuffed against a stone and Mallory drew back his leg and gave vent to his frustration. The stone clattered down the lane and ricocheted from an upturned pail to strike the foot of a nearby door. The sash of the adjacent window shot up and a wrathful head of grey curls poked into the street.

'What d'you think you're doing, chapping at folk's doors, you wee hooligan?'

Head down, hands in pockets, Mallory started to run.

'Don't think I don't know who you are, John Mallory! I'll be speaking to your mother soon enough and then you'll catch it. See if you don't!'

The window slammed closed but Mallory, his hand gripping the now hateful letter, had greater concerns than the sharp tongue of Mrs Mary Dowd. At the end of the road he turned right, made his way past the forecourt of the garage and out into the patch of waste ground that marked the western edge of the village. A muddy track cut diagonally through the tall grass and stinging nettles to the old beech tree. Mallory dropped heavily into the fork between two of its roots and pressed his back against the rough bark. God was surely already out to punish him.

He smoothed the letter out on his thigh and stared in awe at its neat penmanship. Martin Gillis was an educated man, self-made and powerful in the community because he owned the general store. Every Sunday he went to church, sat directly in front of Father McMahon and held his eye for the whole of the sermon. Martin Gillis had no doubt about the righteousness of the Commandments or the deadly nature of certain sins. Mallory envied Gillis the steadfastness of his faith and despised him for it too. In a just world there must be some leeway.

Things were hard for his mam and da, what with him, his brother and his three sisters to clothe and feed. Never in their direst need had they cheated, stolen or envied those blessed with more than themselves. Neither had they lied, although as Mallory understood it they had not told Old Man Sullivan the entire truth. But wasn't that the same excuse he made for having the letter in his possession? He had not set out to steal it, had not even known of its existence, let alone its damning content. All he wanted that morning was to spend his penny on a sweetie. That of itself stirred feelings of guilt. Hadn't Uncle Brian pressed it into his hand, a belated birthday present, and told him it was his and his alone? God would not begrudge a boy spending his birthday money on a rare treat. Why then, like poor Job, had He put such temptation before Mallory?

Martin Gillis had clearly been surprised to see Mallory in his shop, his mam having collected her messages only the previous day. He viewed the shiny coin in Mallory's hand with equal suspicion, motivated no doubt in part by his recent detailing of the sins of the father and mother.

Mallory, under this intense scrutiny, had explained, 'My uncle gave it me, last week, before he left again for England.'

The mention of this other branch of the Mallory family tree had served only to darken Gillis' mood, but he responded to Mallory's request for joob-joobs by climbing the wooden ladder he kept behind the counter to reach the glass jars of boiled sweets. It was then that Mallory saw the neatly folded letter hanging from Gillis' pocket. The grocer had misjudged the position of the ladder and as he stretched across to reach for the jar the letter slipped free and drifted down, as if directed by the hand of providence itself, to land on the counter in front of Mallory. Fearing to disturb Gillis, who was wobbling precariously on the ladder, Mallory picked up the letter for safekeeping. It so happened that the top fold fell open as he lifted it and he saw Old Man Sullivan's address. A little further down, Mallory glimpsed the names of his mam and da and the details of their crime.

Mallory had not thought what they were doing was wrong and even now, as he rested against the beech tree, he still could not see the harm of it. In many ways what they did struck him as a good thing in that it put a little extra food on the table. Perhaps, had he possessed Martin Gillis' surety of faith, matters would have been more clear to him, but he was only a boy of ten years and often struggled with the adult world.

He had not meant to take the letter, but on seeing its content and grasping the consequences to his family should its intended recipient read it, he acted instinctively. Even then, he had thought to give it back, pretending to discover it on the floor or simply drop it on his way to the door, but that other Commandment burned in his heart: "Honour thy father and thy mother". Did the fact that this appeared in the Bible before the command not to steal make it more important? Father McMahon had not given any such indication and the only other person Mallory knew who might supply an answer was Martin Gillis, whom he could not very well ask in the circumstances.

The wind rustled the letter in Mallory's hands and he looked up into the sky for direction. Should he return to the shop, confess and take whatever earthly punishment waited? As good as it might be for the soul, Mallory thought it unlikely to help in other respects. Gillis had no reason to suspect him of taking the letter and even if he did, the shopkeeper had no proof. All Mallory need do was destroy the letter and Gillis would be left puzzling its disappearance. However, he would be sure to write another in time. It was too much for a boy. Perhaps, this being a question of damnation, he should take the letter to Father McMahon and allow him to decide.

Having reached a decision, Mallory felt much of the weight lift from him. The church lay at the opposite end of the village and to reach it Mallory had to pass his home, a thatched cottage little better than a shack. A curl of smoke from the chimney seemed to wave in friendly fashion at his approach and he thought he detected the smell of fresh baked soda bread on the griddle. The urge to go inside and ask his mam for a piece was strong, for he saw her dark hair and peaceful smile in his mind's eye, but Mallory knew if he gave in he would soon be crying into his mother's apron. How then, as she sought to comfort him, could he tell his mam her son was a thief? Resolution straightened Mallory's back and he ignored the welcoming smells of smoke and bread and continued on his way.

The church came into a view, a simple structure built from the stone of the local hills and devoid of a spire, though a simple wooden cross decorated the western gable. Mallory rushed inside, the soles of his shoes slapping loudly on the boards of the floor as he ran towards the kneeling figure in front of the altar.

Father McMahon rose slowly. A tall, spare figure of a man, his cassock blacker than the very pit of hell itself, he fixed the intruder with an enquiring stare.

Mallory dropped to one knee and genuflected. 'Bless me, Father, for I have sinned.'

Father McMahon's lips twitched with an emotion somewhere between irritation and amusement. He pointed a finger towards the booth at the side of the church. 'It is customary, John Mallory, to make use of the Confessional for such matters. What wrongdoing so troubles you that you must seek absolution in this manner?'

Mallory tried to form words of explanation but his fear of the priest was too great. He thrust the letter into the priest's hand and retreated to the safety of a nearby pew.

Father McMahon removed a pair of wire-framed spectacles from his pocket and read the letter. Once finished, he placed letter and spectacles on the altar and looked at Mallory.

'I didn't mean to take it, honestly, I didn't. I went into Mr Gillis' shop and it fell out of his pocket. I was going to give it back but then I saw me mam's name...'

'You feared Mr Sullivan would throw you and your family out of your home,' Father McMahon said into the pause. Mallory nodded. 'You have done a wrong thing, John Mallory, reading another person's private correspondence. However, your mother and father are hardly the first to sublet a room in order to make ends meet. Mr Sullivan might not be best pleased by this, but he is not such a fool as he is blind to it. Martin Gillis would do well to recall the words of the Gospel of Saint John and remember that he, himself, is not without sin. I will have words with him after evening Mass. In the meantime, I think it best I keep hold of his letter.'

'Mr Sullivan won't be angry?'

'You will find when you get older that what a person feels and how they act are not necessarily the same. Mr Sullivan will do what is right by your family, of that you may be certain.'

Mallory broke into a smile and turned to run for home, the letter, its contents and his fears forgotten.

'John Mallory, are you not forgetting something?' Father McMahon pointed towards the Confessional. 'It is time we attended to your sins. You will make Confession.'

BARCODE

My name is a barcode and I live in a utopian society.

I went to check on the progress of my child yesterday at the Birth Centre. They informed me that the foetus had been aborted in Week Seven due to genetic anomalies, but our reserve embryo was developing as per specifications. My partner and I both agreed — we're having a baby boy with blonde hair, blue eyes and a minimum IQ of one hundred and sixty-five.

We are transcendent now, the first species to make sex for the purpose of procreation obsolete. We mix our children in test tubes, choosing their sex and physical characteristics from an option menu. The genes of our ancestors' greatest minds are there for us to splice together at our convenience. Gestation takes place in artificial wombs, relieving womankind of that task. Now they are truly equal.

Menstruation a problem? Give us your ovaries and fallopian tubes and we'll keep them on ice for you until they are required. Are you worried about the side effects? HRT Series 4 will sort you out. You stay fitter and healthier looking for decades to come.

Some people of course will always reject progress. They raise tedious moral objections such as what of a woman's natural right to carry her child inside her womb? Should she not be allowed to feel that kick inside?

These extremists have clearly not considered a woman's right to the agony of labour, swollen ankles, back pain and haemorrhoids. Perhaps someone told them stretch marks were in this season? They say they are proud of their body's natural ageing process. That they are not ashamed to sag, that we should stop augmenting our bodies with chemicals, surgery and bio-electronic implants.

Central brands them dangerous subversives and reminds us of how technology has improved the species, erasing the risk of uterine childbearing. Now there is no danger of miscarriage or of delivery by crude caesarean section. We are living in the age of the *Übermensch*.

We have purpose and function. We live in a utopian society.

What has sex become in our Brave New World? Is it art? Is it performance? Is it the weaponry of the bedroom? It is all these things and more besides. It is the last legalised violence.

I know my partner's body well, the curve of her thighs, the soft round of her belly. Every last little nip, tuck and implant. Every single melanoma scar, piercing and iridescent sub-dermal laser tattoo, that which forms the fine detail, the contour lines, of the map of her body. Her crowning glory is not her soft ash-blonde curls, but the neuro-link socket behind her right ear, the partner to my own interface. Now, more than ever, sex is the beast with two backs. We hack into the other's nervous system, exchanging physical sensation and know if we are truly pleasuring one another. Sex is a woman. Sex is a man. Sex is one glorious unity.

We fuck without begetting life in a utopian society.

I ran into my labour shift associate the other day. He laughed and told me he was HIV positive, and was on his way to Disease Control to have a complete body flush. I play the machismo game and laugh with him, warn him he shouldn't put it about so much. Then I remember that I am due to have a malignant tumour removed from my pancreas next week. It is my sixth cancer this year, nineteenth in total. The dissidents and malcontents say Disease Control could eradicate it completely, but with a 98.72 percent successful treatment rate there is too much profit to be made from selling the equipment, drugs and aftercare. Why eradicate something as harmless as the common cold when it can be treated within a week or two? Central would never sacrifice the other 1.28 percent in the name of profit. I suspect that those who spread such rumours are the same paranoid delusion riddled conspiracy theorists who claim a successful treatment for AIDS was discovered in the last years of the twentieth century, but deliberately withheld for over twenty years to cut down on the world's excess population. As if any government elected by the people for the people could be that cruel or callous.

We are all one race, one colour, one denomination now. The road we had to travel was long and hard, but no one said it would be easy building a utopian society. Sacrifices had to be made. The morally unsound, the genetically impure, theologically unclean, the mentally handicapped, all of them had to be rooted out. These weeds, which threatened to choke the pure flowering of our species, were systematically destroyed. Our ancestors discovered the true cause of war is difference. Now no one is different.

All men are created equal in a utopian society.

THE KNIGHT, DEATH AND THE DEVIL

(Suggested by the Albrecht Dürer line-engraving)

A hush descended over the patrons of the public room of the tavern. Their collective attention focused on the two figures sitting at the table next to the hearth and its roaring blaze. The boy waited for his companion, an old man dressed in monkish robes, to finish his tankard of ale. The only sound in the room the occasional crack of a splitting log in the grate. These staccato cracks marked off the seconds and highlighted a rise in the shared tension of the crowd.

The old man wiped the ale froth from his lips and shattered the silence by banging his tankard down on the table. At this signal the boy could contain himself no longer: 'Please, sir, won't you tell another story?'

The old man met his rapt gaze. 'Very well, young master, you shall have one final story this evening.' He spread his arms wide to encompass the tavern, 'You shall all have a story. There is an old rhyme that has been told in this region for over two hundred years. Many of you are no doubt familiar with von Bartok's story, but what you might not be aware of is that it is based on true events. This, then, is the tale of The Knight, Death and the Devil.

'Count Maximilian, formerly of the Teutonic Order of Knights, was a veteran of the Crusades in the Holy Land. A prime-mover in many of those battles in his youth, as he approached middle-age he became aware that his battle prowess was failing. A wise man, not prone to the delusions of vanity, he decided to return to his native Saxony, where he hoped to assume a less vigorous role in life. These intentions were dashed when he arrived at his ancestral home to discover his estates in uproar. Although autumn now held sway across the land, the crops had not been harvested and lay rotting in the fields. The Count, understandably angered by this waste, demanded an explanation from his serfs, but their oblique answers served only to further fuel his wrath. When questioned the men refused to meet his gaze, pointing instead to the ancient forest that surrounded the hill on which stood the family *Schloss*. They mumbled about fiends and demons under their breath and it was some time before Maximilian came to understand the bare bones of the matter.

'The local peasants had long regarded the forest as a place of evil, steeped in sinister magic. Neither could it be denied that more than one unfortunate had perished within its leafy environs, though whether they had fallen victim to evil wood spirits remained open to conjecture. But such rumours were hardly surprising when one considers that superstition was rife among the local peasantry during this period. That said, the forest's reputation was no worse than that of a dozen similar woodlands in neighbouring districts. The real cause of their fear came from a series of unexplained events that dated back to the spring.

'A young girl had entered the forest to gather the rare medicinal herbs and fungi that grew beneath its canopy. The unfortunate wench had made many such trips in the past and it was not unusual for her to be absent from dawn until dusk. The girl's parents, who were often in bed before she returned from these foraging trips, did not miss her until the following morning. Word of her disappearance swiftly spread amongst the serfs who assembled a large party of volunteers to search the forest.

'The men searched the forest all day until the approach of dusk reminded them of its evil reputation. Thus cowed by the rapidly waning light they abandoned their search. During their hunt they discovered but one clue towards the girl's whereabouts — her basket, which they found discarded beside one of the well-trodden woodsmen's paths. Of the girl herself there was no trace.

'The loss of one of the searchers was only discovered when they reported their lack of success to the girl's father. The missing fellow being a woodsman renowned for his hunting and tracking skills, they thought it unlikely he had lost his way and swiftly concluded he had met with foul play. Such speculations provoked a wealth of dark uttering until his younger brother finally shed some light on the subject when he revealed what he had been reticent to speak of in front of the girl's father. Otto and the girl had been secret lovers for several months, and the woodsman had informed his brother that tales of ghouls and goblins would not stop him searching for his love.

'No more was heard of either for several days, until Otto was discovered by the edge of the forest. His clothing badly torn, his body a mass of scratches, he was raving in the grip of fever. From his babblings, he believed he had confronted the very Devil himself and maintained this febrile claim up until the moment of his death from the fever four days later.

'Since then no man had dared enter the wood. A spate of ill omens plagued the surrounding fields. Hens stopped laying, cows refused to give milk and, most damning of all, a two-headed lamb had been born. Thus the mania spread among the Count's serfs until many came to believe the hour of the Apocalypse to be at hand.

'Realising that no amount of reasoning would be

sufficient to calm his hysterical serfs, Maximilian called for his squire to saddle his horse. Then, buckling on his armour and other accoutrements of war, he mounted his steed and, accompanied by his faithful hound Wotan, rode forth to do battle with whatever evil now commanded the forest.

'The Count's spirits were high as he entered the woodland by means of a small track worn by the passage of generations. The midday sun cast patches of dappled light on the path as he rode along the hunting trails of his youth and Maximilian drifted off into a gentle reverie. But recollection of the events that led him here soon dispelled his carefree thoughts of childhood. With a snort of contempt for his ignorant serfs, he pressed his spurs to the flanks of his steed, determined to disprove the myth of the forest's enchantment.

'He rode for a further hour, penetrating the heart of the forest, where he felt a sinister change in its demeanour. Towering oaks, whose gnarled bark and shadowed boles parodied human features, surrounded him. Tendrils of moss hung beard-like from these twisted visages, while knots of ivy scaled the trunks, rising from the rank vegetation of the forest floor. Most perturbing of all was the absence of any wildlife. Where once the songs of birds and ruminations of wild creatures had accompanied him on his mission, now only an eerie soughing disturbed the tranquillity of the forest. The Count drew rein in this unholy grove of trees. Surely he had found the source of the forest's evil.

'"Indeed you have," replied a sardonic voice in answer to his unspoken question.

'Maximilian started at this utterance, for before him stood two of the most eldritch figures it had ever been his misfortune to behold. The first, tall and impossibly thin, wore the dark robes of a cleric. It grasped a scythe in its skeletal hands and the cold gleam of iron winked from beneath the shadows of its cowl. The Count clutched at the rosary he wore about his neck. If this apparition was the

Grim Reaper, who then his companion? A sense of foreboding gripped Maximilian's heart as he turned to inspect the other. Short and hunched, with coarse matted fur and legs that bent back on themselves at the knee to terminate in cloven hooves; dressed all in silk and velvet of brocaded scarlet, here was no greater foe than Lucifer himself. A most fitting companion for Death.

'At his horse's feet, Wotan lay with his belly pressed flat to the ground. The hound whined as it cowered from the two supernatural entities. Angered to see his faithful companion so distressed, Maximilian drew his sword and bellowed, "Stand aside in the name of Christ and the Father! You who have been cast out have no right to claim dominion over any part of God's Earth. I command thee to depart the forest and leave my lands in peace."

'The Devil chuckled at this proclamation. "You command me? I think not! Clearly you have no idea how precarious your situation is."

'"You cannot threaten me, Lord of Lies, for I know my place is guaranteed in Heaven by all the Holy work I have done in His name." He stared defiantly at Death, "And you, sir, hold no terror for one who faced you a hundred times at the Horns of Hiitan."

'The Devil scratched his nose with a pointed fingernail. "Yes, I can recall much of this 'Holy work' of which you speak. The sacking of several Saracen villages for instance, where you and your fellow knights put three score of women and babes to the sword. All in His name of course.

'"Are you aware that hell is full of such noble adventurers as yourself? All claim that they were carrying out the will of God, when in reality they were indulging their basest desires. You have damned yourself by your own hand, Count von Bartok."

'"If what you say is true, and I doubt it, why have you not claimed my soul already? Unless, of course, you intend to make some bargain for it?"

'Lucifer cackled once more, "You have a sharp mind,

von Bartok, but you have not quite guessed my game plan. I have no need to bargain for your soul, since I already own it. What I am offering you is a chance to escape your fate. In short, I propose a contest. A test of your martial skills against my agent," he gestured towards Death, "Do you accept my challenge?"

'Maximilian frowned; he knew well the Devil's penchant for treachery. "Perhaps," he stalled, "but first, before I make my decision, I'm curious to know why you would offer me the return of my soul."

"'Ennui — the boredom of immortality. Then there is my reputation as a sportsman to maintain, although I leave the chess to my companion. Does that satisfy you, little knight? You are but a pawn in Lucifer's game."

'Maximilian shrugged. "A fair enough explanation. Very well, I accept your challenge. Tell me what the rules of this tourney are and how it will secure the freedom of my soul."

"'Ah," Lucifer sighed, "I do so like a pragmatist. The rules of my challenge are simple — you have until sunset to escape both Death and the borders of the forest. If you are successful in this you will have won your freedom, for Death must first claim a man before I can take possession of his soul."

'The Count snapped his horse's reins while simultaneously digging his spurs into its flanks. "Then I'd best be off," he cried and galloped from the grove. Branches whipped him as he plunged from the path in an attempt to lose the grisly fiend that pursued him. Blood thundered in his ears as he wove between the trees at breakneck pace, driven to greater effort by the certain knowledge of his fate should he lose the race. He heard the baying of his faithful hound beside him as it struggled to keep pace with its fleeing master. This simple act of defiance emboldened the old knight enough to risk a glance over his shoulder. Scant yards behind rode the leering figure of Death, mounted on a white charger. The wind had thrown back his cowl to reveal the Reaper's grinning skull with its serpent-entwined iron crown, his ghastly symbol of office. The sight chilled the Count's blood until he felt certain it must freeze in his veins. He tore his gaze away in time to avoid a low branch that threatened to unhorse him. As it was, his noble steed stumbled and almost threw him as its hooves became entangled in a mass of leaf mould, allowing Death to gain vital seconds against its master. Death swung his scythe in a deadly arc, cleaving through flesh and bone.

'Maximilian stared into the baleful light that emanated from the eye sockets of Death's skull, amazed to find himself alive. Then his eyes fell upon the cause of his salvation who lay cleaved in twain at his horse's feet. The brave hound had leapt between the knight and his attacker to take the killing blow. Death's voice rustled like the falling of autumn leaves, "Flee, little mortal. Run while you may. Thy hound's sacrifice has earned thee but a fleeting moment in which to make good thy escape."

'Maximilian needed no further encouragement. He galloped towards what he believed to be the edge of the forest. Death gathered up a tiny ball of glowing light, which he tucked inside the darkness of his robes. Having discharged his duty, he brandished the scythe aloft and made his mount rear and plunge. The hunt was on afresh!

'One might be forgiven for assuming the Count's luck had turned, but this was not the case. This should come as no surprise, his adversary being Lucifer himself, who was never one to be bound by his own oath. He sensed his victim about to escape and devised a wily plot to halt his progress.

'Dusk had begun to fall when Maximilian came in sight of the forest edge. The prospect of success rekindled the dying fires of his hope and he gave vent to a wild yell before spurring on his tired horse in the confidence that he had made good his escape. Then, in the sun's waning light, he spied the dishevelled figure of Otto's lost love, Sabine. The terrified girl ran towards him pursued by two cadaverous fiends whose rags seemed to merge with their lifeless grey flesh. At the sight of Sabine's distress, all thought of escape vanished from Maximilian's mind. The laws of chivalry bound him to defend the weak and helpless, even if it should cost him his immortal soul. He pulled up his horse, levelled his lance and called forth a challenge to the fiends. Taking their silence as confirmation of their evil intent the Count commenced his charge. His lance skewered the first revenant through the groin and embedded itself in bone. Abandoning the trapped lance, Maximilian drew his sword and wheeled his horse about to confront the other fiend. He stood in his stirrups to deliver an over-arm blow to the creature's head, splitting it from crown to crotch.

'Maximilian wiped his bloody blade before dismounting to attend to Sabine, who appeared to have fainted from fright. He knelt beside her and gripped her shoulder, only to recoil in horror at the sight that greeted him. This was no damsel in distress, but the Devil in a dress. Lucifer laughed raucously at his deception as Maximilian's face turned scarlet with indignation.

'"Sir, I must protest. This chicanery is not worthy of a gentleman. Have you no honour?"

'"Not a jot," replied the Prince of Lies, "but I see my servant Azrael has caught us up. Rotten luck, Count von Bartok."

'Livid, Maximilian vaulted into his saddle and snarled, "I'll escape you yet!"

'The edge of the forest was only a hundred yards away. He ducked low over the horse's neck and raced the steed for its worth. The Dark Angel's mirthless laughter drew louder as he closed the gap. Terror wrenched the Count's heart as Death drew up alongside of him and swung his scythe. In desperation, he threw himself from the saddle, but not before he felt the sting of that cursed blade. It bit into the flesh of his calf, spreading a chilling numbness through the limb as he fell. He landed hard and tumbled down the leafy embankment that bordered the western edge of the forest before coming to rest in a fallow field as the last rays of the setting sun disappeared below the horizon. Against all odds, and in spite of the Devil's treachery, he had escaped. Death had been thwarted and would now never lay claim to him — his soul was saved!'

The candles had burnt low creating thick shadows around the old storyteller. He sighed and reached for his tankard, to salute his applauding audience.

'Well?' asked the boy.

'Well what?' snapped the old man, tired and irritable from his narration.

'You haven't finished. What happened to Count Maximilian? Did the Devil keep his bargain? What did the Count do next? What happened to the real Sabine?'

The old man raised his hands to stem the rushing tide of questions. He laughed, his mood lightening in an instant. 'Questions, always nothing but questions with you, Albrecht. How should I know what happened to the knight afterwards? I'm just the storyteller. I tell the tales as they are. Nothing more, nothing less. Now the hour grows late. It's time you were in bed, my boy.'

'But...' Albrecht protested weakly.

'No buts.' The old man's voice brooked no argument. 'I'll be back this way next week and then you can have another story. Does that please you?'

'Oh, I suppose so.' The boy rose and kissed the old man on the cheek before scampering from the tavern. The storyteller watched him leave before reaching for his staff. He leaned heavily on it as he struggled to his feet. A series of charcoal sketches depicting several of the tavern's clientele lay scattered across the table. Rough as they were, the boy had a great gift. The old man tucked the sketches into his robe and, with his left leg dragging behind him, made his slow, limping way from the tavern.

THE HUNT

The boar snorted and stamped its front leg in the dirt, sending a ripple through its flanks. A magnificent beast, a thick carpet of bristles covered its shoulders and spine. Yellowed tusks curved upwards either side of the snuffling snout, the points of which glinted in the dark of its eyes. One ear stood proud, the other, ragged and torn, lay limp under its own weight. Each sinewy movement highlighted an ancient wound in its hide, testament to the beast's indestructible nature. Many were the hunters who had cast their spears, considerably fewer those who had lived to tell of wounding the Great Black Boar of Iron Wood. Some said it was Freyja's lover, Ottar, abandoned in his beast form; others that it was the trickster, Loki, cast out once more from Asgard's shining halls. Whatever the creature's origin, the greybeards agreed that no weapon forged by mortal hands could slay it.

Karl did not believe this. From where he crouched in the undergrowth the beast, though admittedly impressive, appeared mortal enough. The rich tapestry of scars that adorned its body proved others had wounded it, and anything that bled he could kill. He had been tracking the boar's spoor since first light, twice ignoring easy kills, the lure of the mythic beast driving him on. The fire of ambition burned hot inside his young heart. Killing the boar would earn him fame and renown. The skalds would recite tales of his victory in epic verse for all to hear. No one would be able to doubt his prowess, least of all the Jarl, who would have to grant his request to join the honour guard. Though his beard was no more than golden down on his cheeks, he was tall and well-muscled. The spear he cast always flew swift and true to its mark, and none of the other boys could defeat him at arms or in wrestle. True to say that his arm and his eye were equal to those of many of the warriors and hunters, and still the Jarl refused him a seat at the mead benches.

Karl felt the wind's subtle shift as a soft caress on his cheek. He gripped his spear tight and fear formed a knot in his stomach as the boar turned. Hunter and hunted locked eyes and a silent communication passed between them: To the death!

The boy nodded. The boar lowered its head, appearing to return his challenge, and charged. Twin plumes of steam issued from its snout as it pounded forward, throwing up leaf mulch in its wake as it bore down on its aggressor. Fear riveted Karl's feet to the ground but the instinct of self-preservation made him brace the butt of his spear in the earth. His vision shrank inwards, reducing his world to the beast's tusks, which gleamed like twin crescent moons. They loomed larger and larger, promising pain and ignoble death. Gored, alone in the wilderness, no songs would be sung of his deeds. Fear of ignominy overcame fear of death and Karl's body obeyed his command. He pivoted to the side and drove his spear deep into the boar's chest. The spear bowed dangerously as he pressed home his attack, the boar driving towards him. The snap of the shaft reverberated through the wood and Karl, relieved of its resistance, pitched headlong to the ground.

Pain ripped through his side as the boar tossed him into the air. The unyielding earth knocked the breath from his body as it received him into its embrace. Karl's vision swam before him, darkness creeping in from the edges, but the vibration of the boar's approach jarred him back to consciousness; succumbing now would be the end of him. Fingers made clumsy by pain and shock scrabbled at his waist, searching for the knife hilt he knew must be there. An inner voice cried out for him to look up and meet his death, but Karl ignored it as he felt the polished wood beneath his fingers. Only when the knife had slid free from its sheath did he look up. As the beast's tusks bore down he braced his hands on either side of his head and flipped into the air to land astride the boar. He stabbed the knife deep into its neck, causing the animal to plunge into the undergrowth. Unwilling to lose his prize, Karl seized hold of its tusks and locked his legs around its flanks.

Branches whipped his skin and thorns tore at his hair and clothing as the boar continued its flight. Twin rivers of blood flowed from the spear and the knife, measuring out its life drop by drop on the woodland floor. Rage and adrenaline carried the boar onwards deep into the heart of the forest and Karl began to believe that the Great Black Boar of Iron Wood was indeed indestructible. His own wound burned with each jolting step, making him fear he would bleed to death before his quarry. Battered and delirious, the boy's grim chuckle rose to a hysterical crescendo, sending fresh spasms of pain through his side. Tears streamed down his cheeks with each heave of his belly, fire burned in his lungs and his vision fogged. Everything slowed. Where the foliage and branches had once whipped they now gently brushed. The time between the boar's footfalls stretched, the impact lessening each time until both animal and rider appeared motionless.

Karl drifted on the tide that lapped the dark shore between life and death. Thoughts of glory and valour paled beside the comforting numbness of his flesh. The sea receded, each wave carrying him further from the shore, from life. Where the tide came from and where it went was life's great mystery, but Karl felt the answer drawing closer. The shore had become a pale smudge at the extent of his vision and when it vanished he would know.

A golden light drew him from his reverie. Fresh strength returned to his limbs and he opened his eyes to find himself suspended upside down, affixed to the trunk of an ancient tree by the shaft of his own spear. Such a wound should have been agony but he felt only a deep sense of wholeness, a connection to the fabric of existence, which expanded as he viewed his surroundings.

A ring of mist enclosed the small glade at the centre of which stood the towering yew, its crown concealed by cloud, its bark gnarled and ancient. Three great roots, twisted and monstrous, spread from its base. The first disappeared into a well of sparkling water while the others curled across the grass into the mist where they were lost from sight. Karl had never seen a more ancient or noble looking tree. He felt that his sense of well-being flowed from its heart, that its sap mingled and flowed with his blood through their mutual wounds. Yet this wonder paled in comparison with the three figures that stood at its base beside the well, sprinkling its bark with water.

The first appeared to be a maiden from the manner in which she wore her hair loose, held back from her face by a gold brocaded fillet, but Karl could not be certain as a veil concealed the lower part of her face and a heavy purple cloak shrouded her body. The second woman, though several years older, was equally striking. The tilt of her head and penetrating gaze spoke of noble lineage. She bound her red-gold hair tightly at the back of her head and sheathed her body in a dress of embroidered linen, fastened at the shoulders by two silver brooches. The third stood in sharp contrast to the others. The crone's hair was grey; her face, gaunt and seamed with age, resembled worn leather. She wore no jewellery and clad herself in a shroud-like woollen smock that hung about her skinny shoulders. The only feature she had in common with her companions was her eyes; they were of a deep sapphire blue. The gaze of the first was inviting, the second proud, and the last the knowing look of one who has seen too much. These were the Norns, Skuld, Verdandi and Urd, governors of the fates of men.

Urd, seeing Karl had woken, nodded at her companions, who stopped their task and closed around him. Skuld took another pace forward and reached up to gently cup his chin between thumb and forefinger. She tilted his head back forcing him to look into her eyes. Her skin, soft and warm, smelled of summer. Karl's pulse quickened as he felt the maiden's closeness. Sensing his thoughts, the girl shook her head to imply she was not for him and slipped her veil to the side. A sharp burst of pain tore him away from her gaze as Verdandi ripped the spear from his flesh. She caught him in strong arms and gently lowered him onto a waiting shroud. She smiled kindly before stepping back. Karl tried to speak but no sound issued from his parched throat. His euphoria evaporated leaving his limbs leaden and stiff. The mist that surrounded the glade seemed to creep closer as Urd slowly drew the folds of the shroud over his body, until at last either cloth or fatigue dimmed his vision completely.

As he slipped from consciousness, perhaps even from life itself, he heard Urd say, 'That which is done shapes that which is becoming and sets in motion that which will be, so each man casts the lot cup of his wyrd.'

Gunnar grunted and thrashed angrily about with his sword, sending ferns, twigs and bramble into the air. Wiping the sweat from his brow, he turned to the boy beside him and snarled, 'You're sure he said he was going hunting, Agnar?' Frightened, the boy could only nod dumbly. 'Odin take his fool hide! No one, not even the Jarl, hunts alone. If he's not already dead I'll make him wish he were! It'll be dark soon and wolves are abroad. They were seen the other night. Half a dozen of them, big enough to be Fenrir's spawn, starved enough to be dangerous. I ought to turn back now and leave the young fool to his fate.'

'You can't!' Agnar cried, tugging his cloak. 'Please don't leave him for the wolves. You have to save him. Everyone says you're the best of all the hunters. Only you can find him!'

Gunnar hunkered down beside the boy and ruffled his hair in an awkward attempt at affection. He had known at the time he would regret bringing the child, but he was the last to see Karl and his guidance had saved many hours of searching. Now, with darkness closing, Agnar had become a hindrance, slowing him down, crippling him with a weak spot to protect. They had been lucky the previous night that they had still been close enough to the borders of the wood to be reasonably safe. However, he should have sent the boy home as soon as he discovered the bloodspots. From the scuffed tracks on the woodland floor, he knew that Karl had failed to bring down his quarry, leaving a wounded and dangerous animal roaming the woods. One large enough to have carried off a full-grown man, for only one set of tracks led away from the battle. A notion of the beast's identity played uneasily with him. boar tracks that large could only belong to one animal, the Great Black Boar itself! He would probably never know what had possessed the fool to hunt the beast for the lad must surely be dead. Even now, he could hear his sister begging him to find her son and recall the fear in her eyes. Karl's father had said nothing, though the pain showed clearly in his eyes. Custom and pride forbade him speaking his heart. A good man, he had provided well for Gunnar's sister. Gunnar knew him to be proud of his eldest son's prowess, even if he would never admit to such. A similar pride in combination with his sister's pleas had persuaded Gunnar to enter Iron Wood. Now, as an eerie howl rent the air, his foolhardiness looked set to cost his sister both her children.

Gunnar grabbed Agnar's hand and pulled him to his feet. 'Stick close to me boy, and do exactly as I tell you.' Running being futile, their only hope if attacked would be to fell the leader of the pack. Perhaps, with the Allfather's blessing, it would not come to that. He turned the possibilities over in his mind as he followed the bloody trail in the fading light. The wisest course would be to cut his losses and turn back, but honour demanded he continue while the possibility of Karl being alive remained. Honour also prevented him from sending Agnar home by himself. Even if the boy could successfully navigate the woods, he would be easy prey for the wolves. Hemmed in on all sides by the warrior's code, Gunnar pressed on, the boy following behind closer than a shadow.

Dusk painted the sky a lurid shade of red, the clouds seemingly swollen with blood. Their progress slowed as the undergrowth thickened, though Karl's path, delineated by snapped branches and heavy prints in the leaf mulch, became easier to follow. The blood spots increased in regularity and size. If mortal, the beast could not have gone much further. A balled fist of dread formed in the hunter's stomach as he neared the outcome of his search. Another howl, closer than the last, chilled his blood still further. Without warning, the thickets of bramble, fern and nettle gave way to a gloomy clearing. The stump of an ancient tree stood at its centre, its roots submerged in a pool of stagnant water flanked by three moss clad menhirs. A pair of ravens, sleek and blacker than night, perched on the stump, cawing softly to each other in secret tongues. Their golden eyes flashed as their heads flicked rapidly from side to side in proprietary fashion. Karl lay slumped against the carcass of the Great Black Boar. His right arm reaching out imploringly towards the weathered stump.

All thought of danger left Gunnar as relief filled his heart with joy. Alive, his nephew was alive, and he had slain the Great Black Boar! Three long strides took him to Karl's side. Karl's eyes stared through him as though focused on some unseen object beyond, the impression so real that Gunnar turned his head, a reaction that saved his life. He caught a movement out of the corner of his eye and threw himself to the side. The wolf leapt over him, its front claws tearing cloth and skin from his shoulder as it bore down on Karl. Gunnar snatched for his sword but his nephew already had it in his hand. Karl braced the pommel against the ground and turned his head as the wolf's spring propelled it onto the sword point. Fur and muscle parted as the blade skewered the wolf through the breast. Its violent thrashing showered both men with droplets of blood, its fury to no avail. Howls of loss and frustration ripped through the dusk. With a final shudder the wolf surrendered to its fate and its body hung limp, tongue lolling obscenely between yellow fangs.

Karl shouldered the body aside and looked around as one waking from a heavy slumber. Sight of the boar's corpse shook him from his torpor. Waves of nausea shuddered through him as he stood and he would have fallen had his uncle not caught him.

'Easy, lad, easy.' Gunnar's voice was coloured with wonderment as he led his nephew over to one of the menhirs. He propped Karl against its scarred surface and inspected the gash in his side with a critical eye. A low rumble escaped his throat as he prodded the edges of the wound. Despite its apparent depth a thick scab had formed over the wound. Karl stiffened and the muscles in his jaw bunched but no sound escaped the cage of his teeth. 'Sorry, lad.' Gunnar sat back on his haunches. 'You're either damned lucky or favoured by the gods, for nothing vital appears to have been damaged. As for that wolf... I've never seen the like in my thirty-five summers.' A new respect sounded in his uncle's voice with a hint of fear below the surface. Something dark passed between the two men but before either could explore it further a scream drew their attention.

'Odin's breath; your brother!'

Agnar crouched beside the wolf's body surrounded by a living semicircle of its brethren. Terror froze him as the pack, deathly silent, moved in for the kill. Rippling grey fur, stretched tight across bone and muscle after a lean season, insinuated itself into the night as the wolves stalked forward, eyes glowing, fangs bared. At their centre moved an old she-wolf. Her eyes flicked from the body of her mate to Agnar and back again. They shone with a fervent light that might have been interpreted as hatred in a human being, but what references that lupine mind understood no man could say. A fury akin to murder and vengeance beat within her breast.

Gunnar moved even as he shouted, hauling his spear up and over his shoulder. As it slid free of its rawhide sling he braced his weight on his right leg and drew back his arm for the throw. The she-wolf, flanked by her three companions, also stood tensed, ready to spring at Agnar's throat. Gunnar cast, aiming deliberately high as she sprung. The leap proved more powerful than he expected and the spear took the she-wolf low in the belly, the impact knocking her to the side, where she thrashed on her back and batted at the shaft. But there was no time to celebrate victory for the remainder of the pack had closed with Karl and himself.

'Here!' Karl cried and threw him his sword as the first wolf leapt. Gunnar caught the sword and turned into the wolf's attack with a powerful downward slash. The blade sheared through its skull with a meaty crack that showered blood and brain matter into the night and the wolf tumbled to the ground, ripping the sword from his grasp. The second wolf, seeing the fate of its brother paused, a pair of glowing eyes and gleaming fangs in the dark. A low snarl vibrated in its throat as it attacked. Gunnar instinctively threw up his arms to protect his face from its slavering jaws and red-hot needles of pain lanced up his arm as the wolf's fangs bit into his wrist. His agony increased as the wolf shook its head from side to side, raking his chest with its claws. When he thought he could endure no more the pain faded away. A sense of detachment descended on him as if he were viewing the bitter life and death conflict from a distance. The screaming and howling sounded far away, as did the crunch of bone and tearing of muscle. All that mattered was he was suddenly free. He stumbled back, almost tripping over the body of the first wolf as the hilt of his sword banged against his thigh. Reaching for the sword, he discovered nothing attached to his wrist with which to grasp it. The ragged stump twitched uselessly above the pommel, dark blood jetting from ruptured vessels. The wolf growled as a voice in his head reminded him that a warrior should always die with a sword in his hand, any hand. The sword felt clumsy and unfamiliar in his left hand but such close quarters left no room for finesse. He had time for one blow and one blow alone. Gunnar raised the sword above his head and swung as the wolf sprang, pitting brute strength against animal cunning. Gunnar loosed a scream of rage as the blow stuck home, sending a jarring vibration along the length of his arm. Blood splattered his face and the wolf fell at his feet, its severed head landing beside it. The sword followed it and Gunnar sank to his knees. Pain returned and bile burned in his throat as he retched. It mingled with his blood to form a pool around his knees that grew steadily. Ignoring the pain, he jammed the stump between his side and his good arm and waited for the Valkyries.

As Gunnar cut down the first of the wolves another fierce struggle took place. The final member of the pack, sensing easy prey, leapt at Karl. Quick to react, he fell on his back, catching the wolf with a kick to its underbelly as it passed over him. The blow caused the wolf to land awkwardly and Karl was astride the beast before it could recover. He seized it in a chokehold and pinned its forelegs with his knees. Beneath the wolf's fur the muscles of its neck twisted and tensed, trying to resist the tightening grip. Karl gritted his teeth and applied all his remaining strength to the grim task of throttling the wolf. Veins stood out in a criss-cross of blue relief as muscle and sinew writhed beneath the tanned skin of his forearms. The noose of his fingers slowly closed, crushing the flesh below. A piteous whine escaped the wolf's foam flecked lips, taking the last of its breath, and with a final quiver the wolf lay still.

Karl rose and surveyed the glade. Night proper had fallen during the brief conflict but a full moon and a cloudless sky provided sufficient light by which to see. Agnar sat crouched beside the body of the she-wolf rocking gently back and forth on his knees. To his left sat his uncle with the body of a wolf on either side of him. Head bowed, he emitted a low keening note of pain. Sensing something wrong, Karl ran to him.

Gunnar looked up, eyes glazed with delirium. 'Wrecker of Plans is that you? Have you come to take me to Valhalla's great hall?'

'Uncle, it's me, Karl.' He stepped closer, noticing the dark stain that soaked the older man's tunic and leggings. 'Let me see your hand.' Gunnar offered no resistance as Karl pried his arm from where it lay wedged against the side of his body. A jet of blood pumped forth and Karl dropped the limb, taking an involuntary step back. Seeing the threat to life, he recovered quickly. Ripping the leather thong from the front of his shirt, Karl fashioned a tourniquet, twisting it tight with his dagger scabbard. Gunnar cried out at the pain, his back arching like a bow as the shock brought him to his senses.

'No lad,' he grunted, 'let it go.'

'Uncle?'

'A one-handed man is no use as a hunter. I would only be a cripple and a burden if I survive. Better I should die now than live to face such a fate. Pass me my sword and stand watch over me.'

'I... I can't,' Karl stammered.

'Damn your eyes, boy!' Gunnar cried, ripping the tourniquet free. 'This is no time to fail me. I'm finished as a hunter and a warrior, at least let me die with dignity and take my place among the fallen. My sword — quickly!'

Karl reacted automatically to the harsh bark of his

uncle's voice and handed him the sword. He wanted to turn away but his gaze remained riveted on the pumping jets of blood that marked out Gunnar's life in a growing puddle of gore. The dark ichor congealed rapidly about the stricken figure and his uncle's head sank slowly to rest upon his chest. With a ragged susurration of breath, his hand tightened on the sword hilt before relaxing in death.

Agnar cried throughout the night and Karl had to lie with him clasped to his breast for comfort as they huddled by the fire he had lit to keep the wolves at bay. The new day dawned bright but there was no joy in the sun's return for the two figures as they toiled to build a funeral pyre for their uncle. It was a makeshift affair but as they could not carry Gunnar's body through the woods Karl reckoned it better than leaving him to the carrion beasts. He had died a hero's death and he deserved a send off in accordance; there being no doubt that he would be welcomed among the heroes in Valhalla. Karl placed the carcass of the Great Black Boar at his uncle's head as a mark of respect and piled the wolves at his feet. Some would doubt he had slain the beast but he no longer cared. He knew the truth in his heart, knew the cost. Let them all burn together!

The flames took hold quickly and Karl did not look back as he led Agnar from the clearing. The tang of woodsmoke sharp in his nostrils, the black plume billowed up into the sky, a beacon that the gods would surely see in Asgard. Karl had glimpsed this moment in the slipping of Skuld's veil, his passage into manhood, only not as the conquering hero he had envisaged. The skalds would sing of this evening as he had foreseen. But they would cast his uncle in the role of the hero, not the young fool whose hubris led him into danger.

REFLECTIONS

A breeze flitted across the meadow, set the tall stalks of grass nodding and gently lifted the golden heads of the buttercups. The trees bordering the field were a tapestry of green on green, their leaves hung like prayer flags to some sylvan deity. A pair of rooks stalked through the grass at an ungainly waddle. Earthbound and stripped of the grace of flight, their attempt at dignity no more than a clumsy conceit. Beyond the birds, dense clumps of bracken concealed the wire and posts of the fence that demarcated the far boundary of the meadow. Here a solitary deer stood grazing on the topmost fronds. The white of the underside of its tail flashed in the twilight as it sprang forward and caught the eye of the silent watcher.

The old man's gaze took in the meadow and its inhabitants and stretched to the distant hills, which appeared as shadows of slate blue and grey that slowly faded until they were no more than a smudge on the horizon. The land seemed peaceful and still, a slumbering giant grown child-like with the passing of the years, a notion for which the old man had more than a little sympathy. Progress, once the governor of his thought, now represented only change. Life had become a fast and brutal game, the rules of which were uncertain.

It had been an unsettling day, one filled with too many echoes from the past. Some chit of a girl on the television said that they were at war. As far as the old man recalled there had been a war for the last sixty years: in Europe, in Asia, in the Middle East. The war he fought in was no different. You can read all the propaganda and listen to the lies, but when you are face to face with the enemy he looks a lot like you. The photograph of his wife and children in his wallet could as easily be your own. A different roll of the dice and it would be his hand scribbling a letter with a nub of pencil to the widow of a dead man.

Experience had taught him that there were many wars in life besides those waged with weapons of mass destruction. There was the war of words, the war between man and machine, between man and woman, and the treacherous war inside your body. The mutation of a single cell that grew and spread until it ate away not just the flesh but the mind and the spirit. His wife lost such a battle to the enemy within. Now the seat beside him appears empty to the eyes of others, but the old man knows her spirit rests there, a loving ghost that follows him from room to room in the little cottage where they once lived together. Every piece of its stone and wood is imprinted with her soul, a memory so sharp it cuts. Maybe he should accept his son's invitation to live with him and his daughter-in-law. Perhaps that would be less painful, though he fears it would rob him of all that he has left, bitter-sweet as it may be.

Movement returned his attention to the present. The rabbit was too close. It stared at the old man with an opaque eye that failed to comprehend the darkness. The sound of phlegm-filled congestion unnaturally loud as it groomed, its paws rubbing at nose and chin, stroking along the length of an ear. A wet, choking noise, a drowning sound, myxomatosis, quite advanced. The old man could still recall the first outbreaks of the disease, accidental at first but later deliberately spread by farmers. A pity, he used to enjoy a good rabbit stew when he was younger. Now the thought turned his stomach. The butcher paid good money, too. Not that his catapult or snares ever netted him his prey. But he remembered the braces of fat rabbits hanging in the window and the shiny coins in the hands of his peers.

The cruelty of childhood has since passed away. An old man is allowed his sentimentality, much as he is allowed his petulance and fussy ways. The kindest thing would be to end its suffering. A "rabbit" chop to the back of the neck. But how much force should he use to be certain? He neither knew nor cared to experiment, and left the rabbit to limp its blind way across the drive and into the scrubland below the trees. It would die soon enough, as all things must. A shriek above drew his attention to the hovering silhouette of a red kite. If the rabbit is fortunate, it will die sooner than most.

The old man pushed the rabbit from his mind and his focus returned to the land. Bound unresistingly with fences and pylons, transmitters, aerials and satellite dishes. Signals and noise fill the once quiet air, invisible, insidious, but not quite beyond perception. When he listened hard enough he could make out the thrum of the power-lines, an unnatural sound that lifted the neatly trimmed hairs on the nape of his neck. With a little more imagination, he could picture the waves of deconstructed sound and image that flowed from the television transmitter up on the hill. Were these ghosts more or less real than the memory of his wife?

The old man knows that everything has its season: its finite quality being what gives it value. In youth the summer had seemed endless, following after a lengthy and protracted spring, with all its associated pains of growth. In the bustle of a life being lived it had been all too easy to focus inwardly, to concentrate on the minutiae without ever stopping to appreciate the widescreen of the landscape. Love's first flush, career decisions, the raising of children, they all demanded unflinching attention. Then one day you looked out of the window, or into the bathroom mirror, and saw the approach of autumn. You felt the first hint of frost in the air, saw the turning of the leaves, and perceived the grey that shot through your hair. If summer had meant growth and exuberance, then autumn was a period of taking stock, consolidating gains and laying in a store for the forthcoming winter.

Not that he gave this time over exclusively to labour. He recalls the crisp, clear days; the slanting sunlight adding an extra burnish to leaves already golden brown or ruby red. His wife, no longer young, still beautiful in his eyes. Her figure fuller from childbirth, hair dyed, face careworn, but her eyes as bright a shade of green and as loving as ever they had been.

With the children at university and his wife working full time, the weekends had assumed a slow and leisurely pace. If the woods had previously been a brisk ten minute walk from their home, they were now a quarter of an hour or more, there being so much more to see and appreciate. Everything was a succession of transformations tied to a natural timetable. The unfurling of fresh buds on the trees into leaves, the flowering and fall of blossom, the bleating of new born lambs in the fields, the whistle and chirruping of the birds, the ripening of the corn from green to gold. With the harvest came the first of the brambles. The old man remembers picking them, how they bled purple across his fingers, the tart taste in his mouth. Good days that have become fleeting memories of a love and joy once shared.

The leaves fell and the new pine needles darkened to match their companions, but the woods possessed a stark beauty even in winter. When the first snows fell blanketing the trees in white it brought a sense of purity and magic. The land virginal, as on the first day of creation, and the breath, the vital life, formed clouds that dissipated into the sky. His wife's cheeks flushed red with cold and her hair turned silver, laughed long and loud as she watched the dogs skit across the powdery snow, tongues lolling, tails wagging, hunting some invisible scent. At a certain distance they would stop and wait, until the old man and his wife were once more within the boundary of master and servant. Then the chase began again, every moment born as fresh as the preceding one, spring time in the winter.

The old man sighed and shifted in his chair. Today, even though the canopy was verdant and full, the woods were stark and devoid of joy. The rabbits might hop and caper, the kites circle on the warm thermals above, but the animating life-force had fled. Five years he has been a widower, growing ever more distant and strange, cut off from the bright pulse and flux of life, fixated on a past he could not change. Disease is a terrible and implacable beast, one that consumes its prey slowly, piece by piece from the inside until only a lifeless husk remains. Hope is the only antidote and even that must pass away until it perishes with the dying of the light. Too many ghosts and yet he cannot, or will not, walk away. Everything reminds him of her. The curtains she chose, the flowers she planted, a faded image in a photograph, without which he can no longer see her face in his mind. The image he sees is not the shrunken caricature that haunted the white sheets of the hospice, but the vital, living women who he loved selflessly for almost fifty years. The girl with laughter in her eyes and a bright smile, the one he swore to return to from the war, the one he expected to survive him. His wife was always the strong one, even during her illness. At its darkest point, she was the glue that bound them together. Her consolation for his tears the bitterest of pills. If only he possessed the certainty with which she had faced eternity.

Many were those who came to God late in life, but while his earlier atheism had softened with the years, no longer the fiery brand it had been in youth, still he could not swallow that saccharine fable. That man was bound to the earth and the rhythm of its cycles he did not dispute. In this there was something of the pagan about him, but that worship was not blind but logical. Transcendence was nonsense to him; if any conception of God could rationally be said to exist then he was present within the whole of creation and not separate or aloof from the land, water, plants and animals. The old man knew himself to be as divine as the grass of the meadow, the wandering deer, or the hovering bird of prey. None of which laid claim to an eternal life in the heavens or expected some later resurrection, and that made them all the more precious. A life that was infinite was a life unworthy of appreciation.

Calloused fingers removed a slim pack of cigars from his shirt pocket and there was the faintest tremor as the old man extracted a cigar before returning the pack to its dock. The corner of his mouth twisted as he bit the end from the cigar and spat it onto the tarmac at his feet. The cat, a tawny tortoiseshell, padded out from beneath the buddleia and took up position at the edge of the chair. It regarded its owner as he struck a match and sucked on the cigar, removing it a moment later to blow upon the glowing tip, thin plumes of smoke escaping his nostrils. Judging the moment right, the cat rolled onto its back, exposing the white fur of its belly. Its master, smiling around his cigar, rewarded it by rubbing at the proffered belly. A throaty purr rose from the animal as it scratched its back against the ground, a pleasure that transmitted itself to its owner.

His wife had loved dogs but the old man found the cat lower maintenance. He found its aloofness refreshing and often felt that the cat only allowed him to be its master on sufferance. The last of the dogs had died shortly before his wife's first illness. After its commencement there had been no time for playful walks and on its conclusion he realised a dog would only emphasise her absence.

The cat, having received suitable tribute, turned onto its stomach and left its master to his thoughts. A shrug twitched the old man's shoulders and he removed his cigar and carefully flicked the ash away from the cat. The sun was starting to slide behind the trees but the night remained warm and he felt no urgency to leave his post. Many were the nights he had sat in the hard wooden chair, only a thin cushion for comfort, while his body grew stiff and cold in the gathering darkness. His daughter, on the rare occasions she was able to visit, always made a great fuss when she found him thus. The old man would listen to her words without hearing the content, seeing in her green eyes the shade of his wife. In part, if he were honest, he enjoyed her concern and found it a comfort. His son, he felt, viewed him as a problem to be solved. He had mentioned the value of the land surrounding the cottage often enough that the old man found it impossible to regard his offer to live with him entirely genuine. But if his son wanted to sell the land he would do so over the old man's dead body.

The old man shifted uncomfortably; such thoughts made him uneasy and drove the pleasure from the day. He stood up, disturbing the cat, which shot him a baleful look before slinking across the lawn and disappearing into the meadow, the fence vibrating at its passage. The old man saluted the cat, a predator off to hunt by starlit paths. He, himself, had neither breath nor spirit for the chase.

The interior of the cottage was cool rather than cold, thick stone walls shrouding it in silence. A fire had been laid in the grate despite the daytime warmth and he hastened to light the scrunched up newspaper that lay beneath the kindling. Yellow tongues of fire crackled along the thin wedges of wood and soon smoke, followed by flame, leapt up from the coals and cast drowsy warmth into the room. The old man thrust the poker into the heart of the coals, sending up a shower of orange sparks, then folded out the fireguard across the hearth.

His chair, not unlike himself, had seen better days, but for all that they suited one another. Both were threadbare, with creaking joints and stuffing that appeared to have settled in the middle in a shapeless bulge. There was comfort in such familiarity and when he closed his eyes he did not see the empty chair on his left or the black and white wedding photograph that hung above the mantelpiece. At first he threw nothing away, each picture, every personal belonging, triggering a wealth of memory, often raw and painful. Gradually, his desire to cling to the past faded and his wife's clothes made their way to charity shops and her jewellery passed to their daughter. In many ways this clearing of the house was a preparation for his departure. Piece by piece, day by day, he was letting go of life, withdrawing from the cut and thrust of the race. The process was a gradual attrition, but nonetheless sure for that. His children were safe and secure, and the cat would soon learn to show indifference to another owner. He had nothing to stay for; life's complexities had been reduced to a shadow play, a trick of the light lacking in substance. The old man's fingers rubbed the slim band of gold that encircled his finger. A symbol of unending love the priest had said, but sooner or later everybody died. Nothing was eternal, not man, not beast; even the universe was finite. Why, then, did the pain persist? Better to let it all go. To slow, then stop, and be done with the struggle.

The old man's fingers were still resting on the ring when his daughter let herself into the cottage the following morning. Her hail going unanswered, she made her way into the living room and opened the curtains. She tutted when she noticed the figure in the chair, but her words of admonishment went unspoken. There was smile on her father's face that for all its fixedness shone with heartfelt joy. He might have been asleep, if not for a certain unnaturalness of his posture, which told her of his passing long before she felt the icy chill of his flesh.

Good, she thought, that he did not appear to have suffered. Stooping, she lifted the cat from the residual heat of the hearth. It regarded her through the slit of a yellow eye and uttered a meow of protest at being disturbed, then burrowed into the warmth of her body and returned to its dreams.

SOUR LAND

The shadows cast by flickering torches danced across the flagstones and pillars of the White Castle's Great Hall. This sinister chiaroscuro fitting decoration for a dwelling in which laughter and good company had long been absent. King Janus sprawled listlessly on his throne atop the raised dais, oblivious to the wind that whistled through the gaps in the crumbling walls, threatening to extinguish the already dying light. Blind and deaf was he to the stirring of the tapestries and hangings that decorated his hall. Though not old as men measured the span of their life on this world, Janus' hair and beard were grey and his back bent and crooked. Swollen and arthritic hands gripped the armrests of the throne, and when his courtiers looked into the vacant eyes of their king they saw death not far distant.

Trapped inside a decaying body that mirrored the ruin of his castle, King Janus dreamed of time past, present and future. Those that said the past was dead and the present always dying perceived not the great spiral of time that revolved around the worlds, binding them together as irrevocably as the Axis Mundi. The groaning of that great tree in its distress was audible to Janus as he sat in his tomb of flesh. Land and king were sick and the World Tree moaned in sympathy. Janus had failed his people and his consort, the earth. The corn did not grow, cows gave no milk and hens refused to lay. Where once there was plenty now famine and dearth were upon every croft and holding. Infants and the elderly were the first to surrender, then the strong became weak in their affliction, and still no aid issued from the White Castle.

The memory of man is short when his belly is empty and his children lie in the narrow house. Good deeds and graces are not such gear as can be stowed away. They fade more quickly than the first flower of spring. Mutterings, soft at first, then more vocal were heard. A king that could not stave off famine or pestilence was no king at all, whatever deeds of renown he had accomplished in the past. Yes, short is the memory of man when three generations of a family lay in the earth together. No one now spoke of the time that Janus had ridden from out of the west accompanied by eight fellow knights with the intention of bringing peace to a blighted land. Passion and youth had been his then, the sword in his hand stained red from tip to hilt with the blood of his foes. Crimson rain fell on the battlefields, nourishing the earth so that it put forth crops in abundance. Rotting flesh made the stalks of corn high and yellow in the aftermath of battle.

Despite the slaughter he and his retinue wrought, Janus waged war without hatred in his heart. He found no pleasure in slaying those that opposed him, those who defied his law, even those that lived as brigands and preyed upon the weak. His task the necessary cultivation of a land so that the seeds sown might flourish. Janus and his men mercilessly uprooted anything that choked this flowering and burned it lest it return. Grim and tiresome work but the knights did not shirk their task. Janus proved to be a leader of vision and a brother with whom they shared a common bond of love.

These nine warriors made it possible for a people who had lived life in constant fear of attack to settle, to farm and to build. Nine men who when war was done were not too proud to put aside sword and lance in favour of the mallet and the chisel, the level and the square. They hewed mighty blocks of stone from the earth and mortared them together to build the White Castle. Its walls became a symbol of all that was pure and holy in the land. A light that drew a retinue of ten score knights to the service of the King and saw the borders of his kingdom expand, from the sea in the east to the mountains in the west and the river in the north and the forest in the south.

Tribute flowed richly from the newly conquered lands, and with it temptation. Petitioners brought girls for Janus' pleasure, but he loved none of them and produced no heir. Some thought him too proud to mingle his blood with such simple stock, while others spoke of a terrible wound received in battle. Either notwithstanding, with no battles to fight or wars to wage the king grew listless, discontent and finally feeble. All he had struggled and fought for now had the bitter taste of ash. What good was a kingdom that served only itself? The temporal limits of his achievements worked into Janus' flesh like a thousand splinters, poisoning both spirit and body.

Apothecaries, alchemists, sages and magi examined the stricken king. One by one they made their diagnosis. They cited poison, enchantment and every malady in between, one going so far as to say that the fire had gone cold in Janus' heart. A man with no love or passion has no spirit of which to speak and no defence against the whispering voices of fear and doubt that fill the slumber of every great ruler. All such men have blood on their hands and a weight on their conscience, that being the peculiar burden of leadership. King Janus, perhaps, had more than most.

Whatever the true cause of the king's malady, its effect ran to more than matters of state and warcraft, as witnessed by the barrenness of the land. Without Janus' gentle guidance and purity of heart, many of his knights descended into drunken debauchery and lost themselves in earthly pleasure. Finding the White Castle's cold stone too monastic for their sybaritic tastes, they departed one by one until only a handful remained to haunt its empty halls and tend its dying ruler.

While King Janus dreamed of past, present and future, these last retainers lived only in the nightmare of the present. The grain stores were empty, the cattle as starved as their masters, and the earth had become cracked and dry as old bone. The weaker among them lamented it should be their lot that they live to see such dark times. Surely the end of days had come, a judgement called down upon them from the heavens. While their brothers held a last vestige of hope in their hearts there was but one of their number that openly spoke out.

Ursula was the daughter of Halga, one of Janus' original companions. Though young in years, many held that she possessed an old soul. Of comely appearance and courtly manners, her eyes were dark with wisdom and her head heavy with thought. Of those that still served the White Castle, hers remained the only armour without rust, the only sword with a keen edge. Ursula's father had fallen defending Janus in the Corvine Marshes, passing on that duty to his daughter in defiance of convention. The girl now drew her sword and addressed her companions in misfortune.

'Well you might skulk in the shadows, those who bleat like sheep and cry like babes! Have you no spirit? Have you no honour? Our king sickens and dies and the land fades with him, yet none will leave these walls in search of a cure.'

'A cure, girl? Don't talk rot. We have had the finest healers in the land attend our king and none has been able to effect a cure. Where do you propose to find the cure of which you speak? If the finest analytical minds of our age cannot conceive of the cause of the king's malady what chance does a callow youth have of discovering what afflicts him? None! Disgrace yourself not with these childish imaginings, this unbecoming quest for self-glorification.

Fall instead on your knees and offer up prayer for the king's salvation, as is fitting.'

'It is true that my years are brief, Marcus, but my heart is open and I hear what is not said as well as that which is spoken. The learned sages of whom you speak are all men. Men do not understand the mystery of life. They can only take, not give. Clearly it falls to me to speak of that which you do not speak. The Chalice will restore our king, the sacred cup which holds the blood of the Magdalen.'

'Blasphemy! Foul lies of an abominable nature! That you should even mention that cursed pagan object, that foul excretion in this hall, is a sin against God.'

'There is no sin in love and no sin in drinking from the Chalice, which I will shortly prove. I will seek the Chalice and through its power restore our king and land. I will reunite that which is split asunder and make us whole.'

'All you will find in the Glass Tower is death, Ursula. Mark my words, girl. Death and damnation waits should you choose to follow this path.'

'Then at least my death will be quick, old man. Not the slow rot of fruit upon the vine that you seem to favour.'

Marcus called out a final warning, an imprecation against meddling with the infernal, but Ursula ignored his words, her heart set on its quest. Though she knew not the way, she would travel to the land of Gehenna and seek out the Glass Tower, said to be the resting place of the Chalice. She saddled her horse and struck out westward across the Wasteland to the Mountains of Tor.

For many days she rode, sleeping at night rolled in her cloak for warmth. Each morning Ursula woke to find the brooding bulk of the mountains a little closer, until on the evening of the seventh day of her quest she arrived in the shadow of Mount Ararat's sickle-shaped peak. There she dismounted, for the pass that wrapped around mountain's side was narrow and treacherous. With a comforting word and a soothing hand, she bound Fleetfoot's eyes and led the horse across narrow spans of rock and through the towering gullies. Progress slowed as the air became thin and cold while horse and master ascended the pass. Sleep was impossible and Ursula walked for two days and three nights, sustained only by the waters of the fresh mountain springs and the dark blue berries of the juniper bushes that clung to the lower slopes. More than once she thought of turning back and trying to find an easier, if longer, passage around the range but the image of Janus and the parched earth made her continue.

On the evening of the second day she came down from the mountain and made camp in a small stand of birch trees, where she fell into a deep slumber. Ursula woke not the following morning but the morning after. Her stomach, hollow and empty, drawn in until it felt stuck to itself, growled a loud complaint. Of more immediate concern than hunger was the absence of Fleetfoot. Ursula had forgotten to hobble the horse in her exhaustion. She called the gelding's name three times, the only reply the whispering of the wind through the branches of the trees. She knew her quest futile without a mount and the White Castle too distant to attempt the return on foot. She would not even make it through the pass in her present condition.

More from desperation than reason, Ursula cried for Fleetfoot once more. The sound of a whinny from the far side of the grove rewarded her cry. Unwilling to leave any of her possessions behind, she clasped her cloak around her shoulders and plunged between the slender trunks of the birches. Inside its environs the grove appeared larger than from without, or else time somehow flowed more slowly between the silver-skinned pillars, it taking several hours to reach the other side.

There, perched atop a rock next to a stream by which her missing horse was tethered, Ursula saw a peculiar figure. A tangle of red hair and a bushy beard of the same hue hid most of the man's features from view but this riotous growth was secondary to his outrageous garb. Doublet and hose had started life ordinarily enough, but they had been mended and patched so often that the original fabric was invisible beneath the patchwork of colours and materials. No jester had ever worn such motley, nor had any vagabond seemed so kingly, such was the presence of this curious stranger. On closer examination, Ursula perceived that he was a man of middle years and, from the scars that covered his forearms, had once been a swordsman. Had the stranger grown sick of battle and renounced violence in favour of a monastic hermitage? Such acts were not uncommon, particularly with the increasing influence of the Christ God.

'I was wondering who that fine beast there belonged to and now I know, m'lady.' The stranger's voice possessed a rasping quality as though it had grown rusty through long disuse. 'Careless of you to let it wander, a less honest man than I might have laid claim to such an animal.'

'Then I'm fortunate it was you who came across him first, sir...'

'Bern. I've had other names but that one, I think, has the most favourable reports attached to it.'

'In that case I thank you, Bern. I hope that virtue truly is its own reward for, as you can see, I am a poor knight with only the armour I wear and the arms I carry for my possessions. I have neither a crust of bread nor a rind of cheese that I might share with you in order to repay the service you have done me.'

'In that case will you at least grace me with your name, m'lady? That seems little enough to ask for a reward.'

'My name is Ursula, daughter of Halga, knight of the White Castle.'

'The White Castle, you say? Now that is a name I have not heard in many a year. You are a long way from home, Lady Ursula.'

'Aye, I am that. And I have many leagues yet left to travel for I seek the Glass Tower in the land of Gehenna. Can you tell me the way?'

'I can, though I will not do so willingly. The Glass Tower is an evil place from whence few, if any, return. They say a witch lives there and though fair of face she is steeped in foul necromancy. Better that you return to your home than go to your death there.'

'You are the second man to offer me such advice and I will tell you what I told Marcus. It is better to die while living than to wait for death. With or without your help, I ride for the land of Gehenna.'

Bern hauled himself to his feet by means of the gnarled staff that lay at the side of his seat. As he advanced towards her Ursula saw he was lame in one leg, the result of an old battle wound. Raising a scarred arm, he pointed along the gleaming strip of the river and directed Ursula to follow its course. There, at the source, she would find the Glass Tower. So convinced was Bern that he was sending Ursula to her death that he refused to accept a single word of thanks for his directions. He hunched his shoulders and made his painful way downriver.

Ursula watched until Bern became no more than a distant speck on the horizon, then she slipped Fleetfoot's tether and climbed into the saddle. She had spoken true when she said that her journey was far from over.

The lands next to the river were lush and verdant with no trace of the drought that affected Janus' kingdom. Plenty of grazing for Fleetfoot, but what was good for a horse was not so good for its rider. Yet where the earth flourished animals also thrived and Ursula quickly brought a rabbit down with her sling. The meat, roasted slowly over her fire that night, proved succulent and tasted more wholesome than any flesh cooked inside the walls of the White Castle for many a season. Ursula picked the bones clean and sucked the juices from her fingers. Her belly, shrunken by her involuntary fast, felt swollen to bursting point, yet still she craved more. Finding no more meat, she drank a long draught of the river and fell once more into a deep slumber.

Ursula awoke to find the moon high in the sky, a silver sickle against the dark backdrop of the firmament. It called to her in a language written in flesh and bone and her body responded. She rose, saddled Fleetfoot and continued her journey, riding through the night until sunrise, when she slept. Ursula rode to the slow waxing of the moon, living off the cold waters of the river and handfuls of nuts and berries. At night she was restive, her mind filled with visions and ideas, the flowering of a deep instinctive knowledge. Her dreams were haunted during the day by images of a dark stranger. She responded with fear and suspicion to these diurnal visits at first, but as the moon grew to fullness the man transformed into a trusted confidant. The reconciliation brought fresh illumination and Ursula grew confident that her quest would be completed successfully.

On the tenth night since her passage of Mount Ararat, Ursula arrived in the land of Gehenna and beheld the tall finger of the Glass Tower on the horizon. The black volcanic rock of the broch possessed a brooding quality that sent a frisson through Ursula's flesh. Bern's warning and that of Marcus, the old mage turned priest, returned to her: an evil place. Both had seemed sure of that fact, but excitement rather than fear gripped the young knight. Here was a place of secret knowledge and forbidden medicine. Behind those thick unlovely walls resided a power capable of restoring King Janus and of making the Wasteland flourish once more.

Ursula spurred Fleetfoot into a gallop, determined that she should reach the Glass Tower before daybreak. The river, whose route she had followed since taking her leave of Bern, had petered to little more than a stream. Its waters, translucent in the moonlight, bubbled across a bed of pebbles with a comforting shush. Now the broch's great age became apparent. Its window slits were narrow and unglazed, its stonework cunningly interlocked without the aid of mortar. The ancient race responsible for its construction had long since perished, their customs and language dying with their passing, leaving behind oblique standing stones and their once impregnable fortresses as mute testament. Those that had come after had first adopted and then adapted the stone towers to their needs. The current occupants of the Glass Tower were the latest in a long line of such occupiers and much of their power derived from the ancient wisdom stored there.

Ursula stooped, ready to enter the narrow passage that led inside the Glass Tower, when a hail made her turn. The dark man of her dreams stood before her, his face deeply etched with the lines of a long suffered private pain. Across one shoulder he held a fishing rod while his other hand held a line on which two silver fish hung.

He seemed embarrassed by his catch for he said, 'It is too early in the season to land more worthy fish but it helps to pass the time and keep me from mischief.'

'Fine enough fish they seem to me,' Ursula replied politely.

'For a peasant's supper perhaps, but poor fare for one such as yourself who has ridden long on her quest.'

'You know that of which I seek?'

'Let us say that there is only one reason visitors come to the Glass Tower and it is not for the company. A gloomy lot are we, who labour under the weight of an ancient curse. The Chalice, despite its power, is a heavy burden, as you will shortly find. But my manners desert me. I am Pelles, king of this land, and a poor host would I be if I did not offer you meat and drink after your journey. Come, I will send a servant to attend your steed.'

Ursula followed Pelles through the long neck of the entrance tunnel and into a circular chamber. Although no torches were visible a ruddy glow, both warm and comforting, suffused the whole. A long table occupied the centre of the room, either side of which were arranged benches. The table was set with platters heaped with meat and goblets flowing with wine and mead. Though two score could easily have sat, there was but a single figure. Despite his back being to her, Ursula recognised Bern from his motley attire. He turned to her and smiled.

'I see you chose to ignore my warning, Lady Ursula.'

'And I note you have little qualms about taking meat with those you were so quick to brand as fell and unnatural. You seem to travel quickly, for last I saw of you were heading far from this place.'

Bern shrugged. 'All roads in the land of Gehenna lead to the Glass Tower sooner or later. And they do say that the dead travel fast.' He paused to pick a gobbet of flesh from his teeth. 'Might I recommend the roast partridge? It is particularly excellent.'

Ursula surveyed the food. The banquet had an unwholesome quality about it that made her hesitant to eat. 'I've no doubt that it is,' she said, 'but with respect to my host, after my time in the Wasteland bread and water will be a feast to my stomach.'

Pelles shifted awkwardly at the head of the table. 'I would not like it said that anyone dined like a pauper while my guest. Are you sure you will not partake of the feast?'

'I fear my tastes have grown simple, King Pelles. Please be assured that none will hear from my lips that a received a welcome in the Glass Tower that was less than gracious, or that a kingly table was not set before me.'

Pelles' face darkened but Ursula's reply was such that he could not refuse her. He snapped his fingers and a servant appeared, entering the chamber through a doorway concealed by a tapestry. A whispered exchange took place and after a furtive glance in Ursula's direction, the servant exited with a low bow.

'You intimated that you had knowledge of my quest, King Pelles?' Ursula said.

'Indeed I did, Lady Ursula. However, I do not think it a fit subject for discussion while at table. There will be time for such talk after.'

'Of course, forgive me.'

Pelles ripped the leg from a roast goose and waved away Ursula's apology. As if by some signal, he and Bern fell about the heavily laden platters. They consumed fowl, game and fish, washing down the meat with mead and wine.

Ursula's stomach cramped enviously as she watched the juices drip from fingers and run down chins. The two men tore at the food with an exaggerated passion, as beggars invited to a banquet. Periodically, they offered Ursula a plate or a cup, which she refused in spite of their chiding. When she felt that she could not possibly endure more, the servant reappeared, carrying a silver salver on which rested a loaf of bread and a clay beaker of water. He set the round dish before Ursula, nodded to his master and retreated once more behind the tapestry.

The water proved to be as chilled as the river that had sustained her on her journey and the bread possessed the warm softness of the freshly baked. In spite of her hunger, Ursula ate and drank sparingly, savouring each mouthful and sip. All the while half-picked carcasses and gnawed bones continued to fall on the boards of the table, where their juices mixed with the slops of spilled drink.

Three times three, they asked Ursula to join in the feast and each time she declined. A clap of thunder sounded on the ninth refusal and the hall was plunged into darkness.

The song started as a vibration, a form of static that raised the hairs on the back of the neck. It grew in volume, rising from a low susurration and splitting into three distinct voices. The latter two harmonised with the melody of the first and the song became an eerie cadence. With the increase in volume came the return of the light and in the soft ethereal glow Ursula beheld the Chalice Procession. The three singers were maidens, dressed in flowing gowns of white samite. They proceeded with stately grace to walk across the chamber, the soles of their bare feet treading upon the air as though they walked on solid earth. Ursula, her face a mask of wonderment, looked at her companions but Bern and Pelles remained oblivious to the spectacle above them, even when Ursula gestured for them to look. The procession was for her benefit alone.

The lead figure stepped from the sky-bridge and descended to stand beside Ursula. Her lips were the bright red of the rowanberry and her eyes pools of jet. If this was evil, then evil was not so very terrible, and as with her first sighting of the Glass Tower Ursula's emotion was one of excitement.

The Chalice Maiden placed her hands on Ursula's belly and then rested them on her own. She smiled before she spoke. 'Are you ready to answer the Chalice riddles?' Ursula nodded. 'Then tell me, who does the Chalice serve?'

'Humanity, for without the Chalice there would be no humanity.'

The Chalice Maiden appeared caught off guard by such a ready answer. 'Perhaps my first riddle was too easy, but my second may vex you, though it is clear that you are no fool. The world is in the Chalice and the Chalice is in the world: what is the Chalice?'

'The Chalice is the Moon's influence upon the world and every woman may bring down the moon. This is because every woman is born from a womb and carries one inside her.'

'Two riddles asked and two riddles solved, answer my third and you shall have that which you seek. Where is the Chalice Castle, which is surrounded by water that is everywhere at once and is yet invisible?'

Ursula fell silent. She had presumed the Glass Tower to be the Chalice Castle but now her instinct told her the answer was otherwise. It felt tantalisingly close and yet remained out of sight. The Chalice Maiden, sensing victory, smiled and it was in that moment that Ursula recalled her touch and knew. 'The Chalice Castle is inside me! Its waters protect the gift of life.'

The Chalice Maiden nodded. 'That is so. You have journeyed far and long to discover that which you sought was inside you all along. The path to wisdom is often so.'

A panic gripped Ursula as the ghostly figure of the Chalice Procession started to fade away. 'Wait!' she cried out. 'What should I do?'

'You must make the Wasteland flourish,' echoed the

Chalice Maiden's voice.

Neither King Pelles nor Bern paid Ursula any heed as she slipped from the table, occupied as they were with the feast. No one stepped forward to stop her as she made her way through the narrow entrance hall. Night had fallen once more and a full moon glowed high in the sky, casting its pale light over the landscape.

Ursula discovered Fleetfoot tethered nearby, cropping the grass that surrounded the broch. He looked up at her approach and gave a whinny of recognition. Someone had groomed him and she noted that a waterskin and a sack containing bread and cheese now hung from either side of the saddle. Ursula thought it best not to question the origin of this providence, it being the least of that day's mysteries.

Journeying by the light of the moon, Ursula rode across the land of Gehenna and through the Mountains of Tor to arrive once more in the Wasteland. In her absence the land had grown more desolate, great cracks snaking across the arid soil. A murder of crows circled overhead in anticipation of the feast, for the White Castle remained some days distant and Ursula's food was gone and the waterskin half-empty. Good fortune had preserved her thus far and Ursula shook her fist in defiance of the crows. She had not travelled to the Glass Tower and back only to fall at the last.

The final days of her quest remained forever blank, erased by a delirium of thirst, for she realised that her only hope of crossing the Wasteland lay in giving Fleetfoot most of the water and trusting that he would make his way home. And so it was that a dusty, ragged figured arrived at the gates of the White Castle and demanded entry.

Marcus arrived first to examine this miracle from out of the Wasteland. He seemed displeased by Ursula's return, having prophesied her destruction at the hands of the Glass Tower's foul magic. For the longest time he examined her prone form, searching for the mark of the witch or other signs of the changeling. Discovering neither, he grudgingly allowed that Ursula be brought into the Great Hall and ministered to.

Three days she lay in sleep, waking only to take water and a little bread, while the remaining knights and advisers of the White Castle hung on her every breath in the hope of discovering the great secret of the Chalice, but Ursula kept her own counsel throughout her recuperation. What she knew of the Chalice was for the ear of King Janus and King Janus alone. Only once he had drunk from her cup would the Wasteland again flourish. That was the magic of the Chalice and the Moon, that which restored the king and the land.

KUDRYAVKA

Kudryavka hated the winter. The snow that shrouded the city in pristine white meant biting cold and starvation. While its citizens had rebuilt much in the decade that followed the war, pockets of ruins formed open wounds from which the homeless and dispossessed oozed like pus. Free from command and lacking a protector, they survived by preying on one another. But even thieves and marauders such as these had their foes.

At first Kudryavka dismissed the snatch squads as nothing more than a rumour used to frighten the young. She possessed a phlegmatic nature and trusted only what her senses informed her. No one who told of the uniformed men had actually seen them in the flesh. Always the information came second hand, from someone who had lost a friend or a relative. But fable or not, the survivors' number decreased and the day came that Kudryavka counted her mother among the missing. Caution became her watchword, terror hiding in every shadow.

Kudryavka slunk along the front of a derelict tenement, fearful of the light cast by the moon. The sun had risen and set three times since she ate her last meal of beef scraps from an old bone. She disliked prowling so close to the inhabited houses but hunger made her bold. A few streets ahead lay an alleyway behind a restaurant where the bins overflowed with the leavings of the rich. That it meant threading her way through one of the more populous areas of the city was a risk she had to take.

The same snow that chilled Kudryavka served to soften her tread and she passed along the street with barely a sound. Manic laughter met her as she turned the corner and she cowered from the reeling figure of a drunk.

The man waved a bottle in her direction. 'Don't take on so, little sister, I mean you no harm.' He shook the bottle before upending it. 'All gone and I've not a kopek to my name. That I should live to come to such a sorry pass, and me a war veteran! At least now I have a little company, yes?' He threw his hands up in the air in a comic gesture of despair and Kudryavka, seizing her chance, darted past him.

Kudryavka ran; down one street, up an alleyway, across a bridge, to the left, to the right, heedless of direction, only caring that the drunk did not follow. Panting, her breath forming great clouds of vapour, she came to halt in an unknown part of the city. Panic took hold and she turned in a circle, seeking some familiar landmark. All was strange and unknown, the skyline dominated by the blocky silhouettes of the most recent wave of building.

A hungry growl from her stomach cleared Kudryavka's mind of doubt and fear. If she did not eat tonight, tomorrow would find her too weak to survive. She moved with fresh urgency, heading toward an ugly apartment block. People crowded together meant waste, meant food. Skirting the road, she passed to the rear of the apartments where a set of bins huddled behind a wooden palisade. She crept forward, belly low to the ground to minimise her profile. Having waited as long as she could bear, Kudryavka leapt on the nearest bin and knocked its lid to the ground. She rummaged inside, exposing vegetable peelings and the bitter green shoots of beets. She delved deeper and turned over mouldy bread and eggshells, from which she licked the clinging remnants of the whites. Disappointing fare, but there were others to try.

'Gotcha!'

Kudryavka squealed as a noose tightened around her neck. She dropped to the ground but the man held firm to the pole and kept the cord about her throat as she thrashed on her back in a desperate attempt to free herself.

'Struggle all you like, bitch, you're going nowhere.'

Her captive called out to his comrade. Kudryavka's vision filled with the polished leather and brass of the approaching figure's uniform. Something silver gleamed in the man's hand and a tiny spurt of liquid shot into the air. She pressed herself flat and a spreading patch of urine discoloured the snow around where she lay. Kudryavka felt the needle prick her flesh. As her consciousness slipped away, she wondered if anyone would miss the snatch squad's latest victim.

Compared to life on the street, Kudryavka found life in the camp both ordered and comfortable. Her cell was warm and dry and the uniformed men fed her regularly, demanding only obedience in return. But such luxury could not last. They released her on the third day and walked her down the concrete corridor that led to the laboratory. The men in this room wore long white coats and false smiles. Some wrote on clipboards, some monitored stopwatches, while others carried tools with which to adjust the machines. Kudryavka had never seen such monsters of polished steel and brightly coloured wire. The attitude of the men showed them to be in thrall to their mechanical masters and Kudryavka had no doubt as to the sacrifice with which they would seek to propitiate them. When she tried to back away, she discovered herself held firm.

'Nothing to fear, Zhuchka,' the man soothed. 'The experiment is quite harmless, I promise.'

The technician carried Kudryavka over to the gaping maw of a long cylindrical machine, strapped her into its seat and attached sensors to her body. Stepping back, he gave the thumbs up symbol. The machine shook and shivered as it came to life. The noise increased by degrees, first a groan, then a shout, until it finally became a sense-annihilating roar. Little wonder the men covered their ears as they watched the flickering dials and flashing lights.

Even after the machine stopped, the sound continued to ring in Kudryavka's ears. It made her feel sick and anxious, but whatever the point of the experiment the men were pleased. They nodded excitedly to one another, read tickertape printouts and scribbled notes on their clipboards.

The cell they returned Kudryavka to was little more than a cage. Where before she could walk about, now she had barely enough room to lie down. Mealtime brought another unwelcome change; her food substituted by a small portion of flavourless gel. The knowledge she had eaten worse made it no more palatable, but it quickly became apparent that she must eat the gel or starve.

Days passed and the experiments continued. One day the roaring beast, the next a spinning wheel that went faster and faster until she felt as though some great invisible hand were pressing her into the couch. Each night she returned to a smaller cage until at last there was only room to sit. Unable to defecate, she became constipated. When the laxatives they laced her food with failed to work, they took her out to a courtyard and made her exercise until she produced the desired result. Never angry, always encouraging, she came to suspect their soft voices of concealing some dreadful truth.

One evening her gaolers took her back to the original cell and Kudryavka knew the morning would bring something new. They woke her early, dressed her in a harness, and walked her through the maze of corridors that led to the outside. Kudryavka scented freedom on the freezing air but knew it was not for her. The body language of the white coated men was both anxious and excited as they led her to the foot of the metal scaffold that gripped the side of a tall metal spire. Two of the men took her inside the lift at the base of the scaffold and travelled with her to the top. The wind whistled about them as they walked across the gantry to the conical top of the spire. An open hatch revealed a space the size of her final training cage, fitted with a compartment similar to the whirling machine.

Recognising it for another experiment, Kudryavka clambered obediently inside and sat. Unlike previous tests, the men attached chains to her harness that allowed her enough freedom of movement to sit or lie down but prevented her from turning round. Another unwelcome addition was the attachment of a bag to catch her waste, indicative that this experiment would last for a considerable time.

Having checked the various gauges and dials, the men recorded the readings on their ubiquitous clipboards.

'You see, Limonchik, nothing to worry about. I'm just going to close this hatch and you'll be all snug and secure.'

The hatch clanged shut, leaving Kudryavka in the eerie twilight cast by the winking lights of the consoles that surrounded her. Warm air began to blow from somewhere above, taking the worst of the chill from the air. Kudryavka leaned against the padded rest in front of her chest and settled down to wait.

The days that followed settled into a monotonous routine; the white coated men monitored the machines, changed her bag and made notes on their ever-present clipboards. And so it continued until the third day, when she sensed fresh excitement in the men. They washed her and painted patches of foul smelling iodine on the parts of her body where the sensors would go. The men appeared unusually sad as they attached the pads and checked the machines. Kudryavka grew frightened. Up until now the experiments, although noisy and uncomfortable, had not actually harmed her. Something in the men's attitude told her this was about to change.

The rumbling noise seemed greater than before and the pressure that forced her against the floor of the cabin more intense. Kudryavka had no way of measuring how long it lasted, certainly far longer than the experiments in the laboratory. A bang and a shuddering jolt signalled its end and brought with it a fresh terror. No longer pressed to the floor, she found herself floating free. Her efforts to reach the ground only served to drive her further away until she reached the extent of her chains. After several minutes of struggling ineffectually, Kudryavka admitted defeat, relaxed into weightlessness and began to drift.

The temperature had grown noticeably hotter, the whirring blades of a fan serving only to push the superheated air around the cabin. Water helped at first but Kudryavka soon found herself gasping for air. Her panting increased in time with the racing of her heartbeat, the latter going faster and faster until she was sure it must burst. Why didn't the men come and set her free? What could they possibly learn from allowing this to continue? Hadn't she been good and obedient, done all that they had asked?

Lacking an efficient means of cooling the craft, the result was inevitable. On the fourth circuit of Sputnik 2's flight, Gazenko duly recorded that all life signs had ceased and informed his superior.

'Don't look so downhearted. The bitch was always destined to die — this way she has gone from a mangy stray to a hero of the people. More importantly, we've proved a living being can survive leaving the Earth's atmosphere. Where a dog leads, man may follow.'

THE PAY OFF

Justice — she's a queer old bugger. I beat my old lady to death but served less than twelve years, thanks to a good solicitor and a suitable sob story. Had I sawn off a shotgun and relieved the bank of a few million quid's worth of bullion I'd probably have drawn a stretch twice as long like Big Jim McClusky. Banks being insured and no one being hurt beyond some lumps and bruises, Jim reckoned it a victimless crime. I should know, having listened to him bang on about it for close to nine years.

You get to know a man inside out when you share a cell for that length of time. Not just the face he presents to the world, but the things that lurk below the surface. The petty hates, jealousies and guilty pleasures that make up a personality. Most important of all, where they came from.

Jim grew up dirt poor in Glasgow's East end, eighth of ten kids. A smart lad, he could have gone far if necessity hadn't forced him to leave school at fourteen. After a stint as a butcher's apprentice, his life fell into a pattern of labouring jobs broken by bouts of unemployment, from which it proved a short step into crime. Charges for petty theft, assault and finally GBH followed, the latter earning Jim his first three years in the Bar-L.

His mother and father black affronted, Jim apologised and promised to go straight. Yet he knew deep in his heart that the only way he'd ever get out would be to score and score big. So he started planning the perfect robbery.

Besides some shoplifting as a kid, I've never been much of a one for thieving. As Jim explained it, pulling off a heist involves more than finding an easy target or seizing an opportunity. There's no such thing as too much planning and preparation, but what you need beyond anything else is a team. Any muppet can wave a gun around and is usually the first to do so, which is likely to lead to all sorts of trouble. You want boys capable of keeping a cool head when the pressure mounts. Ones you can rely on to have your back and, most important of all, capable of pulling the trigger. Depending on the job, you might require an explosives expert, and you're definitely going to need a getaway driver. Then there's passports, airline tickets, a bolt hole with no extradition laws, which in turn requires payoffs and the services of a skilled forger. The list goes on and on. All of which is the long way of saying a bank heist doesn't happen overnight.

It was another two years after he got out of the Bar-L before Jim felt ready for the job. A tip from his inside man coincided with some road works diverting the bullion truck along a backstreet where it would be ripe for the taking. But you can never plan for every random element. A blow out put the truck they were using into a skid. The driver and one of Jim's brothers died in the crash. Jim was thrown clear, earning a busted wrist, broken thigh and cracked head in the process. And there the story might have ended if not for the fact that by the time the emergency services arrived the bullion had vanished.

Suspicion fell on everyone from passing drivers to the police and the unconfirmed presence of a fourth man during the robbery. Jim remained silent, refusing to implicate anyone beyond those at the crash scene. The bank, citing a loss of seven point four million, had rather more to say, stirring up a tabloid frenzy of speculation. Any hope Jim had of leniency faded with his silence, particularly his refusal to identify which member of the gang assaulted the driver of the security truck. As Jim put it, 'Ach, it wis only a wee love tap to settle the boy doon.' The judge didn't take so kind a view and handed down a life sentence — twenty years to be served without possibility of parole.

Jim had already been inside for six years when I met him. A large man, as the "Big" before his name suggested, who walked with a distinct limp. Already the wrong side of forty-five, he'd be drawing his pension by the time he tasted the outside air as a free man. Despite the press coverage turning him into something of a minor celebrity, he kept himself to himself. A man committed to doing his time in as quiet a way as possible. I think that's why we clicked, because neither of us had any interest in taking sides or playing games. Although, admittedly, I had my own agenda.

It was six months before Jim started to talk about the job but once he broke the seal he couldn't stop. With one important exception — he always stayed clear of discussing the missing gold and if ever I tried to raise it, a shutter came down instantly, his affable manner replaced by sullen suspicion. I let it drop after the first couple of times but never lost hope that somewhere along the line Jim might let something slip. He never did, and nine years later I was none the wiser on my release.

I might have been on the outside but I was anything but a free man. Back in the day they used to talk about prospectors getting gold fever — men driven mad by their desire. That's what happened to me. I became fixated on the missing gold to the point where it occupied my every waking thought. I needed the gold. I deserved it. Quite why I couldn't say, but that didn't make it any less true. Somehow or other I would get the truth out of Big Jim, no matter how long it took.

A few discreet enquiries revealed that Jim's family had cut him off completely. The fact that Mark McClusky was a wee toe rag with a string of convictions for assault seems to have escaped his mother and father. Jim being solely responsible for his younger brother's death in their eyes, not to mention having dragged the family name through the mud. Any lingering doubt about the possibility of mending fences disappeared eighteen months after my release when the Big C got Jim's sister Kathy; his family making it clear that he wasn't welcome at the funeral.

Jim took it hard, Kathy having always been his favourite. I upped my visits at that point. The man had a lot on his mind and having a friendly ear to listen did him good. Brought us closer. I had enough sense never to mention the gold unless Jim brought it up first. Even then, I never asked questions unless he expected it of me.

Time passed. Five years. Ten years. I kept my head down and drew my dole. Hardly the lap of luxury, as some would have it, but it kept me in fags, booze and the odd flutter down the bookies. Whenever the DSS got snotty I'd get myself a job interview and on those few occasions when being an ex-con with no skills or qualifications didn't put my prospective employer off, I'd find some other means of fucking it up.

The parole board turned down Jim's first two applications but the third time proved the charm. Twenty-three years, six months, two weeks and three days after his arrest Jim finally walked free. I met him outside the prison and we walked down to the Anvil where I bought Jim his first pint. After we'd chewed the fat for a while, I put him in a taxi to the digs I'd sorted out and promised to meet up with him in a couple of days to see how he was settling in. Didn't want to appear too keen in case he got suspicious or thought me some sort of queer.

Most people had never heard of PCs or the internet when Jim went away. Now the world was full of smart phones, tablets, wi-fi and social networking. Jim viewed it with the fear that comes from being out of your depth. Can't say I blamed the man, it having taken me a good while to adjust myself. Once I'd pointed him to the good shit such as free porn and movies, he took to it well enough. From there it was only a short step onto the sites and forums that taught you how to work the system. Before long he had his own flat and was claiming the maximum whack from the government.

A year went by and Jim showed no sign of moving on the gold. I watched closely but Jim continued to live well within his means. He bought supermarket own brand food, wore the most basic of clothes and remained in his council shithole. The man either had the patience of a saint or else, and I couldn't even begin to accept the thought, he had no more idea of where the missing gold went than anyone else.

Six months later, fearing he'd spent all these years making an arse of me, I reached breaking point. One way or another I had to know. Jim not being the sort of man to respond to threats or violence, I called round in the company of Mr Tennent and Mr Bells in the hope of finally loosening his tongue.

There's an art to getting someone else drunk while staying sober. Your glass has to be in your hand or against your lips as often as possible. It doesn't really matter if the level's going down or not. Same as when you pour your man another drink, he has to see something going in your glass as well. Loud talk, big gestures and uncontrollable laughter all help to make it look like you're in the zone. A few lines of ching or whizz will also help to keep you straight, and there's always the option of spiking with a little roofies depending on the result you're after.

Couple of hours in and Big Jim was slurring his speech and repeating himself. I made a show of falling over the side of the armchair as I cracked the seal on a second bottle of whisky. I topped off his glass then filled my own, splashing as much on the carpet as in the glass.

I launched into a story about getting burned on an insurance scam I set up. In on the sweetest deal with two so-called mates who fucked me over and took the lot.

Wasn't so much the money, as badly as I needed it, as the principle. No worse feeling in life than being betrayed. Reckoned Jim of all people could understand that.

Silence. The brittle, dangerous kind. The warm glow from what little drink I'd taken evaporated. Had I just blown years of work?

Jim took another drink and stared at me. 'You been a good friend to me, Dek. Nae doubt about that. Ev'ryone else jist wanted tae ken me on account o' my rep. But you, you listened tae whit I had to say. So I'm going to tell ye something I ne'er said to anither living soul afore.'

Forgetting myself, I took a large swallow of my whisky and leaned forward, anxious to hear every slurred word.

'Ne'er wis ony gold in the getaway van. Pure distraction. Whit there wis, wis a fourth man, richt enough, and access through the basement o' one o' the neighbouring buildings to the auld Victorian sewers. Ah those years o' planning, I'd say the job wis a ba' hair aff o' perfect. Ruined by a bloody burst tyre!'

'But surely the area was searched?'

'It wis but ye see oor man wis polis. A Detective Chief Inspector, nae less. Made the cover up ah the easier. Course I didnae expect the bugger to serve oot the remaining eight years afore his pension an' leg it to Marbella. Probably should hae seen it coming, mind you, but by then it wis too late.'

'So why'd you do the rest of your time? They would have been willing to cut a deal to recover the gold.'

'Because, son, I'm no' grass. Man has to hae some standards or he's nae better than a louse.' He looked meaningfully in my direction. 'Ye dinnae dob in yer mates an' ye ne'er ever lay hands on a woman, whitever the provocation.'

'So that's it? You spent a quarter of a century locked up and now you're out you're content to rot in some council hole? I thought you'd more balls than that.'

'That's yer problem, son. Efter ah the time we shared a

cell ye still ne'er really kent me. Got yersel' hung up on my rep an' built a myth in yer heid.' He took a slug of his drink and cracked a smile. 'How's it feel to hae spent the last twenty years o' yer life chasing a ghost? Reckon that's a fairer sentence than the one the beak handed down tae ye fer beating yer lass to death.'

Jim staggered to his feet and jabbed me in the chest with a stubby forefinger. 'Noo, much as I appreciate the bevy, I think ye've ootstayed yer welcome. Time ye pissed aff back to whitever it is ye've left o' yer life. Hope ye enjoy it.'

I looked at Jim, looked at the bottle in my hand, and thought long and hard about braining him. Then I walked away. Jim's gold might have been long gone but I'd learned enough to plan my own robbery. I'd get it right, too. Even if it took the rest of my life.

LAST EXIT

Pain. A giant hand squeezes my chest, crushing the breath from my lungs. The ground rises up, too fast, all too fast, to meet me. In the distance a woman screams — I think I know her voice. Everything fades to grey.

(I don't want to leave.)

A lazy summer sun hangs high overhead. The sky is the cloudless blue of a child's painting (or memory), shimmering in the heat. Heady scents of flowers, budding trees and new mown grass fill the air. I am safe here, warm, happy, content. The ice cream is cold and sweet on my tongue. It melts quickly in the heat, running across my fingers, dripping onto my shorts. A shadow falls across me. I look up into a smiling face. The image has a name, one I associate with safety — Mother. She squats down beside me and takes the remains of the cone from my hand. The tip of a pink tongue moistens a handkerchief and my fingers, tiny in hers, are wiped clean one by one. She smiles and picks me up.

(I don't want to leave.)

Another summer's day, ochre sun heavy in the late afternoon sky. Another set of lips, the carmine Cupid's bow smiles at me from a mass of blonde curls. I reach out a hand that trembles with uncertainty. Her eyes close as I brush the hair from her face and caress her cheek with a delicate touch. With growing confidence, I put my arms around her shoulders and draw her down on me. Our lips brush once, twice, her body presses against me. I bestow feather-light kisses on her eyelids and at the base of her throat before returning to her lips. This time our kiss is firmer as passion takes hold. Her mouth opens to me and our tongues entwine, probing, teasing awkwardly. What we lack in finesse we make up for in our abandon. She tastes of the strawberries that lie half-eaten and forgotten on the grass beside us. I hold her tighter and wish that this moment could last forever. It ends regardless and the last of my innocence passes with it. I whisper, 'I love you,' knowing the moment for childhood's end.

(I don't want to leave.)

The sun has become a moon. Its light shines cold in the midnight sky. Despite the frost, which sparkles on the ground, my clothing is soaked with sweat. I reek of this fear-sweat. Its stench fills my nostrils. Earth clings to the damp cloth as I cower deeper into the shallow depression that is my only cover. Rounds of tracer blaze across the dark as the enemy attempts to locate our position. For the hundredth time, I ask myself what am I doing on this godforsaken island, squabbling over some half-forgotten throwback to the days of Empire. It's not as if the sheep, which outnumber the people, care whose flag flies overhead.

I inch forward, rifle clutched against my chest, to risk a look over the top. Tiny clouds of earth erupt beside me and an angry wasp stings my ear as it buzzes past. An explosion leaves me temporarily deaf and blind. Mines! I'm in a minefield! Terror grabs me by the scruff of the neck and drags me back into my inadequate hole. My hand slithers in something wet, organic. Palsy grips my body as I dry retch. The bile burns in my throat. I lie back and close my eyes, refusing to look at the pile of bloody rags that are all that remain of my friend. Cold, wet and terrified, I bang my heels together and whimper, 'There's no place like home. There's no place like home.'

(I want to leave.)

No sun. No moon. Just a glowing orb of electric light. I reach out and brush the sweat-soaked blonde curls from her face. My touch is confident, the awkwardness of youth gone. She squeezes my hand as her face contorts with the pain of another contraction. Her breath huffs out and I smile and say, 'You're doing fine, honey. Keep breathing.' I look at the doctor and the midwife but their concentration is fixed on the birth. I look at the blood and wonder how much bleeding is acceptable. Should there be any at all?

'It's coming. Push, Caroline, push!'

My wife's grip tightens, sweat runs from her pores as her body convulses. She screams in pain and frustration.

'Good, Caroline. Just one more push. That's it.'

Suddenly Caroline relaxes and I turn to the doctor and look at the pink, blood-streaked bundle that's our first baby. It's a girl, a daughter. Anxious moments pass before she takes her first breath, crying loudly with newborn lungs. The nurse wraps her in a cotton blanket and passes her to my wife. Her face is so tender that I know a pang of jealousy. Here is a bond that I will never be able to share in its entirety.

Looking at them both I say, 'I love you,' knowing this for a beginning, not an end.

(I don't want to leave).

There is mustiness in the air of the room that the antiseptic cleanliness of the hospital cannot completely hide. Sunlight pours in through the window highlighting motes of dust that dance in the beams. One of them falls across the shrivelled figure languishing in the bed. My father's skin looks sickly grey against the crisp white sheets, his bones show painfully through the skin. Images flash through my head of how he was. I remember him from my childhood as a large man with powerful shoulders and a deep chest. Even in later life he was still a big man, though some of the muscle had run to fat and age was beginning to stoop him. The cancer has taken all that from him. The fat has gone, the muscles atrophied, leaving a wizened figure I can hardly bring myself to look at. We all expect to bury our parents but the reality when it hits is never easy, especially when you have to watch them gradually fade away. Will my own daughter someday visit a cadaverous shell in some antiseptic hospital, secretly wishing for her father's death? I tell myself I only want an end to his pain rather than my own. His head turns towards me and I have no choice but to approach.

'Danny,' he whispers with a grin — a skull has few other expressions. 'It's good to see you, boy. How are you? Caroline and the kids okay?'

He attempts to sit up and I place a hand on his shoulder. A flash of resentment appears in his eyes but he's too weak to have any fight left in him. 'They're fine. They send their love. Sandra still wants you to take her camping. Maybe next summer when you're better?'

'Not gonna happen, son. You and I both know it's the end. You don't have to pretend with me. I'm riddled with the damn stuff. Doc doesn't know how I've held on so long. An' — hurrumph!'

His whole body shakes as a violent coughing fit seizes him. It seems to last an eternity. It passes and he lies there looking spent and even sicklier than before, if such a thing were possible. My hand shakes uncontrollably as I reach out for a tissue and wipe the dark ichor from his chin and the front of his pyjamas. I turn away so that I don't have to see the shame in his eyes. I pour a glass of water and help him sit up while he takes a few pathetic sips.

'No, not long now. Borrowed time's all I've got. That and the pain.' He taps the needle taped into his arm. 'Could have a stronger dose but then I wouldn't be conscious. Want to be awake when your mum gets here. She's coming?'

'Be here soon, Dad.'

There's moisture on my cheeks; I must have something in my eye. Something lodges in my throat making it difficult to speak. I want to tell him I love him but the words won't come. I squeeze his hand, the bones feel brittle, and wait for the end. Unable to say what I feel, I try to communicate as much as possible through my desperate touch. It's not enough but it's all I have. I hope it's enough.

(I want to leave.)

Clapping echoes through the hall as the graduates take to the stage and receive their degrees. A nervous stroll, a handshake, quick smiles, and they exit stage left. My heart fills when they call my daughter's name and she begins her walk. Sandra stares out into the assembled crowd of doting parents hoping to see us, but there are too many faces and not enough time. Her moment is over and she must leave. I turn to Caroline and smile, knowing she shares my pride. Her figure may be fuller and there's some grey in her hair but to me she still looks as beautiful as ever.

Paul shifts nervously beside us. He has just completed his first year in Computer Science and hopes to walk across that stage in his turn. Academically he has always stood in his sister's shadow. Not that he's stupid, far from it. But sibling rivalry can be a difficult thing to cope with. I give his shoulder a squeeze, 'Just stick in, son, that's all I ask. Your mother and I both know you can do it.'

'That's right,' Caroline agrees. 'Now come on. We have to get ready for the photographer.'

(I don't want to leave.)

I float weightless for an indeterminable period in darkness. I cannot remember the last time I felt so completely safe and secure. There is no hunger or cold here, no fear, only peace. It is a return to the primal womb, the timeless void that joins birth to death and death to birth.

(I don't want to leave.)

Everything here is light, a golden brilliance from which all matter stems. I am a consciousness among a multitude. Though we are legion we are, each of us, individual. All of us gathered here on these blessed fields are equal, possessed of a purpose. I instinctively know my own calling, but above the others and myself are the Hosts and above the Hosts is the One. He senses my confusion and raises me to His right hand to seek my answers.

'You are disoriented. It is natural. But now you must continue the Work.'

'The Work? I do not understand.'

He laughs, deep, booming and intense. Despite its good-natured intent there is an undercurrent of warning. 'My Work, of course. The Grand Universal Design. When a soul serves me well it is rewarded by a turn on the Cosmic Wheel. A cessation of its labours, for a time.'

'A holiday?' My voice (if projected consciousness can be referred to as such) shakes with growing horror. 'All that striving to raise and protect a family, to live a good and honest life. Those years of pain and joy, the despair and hope, all that experience was no more than a… diversion?'

Again, His booming laughter fills my being. 'Surely no

one takes it seriously?'

AFTERBIRTH OF DAMNATION

Global war has raged for six years, building a potential of suffering on a scale previously unknown. Now that energy is ready to spark to Earth. Reality is torn asunder in the heat of a nuclear blast and a primordial shape coalesces, a being woven together from the strands of the souls of the one hundred and thirty thousand victims of Little Boy.

Fat Man explodes above Nagasaki three days later adding a further one hundred and seventy thousand to the vortex. As it expands it sucks in the psychic residue of other atrocities, the maelstrom building and gathering pace.

So many incendiary devices are dropped during saturation bombing raids over Dresden that the oxygen in the air ignites, immolating thousands of women and children in their homes. The firestorms caused by a similar raid over Tokyo add another hundred thousand souls to the toll. Psychic residue from the systematic extermination of six million people in the Nazi Death Camps provides further fuel.

The vortex is huge now and as it continues to grow its consciousness expands. But it needs fresh suffering to maintain its momentum. Driven by hunger, even the small tragedies become of interest.

In London a young boy playing on a stretch of wasteland uncovers an unexploded German bomb. A curious nine-year-old, Tommy Doherty examines his new piece of salvage. The vortex travels to ground in a wash of sound, light and fury.

Aware that it will be easier to feast upon humanity's suffering if it moves among them, the creature searches for a suitable form. A face and name with which to interface.

Consciousness returned slowly to Alexandra as she stretched her cramped muscles on the camp bed. The rough woollen blanket slipped from her body and fell to the floor to lie in a heap as she coughed and groped blindly for the packet of cigarettes on top of the bedside table. She shook one from the flimsy packet (American, a gift from one of the wounded) and East met West as she lit it with a lighter fashioned from a Russian bullet casing. Drawing the smoke deep into her lungs, she let the kick of the nicotine relax her before exhaling the smoke in a steady stream. 'Girl,' she said to herself, 'these things are going to kill you.' The acknowledgement of her mortality caused her to emit a harsh bark of laughter. 'Right,' she sneered, her eyes flashing as she tossed her hair over one shoulder. She took another long draw on her cigarette, causing the tip to glow bright in the gloom of the shuttered compartment.

Coils of blue tobacco smoke formed intricate wreaths that drifted lazily upwards before dissipating in the breeze of the ceiling fan. Alexandra sat naked on the edge of the canvas bed and stared at the dark stubble growing on her legs. When had she last shaved them? What did it matter? There were no fashion parades on the Eastern Front. The men she met fell into two categories; those too ill to care or those too coarsened by experience to expect anything better.

Standing up, she started to search for her uniform. Her

patched underwear, blue smock and starched white apron lay where she had discarded them in the grip of exhaustion the night before, across the back of a folding chair. The chair, like everything else in the compartment, had an air of impermanence about it. The same could be said about the rest of the hospital train, or indeed of the world. The war had thrown everything into a state of flux, subjecting everyone to its chaotic whims. Friends, lovers and relatives vanished overnight and unfamiliar homes and faceless ruins replaced neighbourhoods.

She was tired. Tired from working the eighteen or sometimes even twenty hour shifts. Tired of tending the endless stream of wounded, young men who all bore the same crushed expression, the one that begged for the return of lost innocence and the restoration of their shattered dreams. Men, no, most of them were little more than boys, whose lives had been irrevocably warped by the horrors of war. Nineteen-year-old cynics with the eyes of old men, their faces rushed before her in a tide of memory. So many different faces and yet all were branded with that identical expression of pain and loss. Would it ever end? They were like a cancer eating at her soul and when the feast was over she would be ready to join the hollow men. Eaten away by a parasitic composite of fear and disillusionment.

Alexandra sighed and reached inside the bedside table. Time for a little something to help her through the day. The last of her cocaine had gone weeks ago but she still had some Benzedrine. She worked quickly, crushing down one of the tablets and chopping it finer with a scalpel blade before arranging the powder in three lines on the surface of a hand mirror. A further search of the drawer produced an engraved silver snorting tube, a relic of Tsarist decadence. She paused to stare at her pale reflection in the mirror. 'My little white vampyre, how I love and hate you too.'

On the other side of the glass the entity stirs. It has found a name, a pretty face and a weakness to exploit. Humanity will tremble as the White Vampyre exacts vengeance for the millions whose suffering has birthed her.

Klaus Schadows runs through the thick cloying mud, fear clutching at his heart. Drops of sweat run down his shaven scalp and sting the bruises that cover his emaciated face. His malnourished body struggles to work beneath the shapeless grey rags of his clothing. He can hear the baying of the dogs as they draw nearer.

Glancing down, he catches sight of the yellow star pinned to his breast and cries out in horror, 'It's a mistake. Some terrible mistake. I'm not a Jew! I'm a good Party Member. I've given a dozen years' loyal service to the Fatherland! Don't you hear me? You've made a mistake. I'm no stinking Jew boy!'

The pain seemed greater this morning, if such a thing were possible. It cut through the numbing haze of narcotics in sharp, stabbing waves. Klaus gritted his teeth and started to count to one hundred. That was how long he would bear the pain before calling for the duty nurse to administer a more powerful painkilling agent.

His mind began to drift in the mid-twenties. With a dream-like shift of perspective, he found himself travelling back through time to his doctor's office three months earlier.

The doctor's face was grave as he asked Klaus to take a seat, indicating the results of his tests were bad.

'It's cancer, isn't it?'

'I'm afraid it is. And it's already quite advanced.'

'I see.' Klaus swallowed. 'I imagine it can still be treated?'

The doctor looked away for a moment. By the time he restored eye contact with his patient he had composed his features into a suitably serious expression. 'No, I'm sorry. It has already spread to your lymphatic system and is now inoperable. To be strictly candid with you, Mr Sheridan, you have perhaps three months left to you at the outside. 'I really am sorry, but it is beyond medical science at present to cure your condition.'

'I suspected as much. At least I shall have a little time to put my affairs in order, yes?'

'Indeed.' The doctor frowned and chewed nervously at his lower lip. Relatively young, his experience in delivering a terminal prognosis was limited. Some things one simply could not learn from textbooks. There were standard prerogatives, of course, but no physician likes to lose a patient.

The doctor continued, 'I don't wish to be indelicate but do you have any medical insurance? It's just that you're going to require constant care towards the end and the pain is going to get steadily worse. The cost of all this, medicines and care, will not be cheap. Perhaps you have relatives, a son or a daughter, who can help? Possibly provide care for you at home?'

'I have no one, doctor.' Klaus watched the young man's face fall, for a moment he felt a vicarious thrill of pleasure as he watched the doctor's concern twist into guilt and helplessness. Then some gradient within him shifted and he put on a brave smile and hastened to assure the doctor. 'You needn't worry, I have full coverage, plus a little something salted away for such eventualities. But I appreciate your concern. Now, I believe I have taken up enough of your time. I'm sure there are hospices I can contact and literature I can read to provide me with more details. They shall help me organise things from here.'

'Quite,' the doctor replied, sounding relieved. 'I'm glad you're able to deal with it so well. Not all my patients could. But if you need anyone to talk to I have a number you can contact. They're very good at this sort of thing.'

'As you wish. But when you get to my age, when you have seen all the things that I have seen, you will find there is little left to trouble you. Six years of war showed me as much horror as I have ever needed. I have seen death in all its forms. Mine is not so very terrible.'

'Right. At least let me give you something for the pain in the meantime. And if you could just give me the details of which hospital you intend to use everything else will work itself out.' The doctor scribbled a few words on a prescription pad and tore off the top sheet. Handing it to Klaus, he enquired, 'I'll see you again?'

'I think so, doctor. I'm not dead yet. Heh, seventy-five years and it ends like this. Perhaps that is justice of a sort. Do you think God has a sense of humour, Doctor Goldstein? When you get old like me you will find that you ponder such things.' Klaus shrugged. 'Good day, doctor. Really mustn't take up any more of your valuable time.'

To think that he, Klaus Schadows, had to accept the sympathies of a Jewish doctor. God did indeed have a sense of humour, a warped and twisted one.

Ninety-seven, ninety-eight, ninety-nine, one hundred. Klaus stabbed down on the call button, signalling for an angel of mercy to bring him relief from his agony in the form of morphine. He smiled as the duty nurse arrived and explained his discomfort. Consulting his chart, she agreed to his request for a painkilling injection and rolled back his sleeve. Below the gathered edge of his pyjamas' sleeve Klaus could just make out the scar tissue of the skin graft that had obliterated his SS blood group tattoo, a physical reminder of the sins of his youth. It had been an expensive black market operation just after the war but he had the money. Money steeped in the blood of innocents.

He looked away as he felt the pinprick of the hypodermic needle sliding into his flesh, its medicinal compound distancing him from reality. Above him the nurse's features and starched white clothing shimmered and warped until it seemed to him that an entirely different woman now stood over him. This one had piercing blue eyes and long black hair curled in old-fashioned ringlets. Her lips were red and her skin pale as alabaster. Instead of sterile hospital clothing, the woman wore an ornate white dress.

Her shadow loomed menacingly over his bed. 'Time for us to go, Klaus. Time to pay the piper.'

Confused, Klaus asked, 'Who are you?' But the woman had already faded from view and Klaus realised that he had also passed from the environs of the hospital. With transportation came transformation. He was a young man again, wearing the uniform of an SS *Feldwebel*, sitting behind the wheel of a staff car. The wind ruffled his hair as he drove at breakneck pace along the mountain track. In few short miles he and his passenger, SS *Oberst* Anton Steyer, would be safely across the German-Swiss border. Safe with their cargo of stolen gold and art treasures, totalling perhaps a million dollars. Enough wealth to buy them new identities and freedom. But before then he would have to take care of his passenger.

Steyer had been commanding officer at Auschwitz-Birkenau between May and October 1944, during which time he helped oversee the feeding of almost a million Jews to the gas chambers. By the end of September, with the Russians advancing into Poland, plans were underway to close down the camp and destroy all evidence of its function. Sensing the end to be at hand, the inmates organised a rebellion. The majority called it off at the last minute but a group of *Sonderkommando*, the special squads of Jewish prisoners used to process the dead, went ahead and blew up the crematoria using smuggled explosives. They went on to attack and kill several of the SS guards with the hooks they used for pulling the corpses from the gas chambers, before being shot down. Klaus remembered the fighting well; he had personally taken part in the hanging of the four Jewish women responsible for the smuggling of the explosives. The SS personnel had completed the destruction of the crematoria before pulling out of the camp.

Members of the unit were later recalled to Berlin where Klaus had served as Steyer's adjutant. This comfortable assignment had ended two days ago when, with the Allies advancing on every front, *Oberst* Steyer decided it would be prudent to liquidate his assets and run. He had commandeered a light aircraft using forged documents and escaped from Berlin. Landing at an airfield near the border where he had arranged to have a car waiting, Steyer had paid off their pilot with a bullet in the back of the skull. As they approached the border, Klaus was under no illusions as to his own fate if he did not act first. Drawing his pistol from its holster, he waited for a straight stretch of road and turned around. *'Gute nacht, Herr Oberst,'* he said and he fired. The Walther bucked twice in his hand and a pair of nine millimetre bullets shattered Steyer's head like an egg. Laying the pistol on the seat beside him, he changed down a gear in time for the next corner. Home free.

'Klaus, how can you ever escape the guilt of your actions? You participated in the slaughter of hundreds of thousands of people. And now you have shot me in cold blood.'

Klaus turned at the sound of Steyer's voice. His commanding officer sat calmly in the rear of the car, a cigarette dangling between his lips, the top of his head missing from the bridge of his nose up. He wiped brain matter from his right epaulet. 'Do you have a light?'

Klaus started to scream. He continued to scream as the car careered off the edge of the narrow road and plummeted down the high mountain pass. He screamed as the vehicle bounced and crashed its way between the rock walls, the impacts breaking bone and rending flesh. He wanted desperately to black out but could not and remained conscious as the car came to rest at the bottom of the gorge. There, against all reason, he lay alive, trapped in the wreckage of the car. He tried to move but every bone in his body was broken and his flesh pulped. Then he smelled the gasoline and heard Steyer comment, 'Don't trouble yourself, Klaus, I've found my matches.'

Klaus screamed loudest of all when the car exploded into flames, He remained conscious as the flames ate the ruined flesh from his broken bones.

He was still screaming when he awoke almost half a century later in his hospital bed. The White Vampyre listened to his screams without interest as she waited for Klaus to wake fully. Satisfied that this was so she crossed to his bed and whispered, 'They would know why.' Having delivered her statement the White Vampyre returned to her realm.

Pain exploded inside Klaus's chest and he heard the monitor beside his bed emit a steady monotone in place of the regular beeps prior to his coronary. He knew he was dying even as the medical team rushed in with the crash cart to begin emergency resuscitation. It was God's will that he should die. He had escaped punishment for his sins too long. Now he would pay for them in hell.

Klaus found himself standing in a barren marsh. At first he did not recognise where he was, then he spied the barbed wire fence of the camp and realised these were the marshes where they used spread the ashes from the crematoria. He had been sent back to scene of his crimes for judgement.

Standing some yards in front of him stood the young woman from the hospital. She wore a long winding sheet and Klaus wondered if she, too, were dead.

The woman smiled without warmth and said, 'I have been expecting you, Klaus. It is time for you to be judged.'

'Really? And who, young lady, might you be to judge me? And by what power have you brought me here?'

'I am justice and vengeance, the sum of your guilt and fear. That is what has brought you here.'

'Ha!' he wagged a finger at her. 'I was expecting someone taller and more masculine. I find it hard to believe that a mere slip of a girl could hope to punish me for my sins.'

'I'm not here to punish you, Klaus. That's not my burden.'

'No? Then why are you here? Do you know what I've done? I'm a murderer a thousand times over. I deserve to be thrown into the deepest, darkest pit of hell. You should hate and despise me.'

'Sometimes, Klaus, life is the best punishment of all. I couldn't hope to hate you as much as you hate yourself. But we have a little time if you feel the need to confess.'

'Spare me your compassion. I neither need nor want it. I regret nothing. Except, perhaps, that we didn't get the other five million while we were about our work. Look around you, girl. This is Birkenau, the second Auschwitz camp, built solely for the purpose of human extermination. And by God did we do it well!

'The inmates were "processed" in less than six hours after their arrival by train. Their possessions were taken, they were stripped of their clothes, their heads shaved, and then herded into the gas chambers. Then myself and other members of the SS death squads would tip the Zyklon B pellets into special ducts in the walls and ceilings and five minutes later a couple of thousand enemies of the State had been disposed of.'

'Yes. I remember,' the Vampyre replied.

Klaus ignored her remark and continued, 'Afterwards, the *Sonderkommandos* would remove the bodies and extract any gold dental fittings they found. Meanwhile, their clothes and possessions were sorted and packed and along with their hair, which was used for insulation in submarine hulls, sent back to Germany on the same train that had brought them. A truly remarkable achievement, recycling human beings to serve the war effort, and at Auschwitz II we were proud of it. Did you know that we were the only camp to employ specialist gas chambers purposely built for Zyklon B? Camps like Chelmno had to make do with gas vans or carbon monoxide.

'Sometimes our efficiency backfired. The crematorium ovens were a prime example. They were designed to require virtually no fuel, operating instead on the fat from the victims' bodies. But due to the starvation diet the fat content of the corpses was so low that we had to abandon this idea. Still, the company who designed the crematoria managed to patent the method in 1953, so it wasn't a complete waste of time.'

Klaus looked at the Vampyre and grinned. 'There, I am quite unrepentant. Do you hate me now? Will you punish me?'

'Why should I? You've spent the last fifty years punishing yourself. Enslaved by the past, unable to look beyond your previous actions. That's always been your problem, Klaus. You've never had the courage to stand up for yourself or what you believe in. Yours is a litany of excuses. "I was only obeying orders. If I hadn't done it someone else would. I am just a simple man who does not question the decrees of his betters." And so on. The only act of courage you ever committed was blowing Steyer's brains out. Your one chance to grow and escape from your self-imposed limitations and you wasted it. You spent the rest of your life living in fear, hiding the past, waiting for that dread knock at the door in the dead of night. The one that meant they had finally found you out. You shunned relationships, a career, anything that might expose you to the scrutiny of others. The only punishment I have to offer is acceptance, because you and others like you helped father me. I grew strong on your fear and anxiety. Fed off your disappointment and bitterness. I relished watching you drive home the nails of your martyrdom.'

'Whatever you claim, you're a cruel bitch, punishing me with truth. If you are Death then you've allowed me more than my allotted three score and ten in spite of my crimes. But at the last even this seems hardly long enough.' The Vampyre remained silent and Klaus continued almost whimsically, 'Is it true I wonder, as it says in Genesis, that the first people lived for centuries? I once heard a story in Tunisia that told how our lives were reduced. There was a virgin who lived five hundred years before dying. Later, when Moses requested that Allah resurrect her, she complained she was tired of life, so Allah told Azrael, Angel of Death, to free his children from their mortal worries after a mere seventy years. Is that how it happened? Did one sour-faced crone screw it up for the rest of us?'

'In my experience,' the Vampyre said, 'people mess things up for themselves.' She traced a circle in the mud with her toe and then looked up again. 'That's something people like you never seem to understand. You're always looking for someone else to put the blame on.' Her eyes narrowed. 'Time to get back to the business at hand, Klaus. It is time for you to go on. But you won't walk alone. There are some people who have been waiting a long time for you to return.'

She spread her arms wide, revealing rank upon rank of shadowy figures. Men, women and children stood silent in naked shame. Their shaven heads and gaunt bodies an accusation. The task of judging Klaus Schadow's soul had fallen to these shades and they found it wanting.

The White Vampyre walked away as their ranks closed around Klaus, her ears deaf to his pleas for mercy. If his fate troubled her then she showed no sign. She had many fathers, some as yet unborn.

BURDEN

The old man stared through the window, seeking familiar landmarks as the bus rattled and shook its way towards the village. New houses, harled in oatmeal coloured chippings, lined the road in place of the fields and trees of his youth. To him they appeared identical, lacking the character of the old cottages built from the stone of the hills. That much at least remained unchanged: the rising slopes graduating through green to purple and ending in a topping of slate-blue stone. Deceptively close through the glass, but several hours distant, even when measured by a young man's stride.

The pneumatic hiss of the brakes and accompanying rocking motion drew the old man back to the present. He stood and clutched his raincoat about him, acutely aware of his pyjama bottoms sticking out beneath, the paisley flannel resting on the dull leather of his boots. The bus driver opened his newspaper and unscrewed the cup from his thermos. He offered a non-committal grunt in response to his sole passenger's thank you.

The enamel sign identified the location as Market Street, but no one had bought or sold goods here in the last fifty years. Memory summoned the ghosts of the past and stalls and carts surrounded the worn stone of the market cross. The stallholders and villagers called out to one another in a lilting dialect that had almost vanished, haggling over the price of barley, cheese and butter. They seemed real enough to touch, but faded away the moment he stretched out his hand, leaving only hanging baskets swinging below the arms of the cross. Autumn had already wilted the blooms.

A snigger made him look across the street where he spied two boys, no more than thirteen or fourteen years old. As he shuffled away on arthritic hips, the old man felt certain he was being followed. Middle of the day. Nothing to fear. So why did his heart hammer inside his chest? Fifteen years ago — even ten — he would have taught them a sharp lesson in respect, but kids are different nowadays, almost feral. Ignoring the sharp pain in his hips, the old man propelled himself towards the safe haven of the corner shop. Relief flooded through him as his fingers wrapped around the handle and he risked a glance over his shoulder. The boys, laughing and pushing one another, were already far down the street, heading in the direction of the old mill. They no longer looked wild or frightening. The old man's laughter turned to tears. When had he turned into such a silly old fool?

The shop door swung inwards to reveal the concerned features of a woman. Petite, dark haired, dressed in what the old man considered slightly immodest attire for the time of year.

'Are you all right?'

'Ach, I'm fine, lass.' The lie came automatic. He had his pride. Man and boy, he had worked and looked after himself, supported a wife and raised three children to fend for themselves. He didn't want to be a burden.

'Are you here visiting family?'

'My family used to work the McRitchie croft.' Sensing the woman's puzzlement, the old man continued, 'Past the mill, on the south side of the hill.'

'Oh, I think I remember driving by some ruins out that

way. Nobody has lived there for years.'

Further words stuck in the old man's throat and he merely nodded as he stepped aside to let his would-be Good Samaritan on her way. The door swung shut, an implacable barrier. Realising that there was only one path left to take, he thrust his hands into the pockets of his faded raincoat and headed towards the mill. Since those first faltering steps from the care home, he had known his ultimate destination. A return to his roots and the memories of a not always happy childhood. He had been born here and it seemed fitting the circle of life should draw him back.

Awkward steps took the old man beyond the mill and onto the now metalled road. Hard surface or not, it still wound its way along the track travelled by sheep centuries before, its black ribbon passing through the base of the glen and up the side of the hill. The road seemed longer than when he had last walked it in his youth, and he leaned against the dyke at the side of the road to catch his breath. Its raggedness surprised him.

The glare of a low sun silhouetted the croft house in the distance. This shadow of the past wasn't his home. Home had been the bungalow he retired to with Jean. Those years, with the children grown and raising families of their own, had been some of his happiest. Then Jean died, leaving him alone. The doctor told him it was her heart, which came as no surprise. She had always given so much love it amazed him it that it had managed to beat for so long.

At first his children visited regularly, but soon they started to miss this evening or that weekend as the rhythm of their lives took over, until a whole month would sometimes go by without a visit. Stubbornness prevented him from saying anything. If they could not come of their own accord, he didn't want them visiting out of guilt or a sense of obligation. But loneliness eats away at a person as surely as a disease. Walking lost its pleasure and with no one to talk to, he turned to the television for comfort. If he grew forgetful, it wasn't as though he had anything important to remember. He found it difficult to get in and out of the bath and standing in the shower was painful, so there were days when he scrubbed only his face and his oxters. Meal times at least helped break the monotony. What did it matter if he had six one day and only one the next? It amounted to nothing more than the marking of time.

Somewhere, somehow, his children came back unbidden. Not only them but his grandchildren too. Underfoot, poking, prying, and never giving him a minute's peace. Wanting to bathe him like an infant, forcing him to walk around the garden while crowding next to him, making him furious with their silly concern.

Even as he recalled the image of his eldest, Heather, standing there with a red mark spreading across her cheek, he couldn't remember hitting her and wondered if this was a false memory or some other kind of phantasm. Yet her expression, neither sad nor angry, only determined, must have been born of some transgression. Why else would she have insisted on him entering a care home, uprooting him from all that he considered his own?

Respite, not for him, but for his long-suffering children. Six weeks at most, the opportunity to step back and assess the situation. Having company might give him a new lease of life. Platitudes intended to make his children feel better about their decision.

Six weeks among the living dead, shuffling from dining room to television lounge and back again until sleep came as a blessed relief. While it was true that some of the poor souls here didn't know night from day that didn't justify the staff talking down to him. He hated the helplessness, the regimentation, and yet when he saw the hopeful, almost pleading looks in his children's eyes, he resigned himself to his incarceration without further objection.

Such care, even as indifferent as he perceived it to be, didn't come cheap. The bungalow and all its memories of Jean and their happy times together had to be sold. A few ornaments, a pile of old letters and a collection of photographs were all he had space for in his tiny room. What furniture Heather, Sandy and Duncan didn't want went to the dump. Deemed, like him, to be worn out and worthless. He cried after they left, not with sorrow but from frustration and rage at the thought of all he had strived and worked for being gradually erased. That was when he began annotating the photographs, writing down names and places, everything he kept locked up inside his head.

Months, perhaps years, slipped by in dull and repetitive patterns. Strange faces looked back at him from across the breakfast table. Or did he only imagine that, along with the hearses that seemed to continually shuttle back and forth? Some days were better than others. He liked it when Jean came to visit, even when she kept on telling him her name was Heather, same as their daughter. She always cried when he tried to comfort her. On the bad days he was an old man in a home whose sons did nothing but complain about the cost of keeping him.

Yesterday had been such a day and so he had risen early and slipped away through the morning twilight, shivering under his raincoat. They had built a new bus station, a confusing palace of glass and steel, but the impossibly young girl who worked in the ticket office had helped him find the right bus. He tried to give her some money for her trouble, but she insisted on him putting the handful of notes back in his wallet. A small kindness rebuffed, and a reminder of how cold the world had become.

The lack of a conductor on the bus saddened him, for the driver and his fellow passengers had few enough words to spare. It made for a long and lonely journey to the village. Now Shanks's Pony had done the rest and brought him to the door of the croft house, which had suffered the fate of many vacant buildings, its roof removed to avoid paying rates. The hinges were rusted and the wood swollen with damp, but he managed to force the door open far enough to squeeze inside. A nail snagged his raincoat, leaving it torn at the shoulder.

With the interior exposed, nature had worked hard over the intervening decades to reclaim the stone cut from her hills. Moss and lichen covered the walls and weeds grew between the flagstones and out of the mortar. Even so, the inglenook remained visible, rusting hooks jutting from the lintel above. The old man pictured the pots that had once hung over the fire; porridge in the morning, soup or stew during the day, with barley, beef or mutton. The taste of the grey meat was in his mouth, unpleasant but not entirely unwelcome. A full belly was better than an empty one, as the painful contraction of his stomach reminded him.

His boots left imprints in the windblown dirt as he walked through the ruin, remembering. Here the old dresser, there the box bed on which he had slept with his little sister, and by the fire the rocking chair on which his Da' had sat of a night quietly smoking his pipe, worn out by the labours of the day. His circuit brought him to the rear window with its last jagged shards of glass protruding from the frame. The slope of the mountain rose steeply outside, its summit hidden by mist. Beinn something-or-other, but he had always known it as the Big Hill, its shadow the dominating memory of his childhood. South meant safety, his father had often told him, the north-west face of the peak a sheer drop of more than a hundred feet to the jagged rock below.

The old man pushed himself away from the cool stone of the wall and slipped from the derelict croft house. He raised his head and his gaze settled on the summit of the Big Hill. Fifty years or more since he last climbed up there. With the mist having come down the odds were he would see little enough, but he would not be back this way again. He started the slow, painful climb, knowing he had all the time in the world.

They grass gave way to springy heather that turned treacherously under his boots. Stopping on the uneven ground gave no relief from the pain in his hips and so he kept walking, ignoring the wheezing in his lungs and chill in his back. The earth was thin here, its rocky bones worn and exposed. Sight of that stone gave him the strength to continue, even though the summit was always a little further away than it appeared.

He used his hands as much as his feet towards the end, hauling himself across boulders worn smooth by the passage of water. Huffing, puffing, but determined to capture one last glimpse of his childhood, to look upon the country that had given him life. As he struggled to overcome the last few metres, it came to the old man that he would not have the strength to climb back down, not in the cold and dark. The idea of failure so close to his goal spurred him on and he crested the mist-shrouded top.

His father's warning came back to him as he inched towards the unforgiving north-west face and peered through the low-level cloud. All was grey and still in the blanketing damp. The old man cocked his head and listened. Faint at first but gaining volume as it swept up the glen, he heard the soughing of a rising wind. Soon he felt its icy fingers probing at his clothing, seeking some ingress through which to strike at his already chilled flesh. The hills were nothing if not treacherous in their ever changing moods. Those born to them learned respect from an early age or perished.

The mist lifted with the incoming wind and afforded him a vertiginous view of the rocks below. The old man stood on the edge and stretched out his arms. A gust caught his raincoat and flared it open like the unfurling of dark wings. He looked out across the surrounding hills and smiled at the beauty of it all, fresh as the day of creation. Fresh strength flowed through him, drawn from the rock and the sky, lifting the burden of his years and granting the power to go home. A single step took the old man into space and the mountain rose up to embrace him.

FUNERAL GAMES

Wallace fed the tail of the tie through the knot and pulled it tight. He examined it in the mirror; the perfect Windsor knot. A frayed edge showed grey against the black, visible even in the dull glow of the room's naked bulb. A frown deepened the furrows in his brow. Bad enough that the young should lack decorum. He fastened the lower button of his jacket and turned side on to the mirror. The suit hung badly on his gaunt figure, something for which he had no remedy. Some might say his Sunday best had worn considerably better than he had these last few years. Wallace uttered a terse sniff and pulled himself straight. Hair neatly combed, shoes freshly buffed; pride in his manner.

A treacherous gurgle sounded from his stomach, forcing Wallace to retreat to the kitchen. He drank two glasses of water, rendered tepid by the summer heat. The glass rattled on the draining board, catching the light that shone in below the blind. Dry weather, always a blessing on a day such as this. His hand sorted through the change in his pocket, taking in dimensions and the number of edges. Ample time to walk to his destination, if he left immediately. Air in your lungs, wind in your face; you didn't get that on the bus.

* * *

The family were already in position at the entrance to the kirk when Wallace arrived. He paused to check his reflection in the glass of the hearse before falling into line with those who had come to pay their respects. The widow greeted him first, a small woman made smaller by the weight of years hunching her over. His words of sympathy washed over her, nothing but wind. The son caught his hand and held it. Faint suspicion shone in his eyes.

'I'm sorry, you are?'

'James. I used to play bools with Alasdair.'

Wallace released his hand and moved aside as another mourner arrived to offer his condolences. A solemn-faced undertaker's assistant handed him an order of service, which he acknowledged with a slight dip of his head. Instinct guided him to the second pew from the back, where he worked his way along until he sat in the shadow of one of the pillars.

The kirk continued to fill and Wallace soon found himself surrounded by strangers. He inched away from the bulk of the woman beside him, shoulder coming to rest against the unyielding stone of the pillar. An elbow jabbed in his direction as the woman snapped open her handbag and produced a packet of tissues in preparation for the weeping to come.

While Wallace would never be so crass as to pronounce himself an expert, he had attended enough funerals to conclude that they comprised the same constituent elements. A life, no matter how long or short, condensed into forty minutes of song, prayer and eulogy, during the course of which the minister acted as character witness for the deceased. Alasdair Swayne Thomson, pigeon fancier and proud Rotarian, had been a popular man in the community. A fact evidenced by a turnout that stretched across the generations, each displaying different degrees of grief, ranging from the heartfelt to the dutiful. Not that

Wallace came to judge; he left such spiritual considerations to the theologians, preferring to concentrate on the needs of the flesh.

Wallace stood as the pallbearers carried the coffin from the kirk, the family following in its wake. The front pews emptied first, each successive row falling in behind. Standard protocol. Something else you learned quickly.

The hearse had already departed for the cemetery when Wallace emerged, as had many of the mourners. A few, mainly the more elderly, were in the process of crossing the road to the hotel opposite, where the family had invited those attending the service to join them for refreshments after the interment. Wallace calculated thirty to forty minutes before the main funeral party returned. His hand slipped inside his suit pocket and rustled the carrier bag.

One of the waiting staff directed Wallace to a function suite at the rear of the hotel restaurant. Three waitresses were laying out a buffet in the centre of the room. Wallace crossed to a table on the opposite side, taking him past the foil salvers. Sandwiches, quiche, chicken drumsticks and, he noted with approval, a selection of cream cakes. If not high end, certainly a decent enough spread not to be an affront to the departed.

'Tea or coffee?'

'Tea, lass. Thanks.'

Wallace watched her pour. She had the red hair and green eyes he associated, possibly somewhat erroneously, with the Irish. If the girl's spring held promise, he knew her summer would be truly beautiful to behold. He felt a pang then for all the things he would not see, but he had already enjoyed his seasons in the sun.

'I can fetch you a plate if you want?'

'No. No. I can manage, but thank you.'

Wallace spooned sugar into his tea and added a splash of milk. He drank it without tasting it and then went to fetch himself some food. Coronation chicken, prawn mayonnaise, cheese and ham, an unimaginative selection but sustaining. For every sandwich he ate, he placed one in his bag below the table. The cakes were too fragile and messy, and so he ate three accompanied by a second cup of tea before slipping from the function suite.

Wallace passed the girl in the corridor, carrying a fresh pot of tea. He flicked his eyes towards the toilets by way of explanation. The waitress smiled, turned side-on to the door and used her hip to bump it open. Wallace stared at the space she left behind. He stood trapped until the sound of the returning funeral party stirred him towards the backdoor.

A habitual early riser, Wallace often found himself stood outside the library waiting for it to open, an act that usually guaranteed him first access to the local newspaper. He turned to the announcements section — hatches, matches and dispatches — and smoothed out a sheet of paper on the table. The trick lay in knowing which funeral to attend. Wallace had an instinct for it, but weather, public events and the unknown still caught him out on occasion. The son yesterday had presented an uncomfortable moment, but few mourners wished to create a scene, preferring to keep their suspicions of funeral tourism to themselves.

His finger travelled over the death notices. Experience had taught him that the young were best avoided, too much tragedy and heightened emotion, as were those with no family. The larger the turnout, the more accepting people became of a strange face, a fact Wallace relied on. He averaged a funeral a week by his calculation, although the festive season might see half a dozen in the space of a fortnight. By contrast, summer often brought lean times, as now.

Wallace rejected the most promising of the death notices on account of being at the same church as the one he had just attended, which left the funeral of a spinster on the opposite side of town at the end of the week. He hesitated before writing down the details, keeping it in reserve in the event that nothing better presented itself.

The remainder of the paper presented the kind of dull, parochial news typical of the regional press. Wallace found the nationals little better. No matter how great the tragedy or low the depravity, he could not escape the sense of having read it before. The settings and the names changed but the plot remained unaltered. For all that the pace of life got faster and the machines more complex, human nature failed to evolve. In moments of weakness he told himself it could not change, and so excused his own failings.

Come winter Wallace might spend his entire day in the library, but the pull of summer drew him outside a little before eleven. The warmth of the sun on his face lifted his spirits. Unbidden, his feet took him across the square and along by the old railway station. The park stretched before him, a welcome expanse of green amidst the sterile concrete.

Wallace skirted the bandstand to arrive at the pond. A flock of ducks, several of which were now swimming towards the shore, had made the island in the middle their home. A bouncing lump of bread explained their mini migration and Wallace turned to discover the waitress from the hotel sitting on the next bench along.

'Would you like to feed the ducks?'

Wallace stared at the piece of loaf in the girl's hand. Pink glitter covered her nails.

'Some people think it robs them of their independence, you know. But who's to say they mightn't starve otherwise? Haven't we taken so much of the wild away from them?'

'Quite,' Wallace replied.

He reached out and took the offered bread. If the girl recognised him, she gave no sign. Wallace tore the bread in half and placed part of it in his pocket. He ripped the remaining half into pieces and scattered them between the bench and the water, enticing the ducks onto land. Their heads bobbed up and down as they bolted the loaf. Wallace smiled.

'They're part of the Anatidae family of birds.'

'I beg your pardon?'

'Ducks,' the girl said. 'They're related to swans and geese. I suppose that's rather obvious, but ducks are definitely the coolest!' She thrust out her hand, an awkward gesture that reminded Wallace of a child acting out the role of an adult. 'I'm Laura.'

'James. Pleased to make your acquaintance.'

Laura looked at him sidelong, attempting to determine his sincerity. Wallace suspected she might not be the full shilling. She stood suddenly, brushing breadcrumbs from her skirt.

'Work. Got to go.'

Wallace watched her cut across the grass, the sunlight burnishing her hair to copper. Had he ever been that young and carefree? He took the remaining bread from his pocket and broke it into pieces. The ducks quacked enthusiastically.

Wallace smiled at the girl's ambivalence to work. Youth guarded its time jealously, little knowing the day would came all too soon when it wished for some task to occupy it, even as those days ironically slipped faster and faster away. It turned treacherously, the desire to be grown up and the subsequent pining for lost youth.

Finding the sun no longer pleasant, Wallace set off for home. Rather than retrace his steps, he made for the football stadium, a route that took him between the distillery and the cemetery. The smell of the mash, rich and heavy, hung in the air, summoning the ghost of whisky past. Dark days. Dog days. Days he promised never to let return. His own will insufficient to hold him to account, he forced himself through the cemetery gate.

There were many paths to the other exits, but Wallace knew his feet would take but a single route; recognised any attempt at turning aside as a pointless deception. He followed the path to the brow of the hill and through the circle of trees with its benches. A left turn led him back down the hill where he stopped in front of a marble headstone. The action of wind and rain had attacked the gold inlay, fading the image of the teddy bear at the stone's apex. His knees cracked loudly when he squatted to pick up the remains of long dead flowers. The stems rustled in fingers that felt only slightly less desiccated. The lines of the inscription stared back at him in mute accusation.

Wallace turned his brolly against the rain, but the wind drove the drops at such an angle that his trousers and shoes were soon wet. He stopped on the steps of the kirk, lowered the umbrella and shook it out. He noted there were fewer cars than he would have expected. The family appeared to be limited to two female figures, a middle-aged woman and a girl, presumably her daughter. A sense of embarrassment enfolded him as he recognised Laura. He knew he should turn and walk away, but she held him transfixed with her appraising stare. Then the presence of someone behind him blocked any hope of escape.

Wallace straightened his back and squared his shoulders, determined to exhibit grace on his way to the scaffold. Despite this resolution, his hand trembled as he held it out. Laura wrapped both her hands about his, her touch cool but not cold.

Wallace's voice caught and then broke as he said, 'Sorry for your loss.'

'Good of you to come, James. I'm sure it would have meant a lot to Uncle Morton. I hate to ask at such short notice, but as you're here, perhaps you'd take a cord? I'd rather it were you than one of the undertakers.'

'I…'

'Good.' Laura smiled brightly. 'That's settled.'

The service passed in a haze. Twice Wallace found himself sitting while everyone else stood. He wondered how long Laura intended to maintain this charade, and what purpose it served. His tormentor never once looked back, seeming to trust in her ability to hold him captive.

Laura motioned him to follow as she walked past in the wake of the coffin. Disorientated, Wallace found himself sitting between mother and daughter in the rear of the funeral car. It travelled slowly after the hearse, taking the road to the overflow cemetery on the opposite side of the bypass. A small mercy; Wallace knew he could not face another visit to the old cemetery so soon.

'I'm not sure I ever heard my brother mention you before.'

'You must have, Mum. Jim and Uncle Morton were in the Merchant Navy together. Jim's only recently moved back to the area from down south.'

'Ah, one of Morton's old friends.'

Much as Wallace did not care for the inference, he felt relieved that it signalled an end to the conversation.

Wallace had not attended an interment for many years. He had vowed never to again after helping lower a tiny white box into another hole, along with his hopes and dreams. If only he could have laid his anger and guilt to rest as easily, instead of suffering the torment of a life sentence.

To his surprise, Laura stood at the head of the coffin. The black cord contrasted sharply with the pale hand that gripped it. Wallace stood opposite at the foot of the grave. He searched her face for some sign of anger or cruelty but found only resignation.

The gravediggers withdrew the batons from beneath the coffin and the cord went tight as Wallace took up the strain. The rope slithered away, burning the flesh of his hand. A gentle touch on the sleeve from the undertaker reminded him to let go. The cord curled serpent-like on the coffin, amidst the coils of its seven brothers.

They completed the journey back to the kirk in silence. Tea and sandwiches were to be served in the hall adjoining the church. Wallace felt more lost than ever as he followed Laura inside. Despite noisy protestations from his stomach to the contrary, he found he had quite lost his appetite as plates of sandwiches and sausage rolls were set on the table.

Laura poured him tea. 'You really should eat something.'

Wallace looked nervously at Laura's mother, but she was in conversation with one of the serving women.

'Why?'

'Because you'll go hungry otherwise.'

'That's not what I meant. I could have walked away without any of… this.'

Laura picked up a sandwich and handed it to Wallace. He stared at the white triangle, the corners of which were already beginning to curl. Egg and cress, with too much margarine. He ate it anyway.

Laura passed him another sandwich, something akin to mischief in her eyes.

'Sometimes you have to feed the ducks. 'Specially the lame ones.'

CHORUSES

'Scabs! Scabs! Scabs!'

He shouted the words until hoarse, pouring every ounce of his anger and frustration into the chant. Four months on the picket line had left him tired and hopeless, but he would never cross the line. Better not to think of his wife, his son and his daughter waiting at home for him, growing gaunter and more desperate by the day. The thought of accepting charity made him burn with shame, but their meagre savings had run out and the kindness of friends and family, with the exception of his brother, been exhausted. He spat on the ground and vowed he and his would starve before they accepted so much as a penny from Geoff. You didn't cross the line, not when solidarity was the only thing standing between you and your comrades and defeat.

The police lined up in front of the bus, visors down, shields and truncheons raised.

'Scabs! Scabs! Scabs!'

No one knew who threw the first stone, although Big Tom Gellately later claimed it came from the police lines. Wood splintered as the men broke their placards into makeshift clubs. They would hold the line, no matter the cost.

Working the pit made a man hard, but the police were well fed, rested and had discipline, while the strikers had only fury. He saw Sharpe's lad go down on his right, blood pouring from his skull. Sharpe tried to get to him, only for a truncheon to break across his shoulders. He, too, disappeared into the flailing mass of arms and legs. Fists, bottles and stones gradually pushed the police back, but with more than half their number on the ground the strikers knew the next charge would break them.

He wrapped his fists about the length of two-by-four, oblivious to the blood that poured from his knuckles. This wasn't right. They were fighting for their jobs, their families and livelihoods. The men who crossed the pickets in defiance of the strike were the criminals, robbing him and his children of their future. He didn't choose this violence, but wouldn't shrink from it either. They fought today for survival.

The police charged again. He stood defiantly, club held before him, while men broke and ran. One after another, the truncheons cracked off his skull, the percussion ringing in his ears.

The wind whipped the red sands into a stinging hail that scoured Wolf's flesh. Wolf had grown accustomed to it during the long years of his walk, found it preferable to the long dark that had preceded his awakening. He angled his wide-brimmed hat to shield his eyes and tightened the scarf over his mouth and nose. The tattered remains of his cloak snapped behind him like the Colours of some defeated and forgotten regiment. Rags held his boots together, inside of which blistered skin oozed. Wolf accepted the pain with a pilgrim's fortitude. His steps were sacred.

Tears clouded his vision as he beheld the empty wastes of the once proud North, where harmony had become discord, doubt had usurped faith, and despair replaced hope. The crops went unharvested, the basket weavers no longer wove, and men ceased to delve into the earth for its riches. Hunger and want ruled while workers stood idle or drifted southwards to worship in the lavish temples of the new gods.

Wolf remembered and honoured the old ways and their songs. He sang the words of power in a lilting voice that denied the gnarled appearance of his exterior, words that called to the spirits of air, of water, of earth. He sang the sweet lullaby of creation to his ancestors and to the ghosts of fish and fowl, calling them back into being.

In the wake of Wolf's song the green shoots of recovery sprang up in his footsteps. Life, however, requires careful nurturing and the young, the desperate, and the dispossessed worshipped the new gods to the exclusion of all else. And so the seeds Wolf sowed withered and died, condemning him to walk endlessly on bloody feet, crossing and re-crossing the wasteland.

'Come on, man. You know it's not right, living like this. Like some wild animal scavenging for scraps. Come and bide with me and Jane. Get yourself sorted out. We're family.'

He measured the stranger from head to toe, brown hair, brown eyes, grey skin. Dressed in clothes that had seen their best but which he cared for out of necessity.

'You're no family of mine.'

'Ten years, man. Time to let it go.'

He shook his head and thrust his hands deep into the pockets of his coat where they balled into fists. He fixed his eyes on the sky as he walked away. The uniform grey promised rain. You got used to the wet and damp after a time, learned the places you could lie up until the storm had passed. A voice called out to him but he closed his ears and trudged on.

Figures appeared from the shadows, two men lit by the

glow of the cigarette they passed back and forth between them, and a couple of women with a bottle of strong ale. If living like an animal meant sharing what little you had, he found it no insult. The pack survived together.

He slept rough most nights, shunning the offer of temporary accommodation, tired of the merry-go-round of B&B to shelter and back again, never permitted to stay in any one place. Rootless, homeless; at least he could stake his claim under the arches of a bridge or in some fetid doorway. Sometimes he had to fight, but not often. Most of the other rough sleepers knew him by sight and feared his reputation. Quite an achievement that a collection of addicts and meth drinkers should brand him dangerously insane. Always talking to himself and seeing things that weren't there, they said. Fools were blind and deaf to what lay around them; shadows, ghosts, a world that screamed in agony.

Only in the winter, when the temperature dropped dangerously low and he feared going to sleep and not waking, did he break this rule, and only after he found Geordie George frozen to the pavement. Then he would play the odds, sniffing the food for poison and staying awake all night to be ready if they came for him. He promised each time he escaped never again to surrender himself into their clutches. Better a clean death by cold than whatever fate waited in their dungeons. Pain he understood and could endure, like the continual thump-thump inside his skull, but few things terrified him as much as the prospect of being forced to think as his enemies did, to come to share their hateful views. Their mouths were full of wrong and it showed in all their works.

Like all successful monsters they came in the guise of friends, with their offers of food, of shelter, of medication. Nothing but lies and deceit. He refused to take their drugs, though he knew they crushed them into his food. Unwilling to reveal this knowledge, he ate what they put before him and purged himself afterwards. But even this failed to prevent the drugs from building up inside his body a grain at a time, slowly taking control of him, changing his thoughts. It separated him from his dreams, cut him off from his visions, and anchored him to the shadow world a strand at a time through the weaving of a mighty tether.

Some things were inevitable. Some things you could not control, no matter how hard you fought against them. And yet what choice did he have? You had to man the pickets, even if there were no pits and factories left to protect. The invisible lines that remained were the most important to protect. Let the scabs across and where would it end? When you valued nothing, everything had its price.

Wolf sang the song of the river and fresh water flowed along the dusty gully of the dried up riverbed. He sang the song of the mountains and great spikes of rock broke through the parched earth to touch the sky's embrace. He sang the song of the trees and the oak, the ash, the beech and the birch grew tall. These were the songs of the ancestors, ancient as the desert rock. To these he added the refrain of the fish, the birds and the roe deer, naming each and its place in the land.

Wolf looked upon the land and saw that it was good. Yet, when he cocked his head, he heard the cry of the desert winds singing their song of destruction: why settle for enough when you could have more? Gather all the nuts and berries of the earth. Catch all the fish in the streams. Kill all the game in the forest. Grow fat and content while others starved and begged for bones and husks. If they threatened to rise against you, sow discord and turn them against one another. Make fear and suspicion their lot. Above all, never let them question your right to take what belonged to all.

Wolf sang louder, but the desert wind proved stronger. Its sands silted the rivers, ground down the mountains and stripped the leaves and fruit from the trees. The rivers ran dry and the land grew barren. The trees crashed to the earth and rotted to dust.

Wolf wept bitterly at the ruin of his song. He screamed to the sky and at the earth, petitioning their help, a lone cry in the emptiness. Earth tasted his tears and was moved. In her anguish she broke her bones and rent her flesh, leaving Wolf islanded from the empty desert. Sky heard Wolf's cries and he split the heavens asunder and anointed Wolf with sweet rain. Everywhere it touched the land fresh life sprung from the waste, creating an oasis of hope. And for a time Wolf was content.

The road wound before him, a black and terrible serpent. Doorways snarled and windows glared as he ran along the street, the broken soles of his boots flap-flapping. Danger in the concrete canyons, eyes following his every move. He wanted to be elsewhere but some things could only be accomplished in the shadow world. Everything felt wrong here; the light, the buildings, the inhabitants, facsimiles of imitations, no more substantial than dreams. It gave him the itch, the shakes and the ague, creeping night-time terrors that prickled the skin with fear-sweat. Even the echoes of his footsteps scared him, following behind like some approaching monster.

Breathe in. Breathe out. Concentrate. Road, doorways, windows, harmless and inanimate. No dark things. Footsteps and echo in synch, pitter-pattering on the tarmac. Heart and pulse normal.

Light ahead, shining out on the street. Manmade, unnatural, but welcoming in its fashion. Learned responses kicked in, driving him towards the open door. He has been here before, many times. The shadows receded, driven out not only by the light but also by a growing sense of familiarity.

The light made him squint but he welcomed the room's heat as it soaked through his tattered layers of clothing and warmed the flesh below. Benches and trestle tables ran the length of the hall, at which a motley collection figure sat. Male and female, the same lines of hopeless despair etched their faces. They looked without seeing as they supped from the paper bowls of soup and tore at the bread. A couple nodded to him as he passed and one called out a name that no longer held any meaning.

Pain exploded inside his head like the tightening of a steel band. The adrenaline rush made his heart pound. Danger here, a trap for the unwary, if he could remember its form, but the repeated knocking of his fist against his head failed to conjure the answer. Knock, knock, knock. Knock, knock-knock. He repeated the pattern over and over; something learned, something significant. Knock, knock…

A firm but tender hand gripped his wrist, calming his natural desire to lash out. Pale blue eyes appraised him through the lenses of steel-rimmed spectacles. The lips that spoke were pale and bloodless but the smile was natural.

'Easy, big fellah. Don't want to scare the natives. How about we get you a seat and Chrissie will bring some soup. That sound okay to you?'

He nodded, his words rusted stiff through disuse. A woman shuffled along the bench to make room for him, but he still found it difficult to make his bulk fit and his thighs pressed against the underside of the table.

The woman looked expectantly at him and then shook her head, producing the effect of a hundred knotted rats' tails dancing.

'Cat still got your tongue, laddie? Suppose better that than that miserable git Auld Reekie Pants effing and blinding all the time. An' me a lady!' She cackled at her own wit, exposing a set of yellowed dentures. 'Haven't found yer sense of humour either, eh?'

'Leave the poor man be, Agnes. Dare say he just wants his supper.'

Agnes shot a venomous glance at the newcomer but held

her tongue. Time was when she would have given Chrissie a piece of her mind, but it never paid to bite the hand that fed you.

Chrissie set the bowl and a plastic spoon down in front of him. He stared at the broth as though expecting some danger to surface from its depths. Nothing more dangerous threatened than the grey flesh of boiled beef. Hunger won out over suspicion and he spooned up the soup, swallowing meat and vegetables almost whole.

Too late, he remembered the perils of eating food in the shadow world. The light dimmed and a sense of solidity crept through his body, anchoring him to the bench. His muscles strained as he tried to rise, but could not overcome the force that held him. The spoon dropped from his hand and a sensation akin to drowning stole over him.

Wolf no longer sang. He prowled the edge of his island, testing the limits of its confines. Across the jagged cracks in the earth the desert stretched as far as the eye could see, dead and dusty. His island of green, so welcoming at first, became a daily torment, a reminder of his failure. He gave up walking and sat in the shade of the great yew tree dreaming bitter dreams. And then Crow came.

How she arrived or where she came from, Crow refused to say. She said little but laughed much, bringing fire to her golden eyes. No longer youthful, but not yet old, the tracery of lines about her eyes and mouth spoke of experience and wisdom. She made Wolf feel uneasy for she seemed to be in possession of some secret knowledge, as though she had taken sorrow, pain and disappointment and made friends of them. Sometimes he thought her laughter and smile mocked him, but saw only kindness in her eyes.

Clinging closer than his shadow, he found no peace in the shade of the yew, no solitude in the fringes of the island, for Crow was always there, waiting, watching. Sometimes he grew angry.

He would snarl questions such as, 'Why do you follow me?'

To which Crow would smile and explain, 'It's a small island. Can I help it if you walk the same way as me?'

Crow's words, always soft and kindly, would draw the heat from his temper. Sometimes Wolf thought Crow wanted him to touch her, but his courage always failed him at the last. He hadn't known he had been alone until Crow came and now he feared to be alone again. And so Wolf prowled and Crow followed, just out of reach.

One day, when Wolf stood staring out over the wasteland, Crow came up beside him. She looked to the east, to the rising sun that seemed born of the blood red sands of the desert, and sang a single note. A cloud appeared in the sky. Crow waited. Wolf cleared his throat. He had not sung for days beyond count. Crow sang her note again and this time Wolf picked up the song and their voices danced with one another in harmony. Other voices joined in, the singers emerging from the shadows where they had waited. They sang the world, not as it had been in the past but as it should be in the future, everything in balance, perfect and regular.

The clouds gathered overhead darkening the skies and the thunder rumbled, providing percussion for their song. Lightning flashed and the rain poured down, producing fountains of dust where it struck the earth. Where the rain fell the land became fertile again and bloomed with life. It rained day after day, the deluge forming rivers that flowed into seas. And still the wind howled, carrying the song of Wolf and Crow across the land in defiance of the desert wind, drowning out its lament.

Wolf looked upon the land and saw that it was good. He looked upon Crow and knew that she was true. The song required a chorus to sing it, and once sung ended the dreaming.

* * *

Agnes reached over and touched his shoulder. 'You all right, deary?'

He blinked, looked around the soup kitchen and then picked up his spoon. It felt plain, ordinary. He looked at the man opposite and at the woman beside him. Looked to his left and to his right, saw poverty and desperation. But more than that, in the faces of the servers he saw hope, a sense of defiance in the face of oppression. The harder you squeezed the more society persisted, and always would so long as single person remained to hold his or her hand out to the fallen, to speak for those who had no voice.

'No, but I think I'm going to be.'

THE WAKE

Kirkpatrick chopped out two long lines on top of the coffin. The name on the Platinum Card matched the brass plate; Boyd had been very particular in his instructions. Kirkpatrick broke the band on a bundle of notes and rolled up a fresh fifty. He turned to the bullet-headed man beside him and grinned wickedly.

'D'you want the first toot?'

McAlpine stepped back and bumped into the hulking figure behind him. Jimmy "Grievous" Anderson topped him by a good six inches.

'C'mon, Frankie-boy. It's no' like you're on duty. What happens at the wake stays at the wake. It's what Dougie would've wanted.'

McAlpine clenched his fists. From the moment Kirkpatrick had stopped him in the street, he had known there would be trouble. Get Anderson on the deck and he might have half a chance of making it out alive. Not that he cared for those odds.

Kirkpatrick shook his head and bent over the coffin. He snorted half of the first line and let out a yelp. 'Now that, Frankie, is the good shit! Oh yes.' He took the rest of the line, dabbed up the stray powder with his pinkie, and rubbed it on his gums. His glassy stare seemed to look straight through McAlpine.

'Bad luck, Dougie buying it like that.'

'Is that so, Frankie? Y'see, I happen to think we make our own luck in life. It's all about decisions. I'm no' talking about that karma shit, just normal common sense. Dougie,' Kirkpatrick slapped his palm down on the coffin, 'God love him, didn't have the coolest of heads. Didn't know when to leave well enough alone,' he banged the coffin again, 'and that's a fact. Didn't need to be out that night, but he would insist on getting involved, and we all know where that got him.'

The room went silent; Kirkpatrick's eulogy skills perhaps not being all that the mourners expected. McAlpine edged towards the door of The Keg's backroom. Almost every face in the room had a SOCA file; connected with drugs, extortion, prostitution and armed robbery. They had travelled the length and breadth of Scotland to pay their respects to Dougie Boyd, a man responsible for moving so much coke he must have emptied half the coca fields of Columbia. Some were known to McAlpine by reputation alone, others, like Anderson, he knew personally, had helped send down for a stretch in Porterfield. Not a friendly room to be in, but Kirkpatrick's invitation to the wake had been… emphatic.

'Whoa! What's the hurry, Frankie-boy? We've no' even cracked open the whisky. Don't try and tell me you're gonna pass up a dram? Jimmy, fetch DS McAlpine a glass.'

Anderson stood undecided. Boyd's death had technically made Kirkpatrick boss, although there were a number of challengers. Anderson shot a look at the most likely contender, Ian Johnston. Johnston inclined his head in the slightest of nods and Anderson stepped forward.

Kirkpatrick pulled the stopper from a bottle and splashed liberal measures of whisky into a tray of glasses. He handed off a couple to Anderson and motioned for the others to help themselves.

McAlpine sniffed the whisky; peat reek burned in his nostrils, suggestive of an Islay malt. He held it up to the light and turned the glass, the pale amber spirit stirred sluggishly.

'It's no' poisoned, if that's what's worrying you. Ruining a good drop of single malt, now that really would be criminal!'

The joke met with nervous laughter; not so much a case of the elephant as the pig in the room. They had their officers, the ones they owned through blackmail or an addiction to a lifestyle their salary could never hope to support. Frank McAlpine wasn't one of them. That made him dangerous. Kirkpatrick had clearly lost his mind in bringing him to the wake. Hadn't he enough trouble with the day-to-day business without actively seeking it?

'Here's to Dougie! *Slàinte!* Well, it's maybe a wee bit late for that, but you get the drift.'

Kirkpatrick bent over the coffin and took the remaining line of coke. McAlpine caught some angry muttering and saw Johnston pointedly check his watch. The crowd were growing bored with the show. They might owe Boyd a certain amount of respect but it was business, pure and simple, that had brought them here today. They didn't want a sideshow, particularly one with a cop as spectator.

'Dougie was like a father to me, which is to say there were days I could've seen him far enough. But I respected the bugger more than anything else. Taught me all I know about the business, and let's be straight about this, in this town, in this area, he was the business. There's plenty in this room tonight made their money because of him, which is why we're here to see Dougie off in style. But nobody goes on forever, something he knew well enough. That's why he wrote down these arrangements for the wake, so he could die as he lived — in charge and in control. So here we are, standing vigil with his stinking corpse. Having a dram and telling stories. Now most of us have a story about Dougie, but there's one man here tonight who has the last story.' Kirkpatrick raised his arms in a theatrical gesture. 'Francis McAlpine, come on down! Now's your big moment, the chance to tell us what really happened that night. No' the guff you told the media, or the half-truths you fed that ball-breaking boss of yours. Let's hear how Dougie really died.'

McAlpine searched the room and met with a series of hostile stares, the one exception being Boyd's widow. Anne deliberately avoided his eye, hiding behind a fringe of platinum curls. That McAlpine had done most of them a favour by killing Boyd would be of little account when they came to balance the ledger. The scent of blood had them longing for the kill.

'Like I said before — bad luck. He could have run either way at the crossroads, but it so happened he picked the road I was on. Came out of nowhere, didn't give me a chance to slow down, let alone stop.'

Kirkpatrick reached behind his suit jacket and pulled a gun from the waistband of his trousers. McAlpine suddenly found himself standing alone.

'I told you not to bullshit me, Frankie-boy! We all ken fine how you ran Dougie down; the question is what were you doing there in the first place. Wasn't your bust. You weren't even on duty — no' officially, though I daresay that bugger Fleming has you keeping queer hours.'

McAlpine raised his hands, palms outward. His collar felt tight and sweat trickled down his back. He licked dry lips with a tongue almost equally as dry. What did Kirkpatrick actually know and how much was he guessing? Maybe not so much, judging from his comments. Hard to think straight with a gun in his face.

'Tommy, let's all calm down. We both know you're not going to shoot me. So why don't you put the gun away before you hurt someone, and we can talk like civilised people?'

'You think I won't shoot you 'cause you're a cop?' Kirkpatrick thumped the coffin with his free hand. 'There's plenty of room in this box for another body. No' like there's many as would miss you, Frankie-boy. Your ex-wife would thank me for a start, and you're no' exactly on the best of terms with the kiddies. As for that tart from the paper you've been rattling, your disappearance would be worth a week of front pages.' A glass smashed and Anne Boyd uttered a terse apology. Kirkpatrick continued almost without pause. 'So unless you want your last words on earth to be a lie I suggest you cut the crap and tell me about your arrangement with Fleming. It's no secret he's been trying to muscle in on Dougie's business for years.'

'You think Fleming's got me in his pocket? Get a grip. That's the coke talking. Fact is I got a call from DI Wallace asking me to attend the scene; he liked one of Dougie's boys for an armed robbery I was investigating. Thought I'd want to sit in on the interview. Everything would have been sweet if one of the uniforms hadn't got careless and let Dougie make a run for it. Yeah, there was a cover up, but that's the extent of it, stopping the boys from the Drugs Squad looking like idiots.'

'I told you to stop lying!'

Johnston let out a theatrical yawn. 'For God's sake, Tommy, if you're going to shoot him, get it over with. Some of us have businesses to run.'

Johnston nudged McAlpine to the side as he stepped forward, a small man with receding sandy hair, dressed in a three-piece. The sharp suit and cultured voice might have suggested solicitor or investment banker, but McAlpine knew better than to mistake him for anything other than an evil bastard. Smart enough to avoid getting caught though, making him all the more dangerous.

'What are you waiting for?'

Kirkpatrick, confused, stepped from side to side to get a shot at McAlpine before frantically waving Johnston away. Johnston, taking advantage of the distraction, stepped in close and smashed his forehead into Kirkpatrick's nose. Bone and cartilage broke with a loud crack and a moment later Johnston had the gun. He stepped away from the writhing figure on the floor, took a short run up and kicked Kirkpatrick in the head. The body stopped moving.

Johnston placed the gun on top of the coffin and produced a pocket handkerchief. He dabbed fastidiously at his forehead and face, removing spots of blood and perspiration.

'We seem to have a wee problem here, DS McAlpine. While I'm no expert, Mr Kirkpatrick would appear to be guilty of being in possession of an unregistered firearm and a Class A controlled substance. If one wished to be particularly harsh, I imagine there's also a case for unlawful detention.'

'You want me to arrest him?'

'That would certainly be one option. Though I'm led to believe that your colleagues in Professional Standards have been taking rather a keen interest in your affairs of late. Tommy's imaginative little tale might prove somewhat awkward for you.'

The statement hung in the air, giving the impression that, depending on his answer, McAlpine could soon be joining it in a state of suspension.

'Perhaps it would be better to forget about this? A misunderstanding between friends?'

'That would be another option. But would you ever really be safe? Terrible thing to be constantly looking over your shoulder.' Johnston ran a loving hand down the length of the coffin, brushing aside the last traces of cocaine. 'Tommy and Dougie always were near enough inseparable.'

McAlpine walked over to the coffin. He picked up the malt, filled his glass to the rim and knocked it back.

'It's what Dougie would have wanted.'

McAlpine was halfway to the door when Anne Boyd stepped in front of him. He could have blocked the slap easily but chose to let it land. The heat in his cheek proved strangely comforting. Anne turned away and no one else challenged him as he left the room.

IMPERFECT PAST

It's a funny old world when ye get down to it. We've had oor clever gadgies like Einstein and Heisenberg, with their theories and matrices, but who'd have thought me, Stevie Anderson fae Dundee, wid invent time travel? Certainly no' Mr Sturrock, the Heid at Whitfield, where I scraped a "D" in metalwork as my highest grade, or my Da, who always said the most I'd amount to wis nothing. But it's the old man I've to thank for my breakthrough or, more accurately, that horrible Vitalis shit he slicked back his hair with. That oily stink is as fresh to me now as it wis thirty year ago, an nothing taks ye back in time like a smell.

The first time it happened we'd no long put the old bastard in the ground. If I'd had my way the heidstane wid have read "Under this sod lies another" but Ma, as ever, widnae hear a word against him. She wis a woman ye couldn't tell a thing to, cause the black eyes telt ye she'd already been told, far too many times.

Anyhow, Ma had asked me if there wis anything in the bathroom I could use, so there I wis rakin' through the medicine cabinet when I came across the old man's hair oil. I keep my ane hair shaved to the wood, but I still unscrewed the bottle and took a sniff. That's when it happened. One minute I wis standing in the bathroom, the next I'm back in the auld flat we had in the multi-storey. I'm standing in the corner, only I'm also bouncing aboot on my Da's knee, a wee bit of a thing all of four or five years.

Fair shat myself, so I did, thinking what if I'm trapped thirty years in my past with no means of signing on. I must have shouted or something because Da turned at looked straight at me, his foreheid scrunched up like it got whenever he tried to read. I got this sensation of every hair on my body standing up and then I wis back staring at my reflection in the door of the medicine cabinet.

That wis pure mental, I thinks to myself. Some sort of flashback or mibbe one of those post traumatic stress things that sojers huv. Losing a parent, even one ye hated, is bound to mess with yer heid. Only thing is my memory of that day's now different. Da puts me down an goes and stares at the corner, which lets me scuttle off to the bog instead of pishing on his lap an getting a hiding. Except I'm no' so sure he hit me at all. I look at my arm and the scar I've had there since he broke it is missing. Mibbe it wis only there in my imagination?

I didnae ken quite whit to mak of it all, but the one thing I kent for certain wis that there wis free stuff on the go. So I took the old man's Bic oranges, Old Spice and shaving cream, plus a heap of his clothes an bailed without saying goodbye. It's no' like any of the family has had much to do with me these last twenty years, so none of them were expecting me to hing about for tea an sympathy.

I had just enough change in my pocket to catch the bus up the Hilltown. Ma flat wis at the top of a four storey tenement. I took the stairs two at a time, near gieing myself a heart attack in the process. Suddenly I jist wanted to be inside wi the door a'tween me and the world. A minute later I'm blubbing like a bairn. Whit yon psychologist gadgies refer to as delayed shock.

A couple of days go by afore I've the heart to look through whit I've taken. Ripped jeans, faded t-shirts and a cut-doon denim jacket that wis last trendy in aboot 1976. Then there's the belt. Heavy broon leather wi a big brass buckle. It smelled of sweat and, if sich a thing wis possible, fear. I saw dark coloured stains along its length when I held it up to the light. Spent maist of my childhood in terror of that belt, and the speed at which the old man could haul it aff his troosers.

It feels as if I'm standing still while spinning roon at the same time! One meenit I'm hauding the belt in my ain hoose and then I'm in oor auld living room with its woodchip walls an swirly carpet. There's a glass lying on its side, a puddle of red kola soaking into the carpet. The old man's got ma younger self by the scruff of the neck and is hauling doon ma breeks, his belt wrapped roon his fist.

'How many times, Stevie? How many tellings dae ye need no' tae spill stuff? Mibbe this will finally mak' it sink into that thick heid of yours!'

I screamed as the belt landed — both of me did — but the old man wis too far gone to hear either of us. Thwack! Thwack! My arse turned bright red. But that's no' enough, wis never enough, there had to be blood afore he'd stop. Looking straight into my own eyes, I pleaded with myself to make it stop, but I couldnae move.

Ah kent whit happened next, wanted to leave, but didnae even ken how I'd got there to begin with. My Ma ran into the room. No' the auld woman I ken, but a young, pretty thing. She screamed dog's abuse at him, for all the good it did. He went right on battering me until he wis oot of breath. Then he stood up and smashed Ma with a backhand, so casual he didnae seem to think aboot it. Blood sprayed from her busted lip, dripped from the belt, and ran from the welts across my arse and the top of my legs. The kola finished soaking into the carpet with oot anyone noticing.

I found myself huddled in the corner of ma room, shaking like a leaf. The belt lay on the carpet in front of me, nothing mair than an auld piece of leather. Whitever jist happened to me wis some serious Voodoo. I needed a drink to sort me oot. There wis twa tins of Tennent's Super in the fridge. The first one didnae even touch the sides as it went doon. Ma heid started spinning again, but at least it wis in a way I could handle. I killed the second can and cracked open a half bottle of Bells, thinking as to why I didnae change the past this time. I need to experiment, find oot how far back I could go an' who could see me. I now had a memory of seeing myself in the room when Da was belting me, or did I only think I remembered it cause I kent I wis there? It's no' like I could ask Ma if she saw me. The old dear wid be sending roon the yellow van an' the men in white coats to fetch me.

By the end of the bottle I'd a plan, but wis so pished I ended up mistaking the airing cupboard for the toilet and pissing in the washing basket. The postie woke me up the next morning by shoving the mail through the letterbox. The evil sod might as well have dropped breezeblocks on ma heid. It took a minute or twa, but I managed to convince myself that ma brains were nae splattered across the hall carpet and hauled ma splitting heid to the kitchen.

I boiled the kettle an' found a teabag in the bottom of a cup fae the day afore, or mibbe the day afore that. It took a good mashing, but I squeezed something close enough to tea oot of it to be worth drinking. If nothing else, it stripped some of the fur aff ma tongue. Then I put whitever part of ma brain wisnae pickled to thinking.

Plenty of stuff reminded me of the old man, all of it bad. Strong smells an even stronger feelings seemed to be the key, but could I tak' myself somewhere else? Growing up roon here wis maistly shite, but I had to hae some guid memories stashed away. Fair to say neen of them wis going to involve the old man. Friday night wis pay day, a great big skelp of which he spent doon the pub. Ma didn't seem to mind as it kept him oot maist of the night. She'd get nervous towards chucking oot time, although he wis normally so fu' she could handle him well enough. Afore then, she'd gie me ma bath and then tuck me up in bed an' read to me. She had a wee stash of books that ma Granny must hae gied her. Da certainly widnae hae wasted money on them, seeing how ye couldnae eat, drink or smoke 'em. I kent then whit I needed.

The soap wis pale and amber, almost away to nothing. The tap spluttered an' hissed but eventually produced something close to hot water. I rubbed the soap a'tween ma hands an' breathed in. The slightly spicy smell made ma nose, an' mair importantly ma brain, twitch.

The bathroom walls were pink with grey tiles. From the look of me I couldnae be much mair than a toddler, splashing aboot in the water while Ma washed ma hair with Johnson's. She had on a flowery frock through which ye could see an industrial bra and big pants. Dinnae think the old man went in much for lingerie. Something else he widnae hae seen the point of.

I watched far longer than I should hae. But how often do ye get to see a moment of true happiness? Far as I could remember, this wis one of the last innocent times in ma life. Couldnae last, though.

'Ma, there's something I need to tell ye.'

She turned roon, took one look at me an' started screaming blue murder. A pulse throbbed in her neck, the one I remember always used to go when Da came near her. Her eyes flicked between me in the bath an' me in the doorway an' she reached a decision.

'We can go in the bedroom, if that's what you want?'

'No! For Christ's sake, no! Ye dinnae understand. I'm here to…'

To what? Tell ye I'm yer son fae the future an' ye should pack yer bags an' leave the old man 'cause all you an' the wee one hae to look forward to is a life of violent abuse? I so hadnae thought this one through.

'Look, it's ah right. I made a mistake. Got the wrang hoose.'

Her eyes telt me she didnae believe us, but so long as we

were heading away from little me it wis good. I dinnae rightly ken whit would hae happened next if the other me hadnae screamed. Ma ran back with oot a second look at me, an' there I wis, back in my ain bathroom, staring at myself in the mirror.

I reached up and touched the old scar on the side of ma heid. Five stitches from when I banged ma heid aff the taps in the bath. Half drooned into the bargain. Still got aff mair lightly than Ma, though. The old man broke her nose and bust her cheekbone for leaving me alane in the bath. She kent better than to mention her mystery man. He'd hae given her twice the hiding if he thought she'd been carrying on ahent his back. Turned out this time travelling shit wis mair dangerous than I thought.

All I could think of after that wis I needed to mak' things right. I kent how it worked now, mair or less, so I jist needed to wrack my brains fer the right memory. Seeing how I wis skint until giro day, I'd nothing to distract me from the thinking. Ma would never leave him, that much wis clear, which meant one way or another the old man had to go.

Funny thing wis, when it did come to me it proved to be one of the guid memories. Mibbe that's why I kent it wis right, 'cause the auld soak wid be aff his guard. Half cut, relaxed, no expecting any trouble. Didnae mak me feel guid, but I didnae feel bad aboot it either.

First stage of the mission wis a trip to Robson's sweet shop. Got all sorts of shit there I remembered fae when I wis a kid; kola cubes, pineapple chunks, flying saucers, even Wham bars. But I wanted the old man's favourite, horehound rock. Absolutely minging if ye asks me, all aniseed an' cloves, but he swore by the stuff. Fair cleared the tubes, so he said. Well, we'd see aboot that.

I asked the old dear behind the counter for a quarter an' got a smile for my troubles. She chucked a scoop on the scales, picked a couple aff, an' charged me a pound fifty fer the privilege. No like I could say I only needed a couple of pieces. But if this came aff it would be worth the investment.

There wis no way I'd be able to get my hands on a gun, so I decided to mak' it up close an' personal with a knife. There were a couple in the kitchen drawer that still had an edge to them, mainly 'cause I'd never used them fer anything other than cutting up a 9 bar. I thought aboot some sort of disguise but decided there wisnae any point to it. No like anybody wid recognise me fae thirty years in the future.

Some things ye cannae really prepare for, so I popped a horehound in my moo and started to sook, reckoning the double whammy of taste an' smell wid be sure to kick in. It wis horrible, but it worked an I found myself in the shadows of the auld living room. Clock said it'd gone nine o'clock on a Saturday night and Da wis sprawled in his armchair surrounded by empty tins of McEwan's Export. The room wis in darkness apart from the glow of the TV, which wis showing the day's fitba highlights. Couldnae be better — little me wid be in bed too scared to come through fer fear of a hiding and Ma wid be next door with oor neighbour Mrs Henderson.

The handle of the knife felt slippery in ma hand. I asked myself whit I wis waiting fer. No like I owed the old man anything. How many times would I watch him ower the next ten years beating the shite out of my Ma? Worst of it wis the neighbours all kent and didnae do a damn thing aboot it. Black eyes, fat lips, even broken bones, were excused on falls doon the stairs an' slips in the shower. Back then whit happened between a man an' his wife wis their business an' ye didnae interfere. No directly. Though sometimes, if things got too bad, a man might hae a wee accident of his own after chucking oot time. The clever anes took the hint an' leaned to belt the wife an bairns where it didnae show. As to the others… I gripped the knife mair tightly.

I didnae plan it, so I must have got lucky, as the first stab went straight through his heart. Da barely made a sound. Jist sat there with his mooth hingin' open like he wis catching flies. Blood bubbled up an' ran doon his chin to join the spreading patch on his chest. I let go of the knife an' stepped back. Everything changed.

I stood up from the grave an' brushed the grass from my trousers. Ma moved away almost twenty years ago, settled in Inverness with her new fella. Still nae sure I like him tae this day, but he's always treated her well an' never raised a hand to either of us. With her gone, I took it on myself to keep the auld man's heidstane looking presentable. Figured it wis the least I could dae in the circumstances.

The murder wis the talk of the town fer years after. I ken fine people thought Ma had a hand in it, that mibbe she'd got a fancy man hidden away and persuaded him to do the job. Course there wis no proof an' so the investigation became anither unsolved case, on the backburner for thirty year. But like I said earlier, the world's filled with clever gadgies an' it's amazing whit they can get DNA from. I got into the polis car with oot making a sound. The prosecution wis gonnae hae its work cut oot proving a five year old did fer his old man.

FALLEN

The call came in from the Guvnor a little before dawn; missing person's case way out in the sticks. Not my usual thing, but you don't argue with the Guv, not unless you want to find yourself going down; a fall so hard you'll never rise again. I'd seen it before and it wasn't going to happen to me, so I sucked it up and hightailed it to nowheresville.

It would be fair to say I'm not a lover of the countryside, it being comprised largely of mud and shit, the difference between the two often only discovered after you've stepped in it. Suffice it to say, whatever the farm boys had spread across the newly ploughed field didn't smell of roses. Guess today wasn't the day to have worn my new loafers. I added it to the account for later, and believe me, there's always a later.

I took my time walking across the field, because I knew two of the three figures in front of the shack would recognise me. Sure enough, the broad stepped in close to her man and he wrapped a protective arm about her shoulders. Back in the day the pair of them had been tight with the Guv. Living on Easy Street they were, everything they could want at their fingertips. Then the dozy bint had to spoil it by touching the one thing forbidden to them. The Guv couldn't tolerate that. An example had to be made.

The years hadn't been kind to her, pushing out a couple of kids and scraping a living from the dirt will do that to you. Her smile, which had once personified innocence and beauty, now had a brittle quality that threatened to shatter at any moment. I felt a pang of regret, but it soon passed. I'd done a lot worse in my time working for the Guvnor. Some nights I could close my eyes without seeing the dead faces of children.

'So he sent you, Mike.'

'Who else was he going to send? That messenger boy, Gabe? Like it or not, I get things done.'

He chewed over that for a while, weighing old enmities against need. Part of him, the spirit of the young man, wanted to have a pop at me, but the father won out. Pride be damned, he needed me.

'It's my youngest. He was out with the lambs last night and never came home. We looked all over for him but it's as if the ground just opened up and swallowed him.'

'Who was the last to see him?'

He jerked his head in the direction of the surly youth leaning against the shack. The boy was the spitting image of his father with the exception of the eyes, which had a sly look.

'Did your brother say anything out of the ordinary last night? Give you some idea where he might have gone?'

The boy fumbled a cigarette from his pack. He succeeded in lighting up on the third attempt. His eyes narrowed in response the smoke, the cover of which stoked his bravado.

'I'm not his keeper.'

'True enough, but that doesn't answer the question.'

We glared at one another, a competition of wills. To give him his due the boy had game, but he lacked experience and caved in after less than a minute.

'He always took the flocks out to pasture last thing at

night.'

'Where?'

I followed the pointing finger across the field and up into the rolling grasslands. Something in my gut told me this wasn't going to end well, but you can only play the hand you've been dealt. I walked into the hills without looking back. Barely midmorning and the sun was already beating down. Sweat prickled my back and I paused to mop my brow with a handkerchief. The white balls of cotton resolved themselves into sheep as I drew near, the smaller blobs lambs suckling on their mothers. They watched me nervously through slotted eyes. An older ewe led the stampede, the flock following close behind.

The buzzing of flies caught my attention. I knelt down and shooed them away from a fist-sized rock. They circled overhead, ready to descend the moment I moved off. Patches of sticky red goo clung to the rock, trapping the occasional hair and flecks of grey matter. Similar bloody flecks led back across the pasture to the freshly ploughed field.

The father searched my face for clues as I fetched a shovel from the barn. I made sure he didn't find any. He might be low on my list of suspects, but with only three names on that list no one was far from the top.

'Find your wife and son and wait inside.'

'But...'

'But nothing. Don't make me ask twice.'

I felt his hesitancy as I strode off but knew he'd obey. Refusing me was to refuse the Guvnor.

The earth in the far corner of the field was a darker shade, suggesting it had been turned over more recently. My suspicion hardened as I dug down to find the earth disturbed below the plough level. The body of son number two lay three feet down on its face, crushed skull clearly visible. A lead weight settled in my gut. The Guvnor was not going to like this. Better to present him with a target on which to vent his wrath.

I started with the mother. You don't want to believe any parent could kill their child, but after a while you learn people are capable of anything. She'd washed her hair since that morning and put on her best dress. They say grief affects people in strange ways. Maybe she thought I'd be flattered, but she hadn't fooled me twenty years ago and wasn't about to fool me now.

'What happened? Junior get a little fresh and refuse to take no for an answer? Can't be easy being a young man out here with needs.'

I caught her wrist as she tried to slap me and twisted her arm until the pain cut through her anger. Then I twisted it a fraction more to make sure we understood one another.

'I'll take that as no, will I?'

She started with the waterworks, delivering the full heaving bosom, trembling bottom lip version. I gave her a moment and pressed on. Once you start tenderising a piece of meat it's best to keep on beating it.

'Your boy's lying cold in the barn with his head beaten in. If it wasn't you, I'm betting you know something about it. So why don't we cut the crap and get to it?'

The tears dried up and she fixed me with a stare that could have cut through stone. She'd come a long way since I'd made it clear she and her man weren't welcome in the Guvnor's manor no more.

'I've got nothing to say to you, Mike. I've already lost one child today. That's grief enough for any mother.'

Won't deny that I thought about slapping her about, but before you lay hands on someone you have to be certain they're going to go. Whatever she was hiding, I could tell she'd take a beating and more to keep it. I moved on to the father instead.

He sat there silent, with that hangdog look of his.

Always was weak. The first wife the Guvnor set him up with ran out on him. Dumb mope got so dejected the old man took pity and found him the current incumbent. Seemed perfect to begin with, but she soon wrapped the poor sap around her little finger and got him into all sorts of trouble.

'They say mothers love their children more than fathers because they're more certain they're theirs. That kind of doubt can eat away at a man; make him get to all kinds of crazy thinking. It wouldn't be the first time she's had her head turned by a snake in the grass.'

'Is that what you think, Mike? I killed the boy in some fit of jealous rage?'

'Somebody was certainly angry with him. Enough to smash him in the head with a rock. Reckon that's the act of a person who's spent years developing a burning hatred for the vic. Thing about poison is it festers inside.'

'It does. Along with disappointment and regret.'

'Uh-huh. So you're a man with regrets?'

'Haven't we all? You're no different, Mike. Just as scared of the Guvnor as the rest of us, so you do what he tells you, no matter how terrible, and try to convince yourself that it's right. Can't you just leave it alone? Go back and tell him you found nothing. No good will come of stirring things up. I'm begging you here.'

Terrible thing to see a man lose his pride. Destroys what little respect you have left for him. But I haven't survived working for the Guv this long by being weak or feeling sorry for people and, more importantly, he's challenged the authority. I hesitate long enough to see the glimmer of hope in his eyes.

'Send the boy in.'

The boy folded his arms across his chest and glared at me. As far as looks of pure hatred go, I'd give it a five or six out of ten. Given time and sufficient brooding on the unfairness of the world, he'd no doubt perfect it. I fished a stogie out of my shirt pocket and lit up. The smoke curled between us in accusatory question marks. Silence. The interrogator's best friend when sat opposite a suspect. I could feel the boy itching to speak, to protest his innocence in the face of my accusations. I blew a smoke ring instead and watched it slowly disintegrate as it drifted towards the ceiling.

'He was always the favourite.'

'That so?'

'From the day he was born he got the best of everything. I wouldn't have minded so much if I'd gotten some credit, but no matter what I did, how hard I tried, I was always second best. Always the one that got punished, even when it wasn't my fault.'

'That kind of thing can be tough to shoulder.'

He nodded. 'I thought once we were working things would get better, that we'd be judged as men. But all those months of busting a gut in the fields still wasn't enough. More money in grazing sheep than growing crops, you see. But we still need bread to live. Even then I could have taken it, if only he hadn't been so cocky about. Lording it over me like he was some big success and I was nothing. Dirt digger — that's what he used to call me.' The boy held up his hands, callused from the plough and ingrained with soil. 'I worked damn hard to provide for this family. And for what? For them to regard me as a joke. I didn't deserve that.'

'So you decided to get rid of your rival?'

'Yes — I mean no! I didn't plan it, it just happened. Y'know?'

'I'm not sure that I do. Why don't you explain it to me?'

It all came out then, like puss squeezed from a festering sore. A taunt too far sparking unthinking rage, after which it was too late for sorry. During his confession the boy displayed anger, belligerence, even relief, but little by way of remorse. The truth lurked behind his eyes, the knowledge that he'd enjoyed the killing. It made him uneasy, but also hungry for more. Some are born to kill.

'Time we took a walk, boy.'

The mother read it all when we stopped outside. She threw herself at me and clung to my knees. To give him his due, the boy stood where he was. He had no distance left to run.

'Please don't take him away. I'm begging you. He's all I've got left in the world.'

That last statement must have cut the husband deep. He hauled her off me and held her fast. Even so, his look pleaded for the mercy he couldn't voice.

'Got to take the boy to the Guvnor. Ain't no two ways about it. It'll be up to the old man to decide punishment.'

'But you'll speak up for the lad?'

'Not my place. I only catch 'em. I don't cook 'em.'

ABOUT THE AUTHOR

Leon Steelgrave is the author of the Europa City series — hardboiled science fiction that traces its genealogy back to the pulp stories of the 1930s. This dark and satirical world serves as a warning of the dangers of ecological disaster and totalitarian regimes.

Leon's early work includes articles and reviews for music fanzines Take To The Sky and Glasperlenspiel. But it was his attempt to secure a commission for writing one of a series of Judge Dredd novels published by Virgin Books that kickstarted his fiction writing career. Although ultimately unsuccessful, the editorial feedback was sufficiently positive and encouraging for him to complete his debut novel White Vampyre. He has published a further three books in the series and is currently working on the first of a new series set in the wider Europa City universe.

Leon is a member of the Alliance of Independent Authors and self-publishes his work through Ice Pick Books — fiction to make your ears burn!

Writing being a solitary profession, Leon loves to engage with his readers, so feel free to join his mailing list for releases, updates and exclusive material.

www.leon-steelgrave.com